KILL HIM AGAIN

Fifteen Variations
on a
Country House Murder

NIGEL TAPPIN

Kill Him Again:
Fifteen Variations on a Country House Murder

By Nigel Tappin

Carrick Publishing

ISBN 978-1-927114-93-3 Print Edition

Copyright©2014 Nigel J.R. Tappin

Cover design by Rick Blechta of Castlefield Media
(http://www.rickblechta.com/)

First published in Canada and the United States 2014.

Cataloguing in Publication:

Tappin, Nigel John Robert, 1961-

Kill Him Again : Fifteen Variations on a Country House
Murder / Nigel Tappin

**CARRICK
PUBLISHING**

ISBN 978-1-927114-93-3 Print Edition

CONTENTS

Major Bly Takes Charge

What was that dratted shrieking in aid of, I wondered with a start.

I had been doing some investment research while my friend Charles Mortlake worked across the room at his desk. A Football Pools win had put me in funds again. Five thousand pounds, while a pittance to my best friend Charles Mortlake (yes, that Mortlake, the Banking heir), means a lot to me. The railway company prospectus I was perusing fell from my hand.

I looked up towards the door beyond which the unseemly racket originated.

Charles was doing paperwork.

Or at least he had been so doing not long before.

For when I glanced across from the Chesterfield to his mahogany desk, I saw he was not there. It is possible I might have dozed off and Charles stepped out of the room for a moment. The papers were still spread out, though atypically askew, and his fountain pen lay on the green blotter beside them.

Feeling hot and a bit wheezy, I sat up, removed my size 12 feet, from the Ottoman, and wondered where Charles was and whether it had anything to do with the tiresome servant's apparently hysterical condition. I had no sense of foreboding.

The fire was warm in the hearth beside me. I mopped my brow with my handkerchief. My eyes were drawn to the log fire itself, crackling and spitting on the elevated iron grate.

The polar bear hearth rug wasn't there. It had been earlier, hadn't it? But the maids could have taken it for cleaning or some such. Some think me a trifle unobservant.

Deciding the unabated screaming needed investigation, I heaved myself onto the old feet. On rising, I noticed a scrap of white cloth sticking out from the paneling in the far corner. I mention it as it might suggest Charles had taken the not so "secret" passage to the scullery to raid the larder. That would explain why the door didn't wake me. The passage slides back silently. Perhaps seeing me snoozing off, he had gone that way to avoid waking me. Plausible, what?

I rounded round the settee. As I did so the portrait of Sir Essau, the first baronet Parrot, framed by brass candle sticks stared coldly down at me from his position above the mantle-piece. It must have been worthless, or else Letitia Parrot, the former chatelaine, would have sold it off after her husband the last baronet's death. She was pretty well out of resources until dear Charles came to her rescue by taking a shine to Morthead Manor and buying it. I persist in calling her Lady Parrot, because she prefers "Letitia" or "Mrs." Parrot to her proper style as the widow of an hereditary knight.

But I digress. The off-key soprano caterwauling continued as I opened the door and emerged onto the marble floor of the inner hall. What a nuisance. Can't have that sort of behaviour in the ranks. The men didn't call me "Bully Bly" for nothing when they'd done wrong, I am pleased to relate.

I'm Major Stephen Bly, by the way. Devizesshire Foot, Retired. The War's where I met my bosom friend Charles Mortlake. Volunteer. A City financier. Inherited a private bank from the pater. He had spirit, Charles did. He was oldish to start as a subaltern — over forty — but keen to give the Hun hell. Ended up a Captain. A damned good line officer in my Regiment. Since I have retired, and he is semi-retired down here in deepest Devizesshire on the Southwest coast, I keep him company and help out with managing the estates.

Doing it again. Digressing. But got to put you in the picture sometime, you know?

From the echoing, it seemed the miscreant was in the hall. I noticed Professor Lawless had emerged from the library on my right and was standing outside the door, hesitating. Miss Leigh, Charles's private secretary (shall we say), flowed clicketty-clacking down the grand stairway. Her tight-fitting red split dress, showed off her excellent figure and shapely legs to perfection. The Professor may have been admiring the view as we both started across the hall. The voice seemed to be coming from behind the stair, from the direction of the kitchen.

As we rounded the stair and neared the passage between the dining room and ballroom, we converged with the tweedy Parrot woman, probably summoned from tending plants in the Orangerie by the rumpus. Charles puts up with her interference with the garden with apparent good grace. He has no real interest in such matters. It was her principal excuse for intruding on the household's privacy.

The same gale that marooned us on the promontory where the Manor sat had caught her, as usual, popping over the causeway from the Lodge in which she now resided to mind Charles's business for him. As Lawless and I, trailed by the ravishing Miss Leigh, came to the area near the green baize covered door to the servants area, that American chap, Hood, hurried up behind Miss Leigh. An unlit cigar hung from his thick, moist lips. It was at that point all of us came within sight of the miscreant.

Mrs. Brown, Cook, and the parlour maid, Mary, were attempting to restrain and comfort Gladys, the idiot of a scullery maid. She was the one screaming her head off. Gladys and Cook had likely emerged from their lair in the kitchens; Brown from the housekeeper's office off the passage to it; and Mary from wherever her duties lay.

Seeing the Parrot woman about to take charge with her usual presumption, I pipped her at the post, as Charles's proper deputy.

"Gladys! Stop that at once!" I bellowed in a voice that would have done our sergeant major proud. That stopped her. Probably amazed anyone could out shout her, the silly, blubbering fool. She was inherited with the rest of the servants except Brown, Jeffries the chauffeur, and Georges, Charles's valet, from the Parrot woman with the house. It is hard getting servants in the country since the Great War. Brown came with Charles from the London House, where she had been his housekeeper technically also, before Leigh's arrival in Charles's *menage* made it one a *trois*. Despite her bucolic origins Cook, more properly known as Mrs. Stout, was a damned fine chef with a taste for her own handiwork and proportions to match. Mary and Agnes though only girls from the village, were trained properly. Perhaps the Parrot did have some talents. I just can't stand her impudent attempts to rule our roost.

I strode across the marble floor and beat the Parrot to Gladys's side.

"That's better!" I barked in rough soldierly commendation. "What's happened? Cut yourself, or some such?" She was clutching a dish cloth as if trying to strangle it.

"No, it's not that, sir," said Cook, her chubby face lined with concern. "She just come running from the larder yelling her head off. Something about murder! Then she rushed out here past Mrs. Brown's office, and through the second baize door, like one of them axe murderers you see at the pictures were chasing her, and started screaming."

From raiding it after the servants retired, I knew the pantry was off the scullery, where the concealed way from the Office emerged. Could Charles have emerged from the "secret" way and somehow upset the girl, perhaps by pinching her unattractive bottom or more likely speaking harshly to her?

"Now Gladys, isn't it?" I said trying for my best avuncular uncle manner.

"Yes, sir. Major, sir," she got out between sobs.

"Sit down," I commanded, indicating the straight-backed chair just outside the green baize door to below stairs.

Gladys complied giving a shy "Thank you, sir." I was somewhat mollified to see she'd at least had some manners drummed into her thick, chinless head.

"Now close your eyes for a moment, and take a few deep breathes. Think of your happiest memory. Perhaps Mary you would get her a glass of water?" The rest of them, even Parrot, saw my approach was working, and held fire. Once the girl had drained the water Mary brought, she sat more calmly, though both hands clutched the empty tumbler, her knuckles white.

"Now Gladys, you're quite safe with all of us here," I said. "We won't let anything happen to you. Just keep calm and tell us what prompted your extra-ordinary performance."

She took a breathe, gulped, and started. "Well, sir. Major, sir. I went out the scullery way to get some thyme and basil Cook wanted from the kitchen garden. When I came back in and was hangin' up me Mac and head scarf, and wiping me feet, I felt a draft from the pantry. Now you know, sir, the pantry window's never left open. Flies or rats or anything could get in, sir. So I went in and closed it wondering-like who'd opened it. Seemed daft. Specially with the storm and all. After I'd pulled it shut, I turned round to go out and tell Cook, and saw him lying there..."

"Saw whom, Gladys?" Parrot got in before me.

"Why the new Master, milady. It was horrid-like. Him lying there on the floor on his front. His head is bashed in! Blood and bone poking out!" She covered her face with her hands.

"My God!" I said. "Surely you are imagining things girl!"

"No, sir! I'm not, sir! I wish it were a dream like!"

"I suggest instead of berating the messenger, Major," said Lady Parrot, "it might be more productive to investigate. You've done well Gladys and been very clear."

"Oh, thank you milady!"

"Shall we?" she said, pushing past me bold as brass through the baize door.

I was left with no alternative, but to follow with the rest.

Alas, upon arrival at the scullery the scene proved just as Gladys described it. She had failed to mention that a number of items stored on shelves under the window had been disturbed, shoved aside or lying shattered on the floor.

Miss Leigh, a VAD nurse near the front lines before the November 11th Armistice, confirmed what any layman could have seen. My best friend and fellow officer was dead from a blow to the top rear of the head from some blunt instrument. We looked for some appropriate, bloodstained object, but nothing to hand met requirements.

The body couldn't be left there indefinitely — with a bad storm lashing the promontory upon which its immediate grounds were located, the Manor might be isolated for days. We summoned Jeffries and Georges and they carried the mortal remains of my friend off to his bedchamber. Jeffries had been in the Show in our own regiment; Georges had been a batman to a French officer Charles got on with. He took a fancy to them both and offered them employment. Both were used to bodies and, though shaken, behaved well.

Cook wanted to tidy up the pantry floor, stained as it was by my dear comrade's blood as well as the debris from the shelf, but Parrot stopped her, informing the gathering that the police, once communications had been restored to the village, would want to examine it undisturbed.

"Obviously some tramp must have slipped into the gardens intending theft, before the storm struck," I said. "Charles caught the blighter in the act and was killed for his pains. Well we'll get him! Cook, once Jeffries comes back, tell him to lock the iron-gate at the causeway. He and Georges are to alternate on watch to make sure he doesn't climb over and steal a boat. Jeffries can park the Daimler down there for shelter. They're to see to it no one gets off. Better take stout cudgels with them."

"Yes, sir," Cook replied.

Hood, Brown and Leigh appeared satisfied and relieved. Professor Lawless, a mere guest, had the cheek to ask questions.

"Are you really suggesting, Major, a man could exit and enter through that small window?" he asked.

"He's right, Stephen," said the Parrot, probably just being awkward, "only a boy could have got through."

"While that may or may not be true, ladies and gentlemen, I suggest we adjourn to the sitting room. This is hardly a suitable place for rational discourse. Cook! I want tea served as soon as possible!" That spiked their guns and would keep the servants busy too, not getting wild ideas about the death. It's always best to keep the lower ranks occupied in a crisis. The Devil makes work for idle hands and all that.

Most acquiesced in these arrangements, though Lady Parrot and Professor Lawless straggled behind. I wondered what devilry they were up to. When they hurried in to the sitting room some moments after the rest of us, both were a tad out of breathe with cheeks flushed and hair in disarray. Their shoes were wet. So were Lawless's trouser cuffs and Parrot's stockings. I wondered what mischief they'd been up too and started to ask when Mary arrived pushing the tea trolley.

Parrot sat down and acted as mother, brushing off my inquiry with, "Let us serve out in peace, Stephen, before we get down to business! One thing at a time."

I reluctantly agreed that a hot cup of tea, some cake, and a few of Cook's delectable buttered crumpets would be welcome. An army marches on its stomach, what? Must feed the inner man. After everyone was settled with plates and cups and saucers, she started sticking her oar in. So predictable!

"Naturally someone had to look outside the pantry window," Lady Parrot explained, a smug, condescending smile on her well-worn countenance. "There is a bed there and any intruder would have left footprints. Professor Lawless gallantly escorted me as a witness. We should conduct no investigations singly. It will make it more satisfactory for the police."

"Well did you find anything?" I said shortly.

"Footprints? No," she replied with a look on her face like the cat that ate the canary. Was it just her smugness or did I detect an evasion. Perhaps they had found something? The missing hearthrug came to mind. Why keep it quiet if so?

"Anything else?" I persisted.

"Nothing that need signify at present," she said coyly, glancing at the Professor for confirmation.

"That's right," he agreed nodding and took a bite of plum cake.

I think the pressure must have been getting to me. Suddenly I felt very tired and hot under the collar at the same time. Taking a sip of tea, I summoned my reserves and determined to regain the initiative.

"Hmm.... Perhaps he got out some other way, or is still in the house. At least one scullery door would be unlocked. I understand Jeffries comes in and out that way to meals and such and it is unsecured all day. Other doors may have been left open if anyone braved the storm for a constitutional. Mrs. Brown please have Jeffries or Georges — whoever's not on sentry duty at the causeway — search the house including the cellars. I'll search the hidden passage m'self." Brown left the room temporarily to relay my orders just as Miss Leigh helpfully admitted taking a walk before breakfast and leaving by the Orangerie. She thought she'd left the french windows unbolted upon her return.

"Professor Lawless and I will accompany you when you search the passage from the Office," the Parrot said. "After tea and with electric torches. Perhaps Mr. Hood and Miss Leigh will wait for us in the scullery in case we flush out your hypothetical tramp?" I did not take kindly to the skeptical tone in her voice. "We will start from the Office entrance, shall we?" She sipped her tea. "Which brings me to my next question, Major, when did Charles leave the Office?"

"The fact is I'm not totally sure. I may have dozed off over a Bolivian railway prospectus, nothing you ladies would know anything about, but it looks like a jolly good investment! Lucky about the Football Pools win. Five thousand pounds comes in very useful when you are short of capital and pensioned off!"

"Not learned your lesson with the Patagonian and Manaus stock disasters, I see! Poor Stephen, do resist temptation this time! High returns are a red flag for me. They mean high risk. As Charles warned you last time, these South American stocks are reckless investments," said Parrot. "From my own experience I know too well the consequences of such folly. My late husband's father ruined the family in similar ventures! Take my advice, don't throw good money after bad."

You see the damned woman's infernal impudence? Bad enough my having even minor, disagreements with Charles. Those cases were different.

"And why would Charles," she went on getting back to the killing, "have gone the long route to get to the larder through the secret passage? It's his house. He hardly needed to skulk about. Oddly close to teatime too. I've not heard of Charles raiding the larder. Mary?"

"Well, milady," the maid replied as she offered me the cake plate, "someone does at night. We thought it was the Major. Begging your pardon for saying so, sir, but Agnes found the plate in your room. Sometime we find a plate in the kitchen or a mug used for cocoa or milk sometimes with lipstick on it and a sauce pan..."

"I sometimes can't sleep and make myself a hot drink and take a biscuit," volunteered Miss Leigh.

"Me too," added Brown returned from her errand, "if Charlie's still up I sometimes make him some too."

"... It *could* have been the Master as well, I suppose," added Mary.

Drat the girl. Insubordination in the ranks! I frowned. "Well he did, on occasion. Are you doubting my word, girl?"

"Oh no, sir!" she said hastily and went on passing the scones.

"Now Major," said the Parrot, "why did you suggest Charles went for a snack through the priest hole passage?"

Damned the woman's insolence! What an officer and a gentleman has to put up with from these old cats. "As for him going to raid the food stores, well it's obvious isn't it? His corpse was found in the confounded pantry. What else would he be doing there? Besides I noticed a white piece of cloth sticking out of the paneling in the corner of the Office that conceals the entrance, just as I left the room to investigate the commotion. No time to check. Must be something stuck in the secret door. I thought that it must be Charles's hanky or some such. He had mentioned feeling peckish." With the last detail, I felt I was up on points again.

"So your *position* is you don't really know when he left the room or how," the old biddy said. "Then once we have finished tea, Professor Lawless and we two, my dear Stephen, have a date in the Office. While the rest guard the scullery end. Mary will you see to collecting three good electric torches?"

"Certainly, milady." The parlourmaid went off to see to this task.

"I know Stephen, being such a dedicated trencherman, you would not want to go without your tea."

Impertinence again! Implying I eat too much. Nonsense. A big frame like mine needs keeping up. I don't believe I've gained more than two stone, or perhaps three, since active service. With my height, a trifling amount.

I felt hot again. Perhaps it was minding my manners with Lady Parrot, despite her provocations. The stresses of being an officer and a gentleman. Still she was a lady and an officer must treat the weaker sex with respect. But there are limits to even my iron self-discipline!

I mopped my brow with the old kerchief. Her parting shot, of course, deprived me of the healthy appetite an active man like me needs. I practically had to force myself to eat the veriest morsels of ginger-cake and just a sliver of cook's excellent jam sponge after those two lonely crumpets dripping with butter, and all washed down with three refreshing cups of tea, without any apparent hurry or distress. Mustn't let the enemy think she'd hit her target!

Some of the party bravely tried to keep up a flow of small talk during the remainder of the meal. I can't remember much of it, though I believe I responded mechanically to some remarks addressed to me.

After tea I used the facilities on my way to the Office. When I caught up with the rest, I was surprised to see Lawless wearing leather driving gloves and old Parrot sporting evening gloves of all things! The same pair, I suppose, she wore to the dinner party the night the storm descended upon us. I was further startled to see Lawless getting up by the fire irons on the hearth and returning a magnifying glass to his inside pocket. It looked like he had been examining the poker. The gloves, they said were so they didn't leave added finger marks. Neither, I noted mentioned the absence of the hearth rug, and I did not bother mentioning it. They did not frequent the Office much and I expect they only had a sketchy idea of the details of its current furnishings. I was not in a mood to help them in their Sherlock Holmes imitation.

With my entrance the search party was complete, and Lady Parrot moved to the outside corner of the room. The age-darkened oak paneling was carved with a fruit and vine motif along each panel edges. With what I hoped might seem a suspicious lack of hesitation, the old biddy took hold of a certain pear just to the right of the protruding corner of handkerchief and twisted it to work the old mechanism. Charles had restored it to full, silent working order. That's when Professor Lawless became a regular guest. My old comrade wanted all his restorations to be authentic.

The panels above and below the fruit silently moved aside. Charles's handkerchief fell onto the threshold of the passage. With a gloved hand Lady Parrot picked it up. And held it out for us all to look at.

"Its monogram is CM," she commented, before carefully folding it and putting it in the pocket of her brown, blue-flecked tweed jacket.

"Oh, do let Professor Lawless and I go first, Major dear," the old Dragon commanded. "Then we have you as the rearguard to come to our rescue should we encounter *the intruder*. Besides you're not wearing gloves. Wouldn't want to leave finger prints in any incriminating places would we?"

I had no choice but to comply with what good grace I could muster. Obviously the old girl was determined to interfere and I decided to play her game for the present and hold a watching brief.

"Go ahead, Professor," she ordered. He switched on his torch and stepped through the opening. She followed. They disappeared into the darkness. I hesitated wanting to check the poker, but Parrot's imperious voice called out telling me not to dawdle.

As I too passed into the concealed passage, Lawless's and Parrot's lights moved back and forth across the tunnel floor. I retrieved the torch from my jacket pocket, thumbed the switch, and caught them up.

The narrow passage passes inside the manor's thick stone walls, going up a set of steps to avoid ground and first floor windows, and then straight along two sides of the house. At the corner where the passage formed a small room, the two ahead of me paused and focussed their lights on some disturbances in the dust to the side of the passage were it widened somewhat. I recalled Lawless saying this was where a bench had provided a hidden catholic priest a hard bed while the ill-fated if devout Mortheads held the estate. After their execution for suspected involvement in helping gunpowder plot conspirators, Sir Essau Parrot had bought the manor and his baronetcy from King James.

Taking a closer look at what Parrot and the Professor where examining, I saw footprints in the dust. Parrot gave her opinion they were of size 12 shoes. I said they weren't as large. We also noted most of the dust in the center part of our pathway had been wiped clean as if something had been dragged behind, obscuring footprints. We proceeded on our journey. Near the Scullery, Parrot noted what looked like the same shoe marks facing the opposite direction near the wall.

When we emerged from the tunnel, Leigh, Hood, Brown, Cook, and Georges were present.

There concluded our joint efforts at detection.

I wrote the earlier installment of my account for the *Daily Screech* in order to help finance my unsuccessful defence. As the last person known to see Charles, I naturally fell under suspicion. Those blasted police have no respect for gallant service for King and Country, nor for high military rank! Now I have lost the appeal to the Lords, and can only hope for clemency. I might as well write this. You will note I did not actually lie in the earlier account -- an officer and a gentleman until the end, I may hope!

My fears that Lawless and Parrot had found the blood stained Polar Bear rug outside the pantry window turned out to have been justified. I had intended to suggest burglary by leaving the window open. I didn't reckon with the old cat playing detective. Shoving the rug -- on which I'd pulled Charles's body through the passage -- out the window was all I could think of. I had intended to retrieve it and put it over the cliff that night when I could get away from the others. I had assumed we would wait for the police like good civilians.

Lawless and Parrot found traces of blood I'd missed on the poker in the Office. They also found the bloodied handkerchief in my jacket pocket. I hadn't counted on anyone searching me.

My big feet gave me away too. You recall me mentioning them on the Ottoman? Well I was the only big-booted man in the house, worst luck! I hadn't realized the rug hadn't wiped out all the prints. I used the torch from Charles's desk drawer, stuck between my clenched teeth for light of sorts on the way as my hands were full. I had to do a fireman's carry up the steps. I'm not quite as fit as I'd like anymore and I couldn't do it the whole way. Charles was wrapped in the rug. That way I didn't risk getting blood on the floor or my person. I did dust myself down after making it back to the Office without being found out. I was hot as I said, not from the fire, but rather the exertion.

Parrot, Leigh and Brown testified that I had a "mania" for railway stocks and that Charles had been reluctant to bail me out the last time, I had done poorly. In fact he'd said it was the last time he would do so. And I happened to be in a hole again. Charles hardened his heart and was refusing to help me. There was no way I could meet my obligations on my pension.

The Football Pools win wasn't mine. I bought the tickets on Charles's behalf. I saw no alternative solution to my little difficulties than to dispose of my erstwhile friend. Besides, I got a decent income under his will. He left me an annuity so that I couldn't touch the capital and "invest" once more.

After his last lecture I was so angry that I lost my self-control. He had so much and wouldn't share it. To him it was a mere pittance. That's what really got me. He sat down at the desk again after delivering me a lecture on prudence and economy. I was standing before the fire near his side and behind him. I found my hand reaching out for the poker. I hefted it in both hands and struck downwards on the top of his skull.

The shock sobered me up and I tried to plan how to get away with it. It was temporary madness. It wasn't really me. I wasn't really responsible. Insanity overtook me for one cruel moment. You must believe that. I'm not naturally vicious. I just lost my temper. They won't hang an officer and a gentleman for that, will they?

— **Major Stephen Bly, Devizesshire Foot regiment, retired.**

Parrot's Call

Just before the kerfuffle started, three of us were in the kitchen. Cook, me, and the Scullery Maid, Gladys, that is. I'm Mary, the Parlor Maid. I'm below only Cook and Monsieur Georges, the Master's French Valet, amongst the inside staff as there's no butler.

That is if you don't count "Mrs." Brown as staff, and she sure enough don't—takes her meals separate, or with the gentry and everything, even though she used to be a music hall singer! She's called the housekeeper, but that don't mean she does much other than lord it over those who does the work. Used to be a lady friend – using "lady" loosely if you get my drift -- of the Master's.

Agnes – she's the chambermaid – was with Mrs. Brown in the dining room laying things out for supper. I said "'bye" to Cook and Gladys, picked up the tray with the ice bucket on it, passed through first green baize door to the old Butler's Pantry—now it was partitioned into a narrow corridor and Mrs. Brown's "office"— and shouldered through the second door into the inner hall.

I was on me way to lay out the drinks tray in the drawing room. The gentry would be finishing dressing for their meal. Once all dolled up in evening dress, they get together and drink them newfangled American cocktails, sherry, or something stronger, just before supper. So I makes up the shaker, gets it ready and puts it, the sherry decanter, and the glasses in front of the drinks' cabinet before they come down.

As I was crossing the hall, the Master, Mr. Charles Mortlake, and his "secretary" Miss Leigh, walked down the grand marble staircase from the portrait gallery all dolled up. Miss Leigh was a nice enough young lady, served as a nurse near the front she did, during the Great War, and from a respectable family too. The servant's hall liked her, except with Mr. Charles you got the impression she didn't act any better than she should be, if you get me meaning. The upper orders say "The *servants* always know." They talk of us like we were one of them different "species" that there Mr. Darwin who caused all the fuss wrote about. And they're right too! Most of the time we've got a good idea of what's going on upstairs, anyhow.

The Master and company were early, so I picked up me pace a bit, but they never did come into the drawing room, while I was making up the cocktail shaker and putting out the other stuff. Maybe he'd something to show her in his Office. Her little office and sitting room was near the top of the grand stairs, just past the gallery in the right corridor.

I finished in the drawing room and was on my way to the dining room to help Agnes finish up. I was a bit surprised to see Miss Leigh coming down them marble stairs again, this time alone. She was on the left side, right hand on the banister. As she came into the light of the chandelier, I noticed she was heavily made up. Maybe the Master'd been a bit rough again. Nasty temper he has. Usual, she don't wear much face paint. At the time I didn't make anything of her coming down a second time. She'd likely left her bag or shawl in her bedroom and gone to fetch it.

I'd barely got through the dining room door when the screaming started. I recognized the voice. Aggie and Mrs. Brown looked at each other. They were as taken aback as me by the looks they gave. We hesitated a minute then all three of us headed out the door. Safety in numbers, like.

The poor lady was standing at the bottom of the stairs staring in the direction of the passage between the games room and the ballroom with the Orangerie door farther along. When she saw us, she looked our way, stopped screaming, and swallowed hard. Her right hand was grabbing the banister so tight, all her knuckles were white.

"What ever's the matter, Miss?" I said. Brown gave me the look for speaking out of turn, but was too curious to tell me off.

Miss Leigh pried her hand loose from the banister and pointed towards the gap between the ballroom and the games room. "I think it's Charles. Mr. Mortlake," she said.

When we got closer, we saw "it" was a man in evening dress lying on the floor with the top of his head and shoulders visible sticking out into the main hall from the corridor. There was a red pool on the marble beneath him. A clatter of shoes on the stairs announced Professor Lawless. He put an arm round Miss Leigh's shoulder and brought her down the remaining stairs with him. Lady Parrot and Major Bly came close behind them. The Professor asked Miss Leigh -- "Grace," he called her -- what had upset her. He sounded like that was the main thing. If you ask me he was head over heels about her, and I'd been starting to think lately that she was falling for him too. A sticky wicket, what with the Master fancying her too.

We all stopped just before the bleeding man, the staff to one side and a little back, the upper orders ahead to our left.

"He said something about checking if he'd left his pipe in the Orangerie or the games room or somewhere. We'd met at the head of the stairs and walked down together. Just then I realized it was chilly and I'd left my wrap in my room. I went back up for it. As I came down again, I wondered what a bundle of clothes was doing there, before I saw it was a man. Then I lost control and screamed. Sorry everybody! After all it's not the first time I've seen a dead body by a long chalk, after nursing during the War," she nattered on. Nerves, I suppose. Well, it's to be expected isn't it? She'd pulled a cigarette out of her bag, the Professor lit it, and she took a drag as if her life depended on it.

At this point Mr. Hood came out of the games room, dressed in a white diner jacket with black bow-tie and pants. He had one of them nasty smelly Havana cigars unlit hung from the corner of his mouth, and a billiard cue held in his left hand. "What's the noise about . . ." he started to ask. He looked to his right, where we were all trying not to look, and failing. He must have had a clear view of the body. "I guess I see," he said slowly. "Who's the stiff?" He gestured at the body with the butt of his cue and peered closer. "Charles Mortlake, I'd say. Hardly any doubt about it. Who topped him?"

"That," said Lady Parrot, our old mistress, "is not immediately apparent. Am I right in assuming he has been stabbed in the throat?"

Hood took a step closer and crouched down. "Yeah. You hit the nail on the head. Under the right ear. I'd say he was stabbed from behind. Caught off guard, you know the deal. Got the artery. Maybe a professional job. Know anybody who'd put out a contract on him? Rich guys can't help making enemies. Who were his?"

"This is outrageous!" protested Major Bly, puffing up like a pouter pigeon. "Charles killed in his own home! Of course he didn't have any enemies! Or not any who would do this. He was an officer and a gentlemen!" He paused for breath. "Besides none of them could have got to the Manor any more than we can get away, or even telephone at present. Morthead is a decidedly pleasant country seat, but not conveniently situated in a storm."

"The guy who did it – if it weren't a dame – could've got out on this here headland before the gale submerged the causeway," Hood argued. "Of course it could be an amateur job. One of us." He looked the rest of us over, sizing us up, looking at the gentry and old Brownie too.

"Now that the victim is established to be Charles," said Lady Parrot, "Brown, get Georges and Jeffries.

Have them get blankets and take him up to his room. We can't leave him there until who knows when."

"I'd better bandage the neck first. Probably most of the blood's out by now but..." Miss Leigh trailed off.

"Agnes, get bandages. Oh, also inform Mrs. Stout. Have her keep supper warm," Parrot ordered. "I shall help you, my dear. Then I suggest we search the Orangerie. Mr. Hood, did Charles come into the games room? How long were you there, bye the bye?"

"No. No one came in. I've been there maybe fifteen minutes. Twenty max. I was dressed early and seeing how the drinks tray wasn't laid out, I thought I'd shoot a few balls till Mary did her stuff. She makes a wild Manhattan, now she's got the hang of it!"

"I'm so sorry. I shouldn't have screamed. Only it was such a shock," said Miss Leigh.

"No need to apologize, Grace," said Lady Parrot in that no-nonsense tone she uses in crises. "You are behaving very well."

Once they'd bandaged the poor Master's neck and Jeffries, the chauffeur and handyman, and Georges, the valet, had removed the body, Lady Parrot said they'd better follow the trail of blood. It led in the direction of the Orangerie doorway and passed through it. Warning everyone to avoid stepping in the spilt blood as much as possible, Lady led the way, though the old Major tried to "take charge." She soon saw him off, she did. A treat to watch. Just like the old days, 'fore she sold the Manor to the new Master. Not being told otherwise, I trailed behind the others—Lady Parrot, Professor Lawless, Miss Grace, the American, Major Bly and Brownie —trying to be inconspicuous like.

There was blood all over the hall, mostly to our left and some splattered on the door to the ballroom and the wall near where he fell. It was difficult not to step in it, but you just about could by keeping to the right going down the hall anyway. Miss Grace said in a deadened voice that it would have been the blood pumping out of the carotid. Sent a shiver up me spine, it did. I guess "cartoid" is that artery the American said was cut. The trail led to one of the raised plant beds along the outer, glass walls. Them french windows on the opposite side were open letting in the wind and rain on the marble floor. Sometime I'd have to get me mop, sponge, and bucket and clean all the gore and wet up, I thought, my stomach turned over just thinking about it.

"Looks like an intruder," said the Major in that stuffy voice of his. He was examining the door. Once he'd said something, he didn't take kindly to anyone disagreeing with him. Lady P. often disagreed with him, so he didn't like her. He reached towards the handle of the door to close it, but Lady put a hand on his arm to stop him, warned of fingerprints, pulled out a lacy handkerchief and closed it herself, touching as little of the handle as possible. There's no flies on Lady, and she reads the papers like all the gentry, and not the *Daily Screech*, neither. She likes them detective books too. She had a lot of them in her room, she did, when she was still real Mistress here in the good old days.

I'm not saying nothing against Captain Mortlake, mind, excepting his rough treatment of women. He was in trade, though, even if it were money trade, and inherited. Not real gentry like Lady Letitia and Sir John. Still the piped water and the electric light and the Agga stove and all makes for less work and we appreciated him for that. Not that Lady didn't want it, but Sir John wasn't well off for gentry. His father had no head for business. There were hard times on the estate then in his time and he was good-hearted, too much so for his own good, we reckon in Morthead Minor, the village across the causeway where me family's from.

"We'd better lock the door to the room and leave it as it is. You'll have it seen to, Mrs. Brown? I shall take charge of all the keys to this room. Collect them and bring them to me. Oh and don't touch the handle when you lock it. Test that it's locked with a handkerchief over the handle or a glove on. The police will want to photograph the blood whenever we can get them over. Leave that in the passage also." Were I relieved! I'd not have to clean the mucky mess right away. Course it would dry on later, but at least we'd have time to get used to it.

"Yes, ma'am," Brownie replied. She talked right to her betters, for all them la-di-da airs she put on about being above common folk, even the upper servants like Cook, Monsieur Georges, and John Jeffries. She knew which side her bread was buttered on, she did.

"Lock all the doors leading into this corridor," milady continued. "And better have Jeffries rope off the area with the blood stains in the passage.

"I don't think there's much we can do except register any oddities. Don't move about, but from where you are everyone take a look about the room and see if you notice anything unusual." Lady, the rest of the gentry, Brownie, and me looked around. I noticed Miss Grace, the Major, and the Yank, had got blood on their shoes. Some of it looked as if it was drying on already. Miss had even got some on the side of her fancy evening slippers. I clean the shoes and I thought it would give me the devil's own job to get that off. I saw that old car coat of Lady's that's normally hanging up near the door weren't to be seen. Lady uses it to protect her clothes while working on the plants, like she still does, for Mr. Charles.

After a few minutes, Lady said, "For myself, I only noticed one or two things other than the blood and the formerly open french windows. Anything else?"

I hesitated. Lady saw it and told me to speak up. I told her about the coat and the blood on people's shoes. "Best give them to me to clean before it dries on once we're back in the main inner hall," I added.

"Very good, Mary! Anyone else?" No one added anything, though the Major insisted it was all a waste of time. Clearly an intruder. Like a stuck record on one of them newfangled phonographs, the poor old horse's derriere, if you pardon my French. Sometimes I wonder if he's not a bit gaga.

"The only other things," Lady Parrot continued, "I can see missing are a pruning knife, some secateurs, and a trowel from that tool rack." She gestured to shelves for gardening tools with three slots empty. "I remember I was using them this afternoon. Mary came in with a reminder about dressing and I may not have cleared them up properly. I hadn't quite finished. I certainly didn't wander off with them. Oh, there are the secateurs and the trowel on the marble edging there." She gestured. "But I have an idea I might have absently put the knife in the pocket of the coat before I pushed my old bones up. I have Jeffries keep all these tools in good condition. The knife was nice and sharp, as it should be. I may have forgotten to put it back in the rack when I took off the coat and hung it on its peg. I sometimes do. Where can it have gone?

"Now I think we should all have drinks and then our dinner. Mrs. Brown, do see to locking the doors and having the area around the scene of the crime roped off, immediately."

At Lady's suggestion, we all checked our shoes for blood once we were back in the inner hall proper. The Major, of course, had walked right through it; Mr. Hood, Miss Grace, and Professor Lawless too a little. They all took their shoes off and left them in a row in the hall. I went to get a tray to take the shoes to the scullery for a good scrub and polish, while the gentry went to drink cocktails, some of them in their stocking feet.

While I cleaned the shoes, I noticed that the blood seemed almost caked on one pair. Some had dried and yet some was still fresh like on the others. Almost like two layers. That and one or two other things made me think, I can tell you! I decided I'd tell Lady P. about it later, quiet-like. She'd know what to do.

After finishing the shoes, I took off me apron, scrubbed me hands, and arrived in the dining room a little breathless just afore the gentry. Nothing much that came up over dinner or during the evening seemed significant. 'Course there was a lot of speculation amongst the above stairs crowd.

We gossiped a good deal downstairs too, as you can imagine. Some of it was quite funny. M. Georges and John Jeffries do carry on! Cook had to quiet them down when they got too frisky. I guess we were all covering up the worry about our situations and joking about it helped. After all, Mr. Charles was our employer.

With everything being late, I offered to help Agnes turn down the beds, layout nightclothes, take up hot water bottles, and such. I wasn't just being helpful like, though I'd have lent a hand anyway given the emergency. I made a point of arranging to see to one room in particular. After all that thinking I'd been doing earlier, I wanted to have a nose around a bit before the "occupant" got to clean things up. Ain't I using a lot of fancy words? The toffs ain't the only ones with education, or who read, though a lot of them'd be surprised at the thought.

I found something too. It were soaking in cold water in the chamber pot under the bed.

Not that anyone but the Major, dirty old man, uses them now we have water closets. He has no consideration for making extra work. But the slop pots, the wash stands and jugs are still left in the rooms. Who'd have thought of it a few years ago? Often the gentry still wanted hot water delivered for the basins if they're just washing, shaving, or the like. But no more endless cans to fill the old hip baths. The new master gave them to his tenants. He even gave us servants a bathroom near our quarters, and a toilet and washstand with running water and another W.C.s off the scullery! Just like grand folks in London.

After the gentry had retired and I had checked all the windows and doors were locked as I do last thing, I went up and knocked on Lady P.'s door. Earlier I'd hid the chamber pot and its contents in the bottom of a broom closet covered by a dustsheet. Aggie wouldn't have cause to go into the closet till morning. I'd brought it along with me to outside Lady Parrot's guest room.

"Come in!" commanded Lady P. calm-like.

I gulped and opened the door. Lady was propped up in bed reading, her hair in braids. She had on a lovely quilted bed jacket with a wallflower pattern.

"Mary? What is the matter? Shouldn't you be locking up or readying for bed, girl?"

"Well, Milady, there's a couple of things about Mr. Charles, like. Things I've found or noticed. I think I know who killed him. One piece of evidence's outside the door in a chamber pot."

She put her open book down on the bed. "Well, don't leave it there. Bring it in."

I brought it in. Then she had me explain about what I saw in the hall and about the pair of shoes and where I'd found the coat soaking in cold, bloodstained water in the chamber pot, and what I'd found in the coat pocket when I'd steeled myself to check.

"You always were a clever girl, Mary," she said when I'd finished. "Let me think for a few minutes about what's best to be done. Sit down." With an absent gesture she indicated a chair near the bed. She lay there staring into the coals of the fire I'd banked up for the night earlier.

"Well Mary, I think before making these things public, we should give the suspect a chance to make an explanation." She told me to summon "the suspect," and I did.

The things we heard that night still give me the shivers.

Lady had said more about "the suspect" than I told you before. It was Miss Grace Leigh.

"She might be covering up for someone else. She might have been provoked. Go to the room where you found that thing," she waved at the chamber pot, now on the carpet, "and ask her to come to me. If she refuses, say it's about Mr. Charles. She'll come."

She came all right, Miss Grace did. I'd found her pacing in her room. She hadn't even undressed. The blood drained from her face when I gave her Lady P.'s summons. She'd missed the chamber pot.

She told Lady Parrot with me standing there how Mr. Charles had been getting very possessive. Insisting she go to his bed when he felt like it, with no talk of marriage too, even though she wanted to stop. He'd started hitting her if she resisted, too. And lately even when she didn't. She said he seemed to enjoy it. He said he'd learned tips on how to bash up people without it showing from a French pal of his during the war who used to be a gendarme in North Africa. It seems they don't treat the natives proper there if they think they've done anything wrong. But you've got to keep how you got the confession from the magistrate, so no marks can be left, or no visible ones. It seemed to fascinate Mr. Charles, she said. But sometimes he didn't bother, as long as it was under clothes. She showed us some green and blue and purple bruises all over her belly.

She was in love with Professor Lawless—Patrick, she called him—and had given her notice. That's when he really beat her. Tonight when they met at the head of the stairs, she said she wanted her freedom, or she'd go to the police. The Master frog-marched her into the Orangerie to "discuss" it. She put on the coat because she was cold and feeling pretty sick with the bruising. Then he started slanging her. Calling her his woman, bought and paid for. His whore. His slut. He threatened to make sure neither she nor the Professor would ever get a post again. He said he'd get Patrick removed from the University and that he could do it too, as a big donor. He'd spread rumors about his scandalous behavior while at Morthead: sleeping with the Master's secretary; stealing from the petty cash; not doing the work he gained admission by promising to do—all sorts of vicious rumors. He'd ruin her reputation and let everyone know what a devious, liar, and a thief she was. Then he gave her another few slaps.

After that he turned his back on her. She put her hands in the pocket and felt the knife. She saw her future as one of being battered or impoverished. Patrick and she ruined, even if he'd stick by her. She found herself lifting the knife and plunging it under his ear where she knew the carotid was while his back was turned. Death would be within a few minutes, consciousness lost much sooner. He seemed a monster to her. She had to fight for her life. And for Patrick. She said it felt like someone else was doing it not her, as if something snapped. The Master staggered to the door—spurting blood—and down the hall a ways. The coat protected her evening clothes. She hadn't noticed the blood on the shoes, which had a red pattern. She opened the french window, hoping someone would think it was a tramp and then bundled the coat up and made it back to her room, shaking with the realization of what she had done. The bathroom was by her room. She drew cold water into the chamber pot, in order to get the stains out before they set. After checking her clothes and plastering on makeup in case the Master's slap had bruised, she went down stairs again and "discovered" the body.

"I believe you," Lady said, once the story had finished. "I've noticed you moving stiffly recently. Haven't you, Mary?" Come to think of it I had. I'd hoped it was a touch of the rheumatism with all the wet weather. I nodded.

"I think this conversation never happened, Mary. Nor did your discoveries. Neither of us will lie directly to the police. But they won't know what to ask, will they? Do you agree?"

"Oh yes, Ma'am," I said. If I didn't have a face like a horse and no figure to speak off, the Master might have done it to me. Besides I'd back up Lady Parrot anyhow.

"Well then, take the chamber pot back to the bathroom for Miss Leigh. She can wring out the coat there, after scrubbing it and rinse away the blood. She will probably throw the knife and coat over the cliff tonight. Unlock the scullery and get up early tomorrow morning to secure it so Gladys doesn't notice."

I did as she said. The police never could pin the murder on anyone. And they couldn't prove it wasn't a burglar, or what Mr. Hood of Chicago called a mob "hit" neither. He could have snuck off the island or swam off when the storm died down before the police arrived.

—Mary Forelock

Hood's Take

The scream didn't wake me. This joint is built solid. Like San Quentin. The dance hall they call a ballroom where the racket started's not exactly under my bedroom floor either. Don't think it woke anyone else. Me and most of the rest of this here enforced house party only heard about it with our morning tea. Only mine was coffee. I don't drink tea. It comes with the shaving water between seven-thirty and eight, unless you ask to get it later.

Me, I take things as they come, so I got coffee and the news about twenty-to-eight. I checked my watch after the knock woke me and I grunted it was okay for the maid to come in. No orgy going on or anything. I wasn't even particularly hung over, though I do like a drink during the evening. Especially when I'm trapped in a house by a storm with the dullest set of guys and gals I ever set my baby-blues on.

Except the chambermaid and the Leigh gal, there ain't a decent looking dame in the place. The guys are boring, especially that old windbag of a Major. Thinks he owns the place. Likely invented his stories about shooting uppity natives in Africa or India, potting Boers, and ordering Tommies to get themselves killed charging "Huns" across no man's land from somewhere warm, toasty and safe in the War Office. They're all Limeys too. After a few months in England I'd got bored with the accents. The stuffy ones, like this bunch, are worst. I'd come down to talk to the owner -- Chuck Mortlake—on mutual business.

He's—should say was—backing the expansion of my nightclub business from the States over here. I got speakeasies all over the States from Chicago to New York and down the East coast to Philly and Washington.

I figure the Brits have dough too, so why not get some of theirs? I just finished getting them going. We were settling the guys who'd manage them, now I'm heading back to the States. Been here too long anyway. My guys tell me some heavies are trying to cause trouble. Nothing serious yet, but you have to be there to really keep that stuff under control. It's delicate.

As I was saying, the looker of a chamber maid sashayed in with my coffee and cookies on a silver tray. Mortlake kept the joint fancy. It's called Morthead Manor after some family who got axed for some Catholic plot way back. Bloody guys them English Kings, from what the Professor tells me. Something about gunpowder plots and hiding priests in holes in the walls. Sounds a bit like the Chicago mob to me—all these "noble" guys and royalty. With kings and queens raking in the biggest take and rubbing out two-bit bosses who cross them.

I was still a bit groggy, getting a good look at Agnes' fanny as she bent to put the coffee down. Then I realized she was saying Chuck Mortlake'd been found dead by the other maid, Mary. Mary's a bit old, scrawny and sour faced too. For Pete's sake, I can't think what she was doing in the ballroom at 6 a.m. Something maids do I guess, like dusting or getting fires ready, maybe.

Anyway she found him. Mortlake. As a corpse. Dead. Not very funny.

After screaming – didn't think she'd had it in her -- she woke up the housekeeper, Mrs. Brown, from her bed. She looks as if she might have been fun in the sack once -- Brown I mean. Then Brown got the Parrot woman. Lady Parrot used to own this pile and lives across the causeway in the Lodge. She's marooned here on this spit of land too by the storm. Nobody can get across to the mainland. And besides, my wheels are here. The sea's too rough for a boat. The telephone's knocked out. Lucky the house has its own generator, or we'd have no lights.

The Parrot dame told 'em nothing was to be touched, the doors to the ballroom were locked, and the keys brought to her. The party would inspect the scene of the hit after breakfast.

Very civilized these Brits, I'll say that for them. An American dame would've started screeching up here and woken all the guys and demanded they "do something." Immediately. My appreciation of the old dame went up several notches, even if she looks like a well-fed goat in tweed suit and pince-nez.

So we enjoyed our full cooked breakfast buffet style from chaffing dishes on the sideboard and polite chitchat. After my coffee I'd figured if we didn't finger the hit artist, the cops might prevent me sailing back to the States next week. And that could negatively impact my business affairs, with the thugs making a move. I tried to ask a question on the subject everyone was thinking of, and I got slapped down with a polite "After breakfast please, Mr. Hood!" in scandalized tones from the Parrot. That old dame could teach old Scar-face a thing or two, I tell you. I did notice, however, that the conversation was confined to comments like, "Would you please pass the butter, Professor?" from the sexy Miss Leigh, who toyed nervously with some toast and jelly. Or, "Can I help you to more of this excellent ham Hood? Sausages? I'll be topping my plate up so it would be no bother! Must feed the inner man!" from Major Bly, the only one of us with much appetite. Maybe the maid had forgot to tell him. More likely he was just a greedy guts. The guy was tall, but fat, and sweated like a pig.

While the meal seemed long, it was really over in about forty minutes. I timed it. Lady Parrot stopped Bly from taking thirds, with the threat of being left out of the inspection. She summoned Mama Brown and Mary and we all proceeded to the ballroom. Parrot unlocked the door nearest the dining room. Her having the keys meant only she, the horse-faced maid, or Brown could have interfered with the room after the body was discovered. Unless someone else had a key of course.

I hadn't seen that dancing parlour of Chuck's before. Impressive! The room probably wasn't used in years, but was dust-free and the sprung wood-floor and chandelier gleamed. Mortlake sure knew how to keep the help busy. There were chairs here and there along the walls and a grand piano near one open glass door. Parrot warned everyone to not touch a thing.

The rain blew in on a gust of wind. On Parrot's orders I closed the french door, covering my mitt with a hanky. The Major said it was a burglar, despite our being trapped on the headland by the storm.

"Very interesting, Major," said Parrot like she was humouring a kid with a few cards short of a full deck.

Mortlake's body lay sprawled face down on the shiny wood floor. It lay just to the right of the french windows and a little way into the room. I could see half of his face as the gang gathered round. It wasn't a pretty sight. There was a smell. His bladder and bowels must have let go. The eye I could see bulged and was dotted with red, the swollen tongue stuck out of the mouth, the face had a blue-tinge. You didn't have to be an M.D. to say he was strangled. There were red welts about his neck. He'd been garroted with a rope or cord.

The Parrot pointed out a red and blue braided silk dressing gown tie lying about six feet from the glass doors on the far side of the stiff. The floor by the windows and the body's clothes were soaked. There was a big pool of water. The drapes at them french doors were open and the other set too. Mary said she had closed the drapes last night and made certain the doors were shut when she locked up last thing. She had drawn back the drapes nearest the door after she came in, before she noticed the corpse.

Lady Parrot bent down to pick up the red, yellow, and blue braided cord. Straightening up she held the tie out at arm's length and looked at it through her pince nez glasses as if it were something the cat brought in. Her eyebrows hit the roof and her lips looked like she'd just sucked on a lime. "Most peculiar!" was her comment.

"Brown," she went on, "you will recall my asking you to have the staff keep an eye out for my silk dressing gown's cord the evening before last?"

"I *think so*, ma'am," said Brown, in a voice that sounded like she'd forgotten all about it, if it happened. Mary looked as if it was the first she'd heard about it. Parrot stared hard at Brown, but didn't reply except with a genteel sniff.

Was the Parrot lying? If not, was Brown forgetful, or had she deliberately failed to put the word out?

"Well, now I have reminded you, you need look no further! And yet I have not been in this room in months and certainly not in my dressing gown."

"The impudent blighter must have been leaving with his booty when Charles discovered him," pronounced the Major. "Perhaps he was using it to tie his booty in a bundle after rooting through the bedrooms for jewelry. When my friend Charles, a man of noble physique, cornered him, he used surprise to overcome him. He may even be an ex-servicemen. There are a lot of the poor wretches out of work and he may have turned in desperation to crime!"

I guessed the Major must have whiled away the odd hour reading trashy dime novels, or whatever they call 'em over here. Not that I bought his story. It was just possible if the guy he imagined had got here before the storm. But who was I to pour cold water on any idea that might get the cops to let me go home on schedule?

From her face, the Parrot wasn't buying it neither. She walked back to the body, waving at me to come with her. When we again had a corpse-side view—and the eau de urine to match—she squatted down stiffly and I followed her example. The others crowded round us to get a ghoulish look-see. Parrot looked closely at the fancy cord in her hand and then at the stiff's neck. The

Parrot nodded. "You see," she said pointing, "Here's a pattern on Charles' neck. Note it matches the cord's braiding. I fear it is either the murder weapon or something very like it. It appears someone has had the unmitigated gall to kill our host with my dressing-gown cord!" She straightened up and I did too.

"Why your cord?" asked the delectable Grace Leigh, mystified.

"To make it look like I did it, my dear!" Parrot replied, as if to a small child or an idiot. She flashed that smug smile of hers. "Unless you prefer the Major's penny dreadful scenario!

"Needless to say, I had no desire to harm him. In fact, whatever Captain Mortlake's peccadilloes, I am much in his debt. His purchase of the Manor allowed me to retire to the lodge in some comfort. He has supplied most of my valued servants with continued employment. Soon I would have had to let them go without appropriate pension arrangements or gratuities. He has carefully restored the property to its glory, always consulting me, as well as experts such as Professor Lawless." She nodded approvingly at the highbrow. "Exactly as I am sure my dear Sir John would have, had he been in a position to afford it. And he has generously allowed me to retain the Lodge and more or less have the run of the place. No, I had no reason to kill Charles Mortlake!"

What the dame said made sense. It might be a clumsy frame. Unless she was just plain crazy. Maybe the old broad hates anyone standing in her old man's shoes and wants revenge. Don't think so, but stranger things have happened.

Or she could be trying to be clever? Might she think that would be the way it would look to the cops? Anyway she has a lot of pull in Devizesshire, knows all the key locals. She's bright enough to know that cops know who they can pull in, and who's in the social register. They'd need an airtight case to act against Lady Parrot.

Oh sure, there's a fair number of no-brains like that Chicago Lieutenant who tried to get me to pay protection direct when I'd paid Capone's boys and they had him on retainer already. They never did find the body. My guess is it's at the bottom of Lake Michigan in comfy cement overshoes and with a bullet in the head. It don't pay to cross Scar-face. Anyway, cops like that jackass are in the minority in my experience. Even the bent ones have some brains.

Don't know what Brown's angle would be. Been with him a long time, I hear. Maybe the two of them had something going once. He may have been two-timing her with the lovely Miss Leigh. I sure wouldn't blame him. Maybe it's a crime of passion. Brown might've gotten mad and done it. The old gal probably didn't look bad once, before she'd put on weight and let herself go. You never know about a guy's taste in broads. I've seen plenty of odd couples in my clubs. Or maybe the professor's hot over Miss Leigh and got jealous. Or Major Bly or someone gets something he needs bad in the will.

I can't see Mortlake—who wasn't that old and was pretty well set up—being Parrot's lover. Or the Major's, for that matter! Maybe if he was like that, the Professor might have interested him. I hear a lot of that stuff goes on at these English private schools they call public, just to confuse a guy.

Parrot shooed us out of the dancing hall. She then checked the doors were locked behind us and had me verify it. Then she dropped the keys into her jacket pocket. She had the staff give her all the keys they knew about. I'd checked the corpse's pockets and he had none on him. The Major pointed out Charles kept a complete set on a ring in the desk in his office. The whole party detoured there. They weren't where the old guy said they should be. The old gal herded us along to the sitting room and ordered some tea. When we were all settled, she started asking questions again.

I had no complaints as I wanted the case closed soon. An enforced stay as a murder suspect in this rainy country—even if the booze biz was legit— was not in my plans. I was no crook, but if you're in the club business during this Prohibition, you gotta have connections with the mob. If the local cops checked with their "colleagues" back home in the Windy City, they might get the idea I had something to do with it. I didn't, but plenty of guys've been framed and plenty more will be just 'cause they're handy.

"Mrs. Brown," said the Lady, interrupting my musings. "Charles is still in evening dress. It seems this happened before he retired. Do you know when that would usually be? When did you last see him?"

"After checking no one wanted anything, I ask Mr. Charles for any instructions and give the staff any necessary orders. Last night was no different from usual. It might have been shortly after ten but not many minutes. Then I went upstairs, checked the beds had been turned down, and went to my rooms. I read a chapter of Mrs. Christie's new thriller about Roger Ackroyd, by the fire. I got ready for bed and turned out the lights about eleven. Mr. Charles often stayed up until the wee hours. Always has ever since I've known him. That was before the War when I was in the theatre, ma'am."

"What about Georges, his valet? Would he not have known something was amiss last night?"

"With Mr. Charles' habits, he does not keep Georges up waiting for him. If he's not up by eleven, he undresses unassisted."

"Mary," Lady Parrot said to the maid, "when did you lock up last night? Describe what happened. Was there anything unusual?"

"About eleven, Milady. I'd check all the windows were shut and bolted and that the outside doors were locked. Mr. Charles was in his Office reading with a whisky as usual. Told me he didn't want anything more.

From what I understand, he usually goes to bed between midnight and two. Doesn't sleep as much since the War. The Major was still with him."

Seeing the Major was about to intrude, Parrot asked, "What did you do then?"

"I continued my rounds till I reached the kitchen quarters—I checks them last you see—and goes up the back stairs to me room. It's the same one you'll remember, Ma'am. Under the roof."

"And you are the last of the staff to go up?"

"Usually, Ma'am, unless Gladys got behind with her cleaning up and had things left to do. She did get behind last night. But she was almost finished when I went up. Said she'd make herself a cup of hot milk or something and be up soon."

Now speaking to the company in general, our lady detective found out when we'd all gone up. Leigh said she'd had a headache and gone to bed about nine, after getting a book from the library. She'd taken some aspirin, read a little, and then slept. Professor Lawless said he'd seen the Leigh gal about the time she claimed and left the library about ten-thirty. He looked in the sitting room and, finding no one to shoot the breeze with, walked up the grand staircase and went to bed. Parrot herself said she had gone up just before the professor. I admitted fooling around with a pool cue till about ten-fifty. The joint never was exactly jumping. The Major admitted being with Mortlake like Mary said. He'd finished his nightcap in the Office just after Mary checked the windows, said goodnight to our host, and then gone up. He confirmed Mortlake often stayed up till well past midnight. Occasionally when they were talking about the War, he stayed up too. Mostly he was changed and in bed by eleven-thirty or quarter to twelve. He said that's what happened last night. No one was around when he went upstairs round eleven fifteen. Brown said she'd gone up as usual at ten after consulting Mortlake. The Major also witnessed this interview.

The phones were still down, but Parrot thought the storm would soon be played out. The mechanic and chauffeur who slept over the stables, Jeffries reported it was still too rough to get across to the village by boat, but things were calming down. Parrot decided we'd be able to contact the cops by evening, or at least tomorrow morning. She retired to the library to write out an account of our investigations so far for them, announcing we were each to read and sign it if it was correct when it was done.

There was a lot in the old dame's approach, but I wanted things wrapped up before the cops came into it. No guarantee we'd get a smart officer in charge. My boat sailed on the weekend and I had things to finalize before I went home. I didn't want some police numbskull messing up my business arrangements. So I headed for the kitchen and the most promising lead I could see.

Mrs. Stout, the Cook and me got on. I'd buttered her up and often had an early or late snack over tea in her stone flagged kitchen. You get the real McCoy from the servants in these English upper-crust places, I'd learned from experience. The servants didn't think of my kinda Yank as gentry, so were willing to gossip.

Mary had just got going on retelling the upstairs news when I came in and put a bit of a damper on proceedings. Brown was in her office. But I soon got them to treat me as one of the family again and I listened with pleasure to her uncensored account. I'd only missed her finding the body. Their nicknames for their so-called betters, except Lady Parrot, were not complimentary and they trusted me enough to use them. They always called the Parrot Lady or Milady, showing their respect for her, same as they called me Mr. Hood (when I was there). They were a bit naughty about the rest though, suggesting they knew where the bodies were buried.

After Mary had finished, Cook delivered her verdict. "I know there's a woman in it somewhere! Mr. Charles was a good master, but he wasn't exactly a total gentleman with the ladies." She glanced over at the thick baize-covered door to make sure it was closed. It fitted tight, so probably no one beyond the room except the other way in the scullery or pantry could have heard her. "Why look at how he treated Brownie! Mr. Jeffries done told me, as most of you know, excepting perhaps Gladys and you Mr. Hood, sir, that she'd been his mistress and housekeeper for years up in London. Expected to be made respectable, she did. Then when they come down here he hired a lady secretary and Cockney Hettie—that put-on accent don't fool me; you all know how she sounds when she's riled—wasn't good enough. Probably never was. Besides getting long in the tooth and putting on weight. He likes them young and pretty and now with a middle-class young lady to turn too, well, she didn't stand a chance, unless the Leigh girl resisted his advances. She might get him to marry her, but there again she might not. Just a respectable background. I think her father's a post office clerk. Not much for the rich Mr. Charles. I wonder which of them it was?"

"Ouch!" screamed Gladys, who'd been pretending to cut up the greens for lunch while listening. She'd cut herself. But I had an idea it was something Mrs. Stout had said that triggered her clumsiness, recalling that she was the last who admitted being down here.

Sure enough, once the wound was washed and bandaged and Cook had scolded while getting her a cup of sweet tea and a cookie for shock, she told a tale. That night she'd pushed past that inner baize door because she thought she'd heard a noise. She'd been drinking her cocoa not long before midnight. When she got there, she saw the baize door into the inner hall was swinging back. This confused her 'cause Brown was never up after "half-ten" if she could help it. Her taste in Motion Pictures went in for cops and robbers I guess, so she imagined a burglar had been hiding out in Brown's office or something.

So she took up her courage and softly pushed open the door to the hall. She heard raised voices that she recognized. One was "the Master's." She didn't dare open the door further and take a look, but what she heard darn well settled the case. Then a door had opened and closed nearby. She couldn't hear anything more, was bone tired, went back to the kitchen, washed up her mug, and dragged herself upstairs. She hadn't thought of it till Mrs. Stout had said what she'd said, but the closest door led to the ballroom. What Mrs. Stout said made her realized she'd overheard the killer just before the crime.

Gladys was a bit "slow," as Cook kindly put it. But once the cops got onto her, I'd be steaming for home on time. I went upstairs and informed the Parrot of Gladys' interesting information. Her only remark was that she'd thought as much. She went off to see Gladys herself, on the excuse that she must make sure they put iodine on the cut and otherwise play Lady Bountiful. The killer really made a mistake by trying to frame that old dame.

The other voice Gladys had overheard was Brown. By what the girl heard, Brown was jealous of Leigh and of the Major, too. Charles had promised her marriage, or something like it. Eventually. Now he trades her in for a newer, firmer model. She finally cracked. She had found Lady P.'s dressing gown cord and was going to return it in the morning. She saw her hands putting it over his head as he started to turn away and pulling it tight with strength she didn't know she had.

Brown probably resented Lady P. like hell too. All the servants thought she walked on water and Brown knew they barely concealed their contempt for her pretensions and easy virtue. Anyway, while she likely didn't really think someone like Lady P. would be arrested—she'd mentioned she was friendly with the Chief Constable—she'd sure have liked that as a bonus.

Besides, Chuck Mortlake still slept with Brown and roughed her up as part of it. He got his kicks that way.

She'd taken it too long and wasn't gonna take it anymore. With him dead she'd be free and financially independent. If she left him alive, she'd have nothing. No reference. No annuity when he died. No acting career at her age. She wasn't any Sarah Bernhardt to begin with. It was her looks that got her jobs.

—Jack Hood

Parrot's Chase

Agnes knocked, and I answered readily. I had been reading by the bedside lamp, too lazy to get up and draw the curtains. As I age I rarely sleep late or long.

By-the-by, I am Letitia Parrot. My late husband, the sixteenth and last Baronet of that ilk, owned this Devizesshire house, Morthead Manor, jutting out into the sea on the southwest coast on its spit of a headland. I had been forced to sell, fortunately at an advantageous—even generous—price to Captain Charles Mortlake, the current master, from a family of city financiers. I was his guest, having been caught on the headland by one of the too frequent storms that prevent use of either boat or the low-lying causeway to get back across to Morthead Minor, the village, and my new home, the rebuilt Lodge.

The door opened and she came in with my morning tea. She seemed more animated than usual, as if pregnant with news. She drew back the curtains, revealing a view of the rain-lashed window. The storm, if anything, seemed to have intensified in the night, extending my sojourn as guest in my former marital home.

Agnes then approached the bedside and transferred the cup and saucer from her tray to my nightstand, much as she had for the few years before and after my husband's untimely demise. He was struck down more than anything else from grief at the deaths of both our sons in the service of King and Country in the late Great War. I was fortunate to have found as congenial and wealthy a purchaser for my husband's family seat as Charles Mortlake. There was no alternative to sale. With John's father's poor management, wartime taxation, death duties, and the

Manor's bad need of repair, what was left of income and principal would soon be exhausted. Now I was able to stay on in comfort and with an easy competence left over for my modest wants at a thoroughly modernized Lodge and be about the village people. I even had a pretty free run of the Manor, was constantly asked to dine, and my advice and views were sought for the extensive repairs and modernizations. No expense had been spared to restore my old home to its former splendor, with tasteful modernization including sanitary facilities, electric lights, and even central heating with radiators in all significant rooms. Even the servants had their own W.C.s and bathroom. Such nice consideration. Who could ask for more in a purchaser?

I put down my book and, with a tolerant smile of long familiarity on my lips, asked her what had occurred. It turned out to be somewhat disturbing—Charles appeared to have gone missing. His bed hadn't been slept in and his pajamas and robe were laid out as his valet, Georges, left them when he retired. None of his coats or other clothes appeared to be missing, and I need hardly say that wandering about outside in evening dress would hardly be conducive to comfort or health, given the gale. Still, he might have borrowed someone's Mackintosh or some such.

After ascertaining the inside servants had already searched the interior rooms, I asked that Agnes pass my compliments to Jeffries and suggest he search the outbuildings and failing that, the garden pathways, check the boats, or places where one might slip or fall and so forth.

After breakfast there was still no news of Charles' whereabouts. Jeffries had reported no sign of him in the outbuildings. No boats or cars were missing. The conditions still seemed to be unsuitable for use of a boat, much less the causeway. He was presently checking the paths with Georges' help.

Perplexed, I accompanied Professor Lawless to the Library. He was also distracted, and wanted to retrieve a reference work he required for his monograph on passages and priest-holes in the southwest for forthcoming publication. I desired to look up details of a remedy for spider mites I recalled in the bound back issues of the Garden Society's *Proceedings* as those pests had made their activities apparent in the Orangerie. Life goes on, as I have learned, even under trying circumstances. Professor Lawless made a disturbing discovery: by one of the shelves there was a brownish stain bearing a close resemblance to dried blood visible on the cream background of the carpet's floral pattern. It was not extensive, but under the circumstances, we could not help but wonder if it had any connection with Charles' whereabouts.

I pulled the bell cord by the window to summon Mary. She arrived with her usual dispatch, looking starched and neat as nine-pence, as always. You would hardly think anything was amiss, nor that she had been up and doing since at least six—the sign of an excellently-trained servant. And if I do say so myself, Mary is one of the best, despite being born in the village. I would have not a moment's hesitation about delivering a glowing reference for any of my former staff should they want or need it. The kitchen maid, Gladys, is a bit slow, but she is a conscientious creature and doesn't slack once she knows a task. Not that Cook, our redoubtable Mrs. Stout, would let her do so, of course. The bloodstain had started me thinking the unpleasant thoughts that I should be turning my mind to arranging new posts for them all. I believe Lady Lacey will be in need of a good cook shortly . . .

"Mary," I began, "is this stain on the carpet new?" I stood beside it near the bay window, with Professor Lawless close at hand.

"Why, yes Ma'am. I never saw it before. It certainly wasn't there yesterday morning. And while the electric light's a bit far from the window, I don't think it was there last evening when I checked that the french window was locked and closed the curtains.

"I'm ever so sorry I didn't notice it this morning when I drew back the curtains, but we knew Mr. Charles was missing by then and everything was rather a rush, what with searching the house for him and still keeping the household running proper-like."

"I quite understand Mary," I reassured. "I don't want you to clear it up quite yet. And pass the message onto the others. Just in case it proves to be . . . of significance."

I could tell from a slight widening of Mary's eyes and an intake of breath that she had got my meaning. But she showed no other outward sign and her proper servant mask was not affected. I then asked her to outline the extent of the inside search. It seemed there had been two significant omissions. These were based on neither ignorance nor negligence but standing orders, and I had expected them. After her account was complete, she asked, "Is there anything more at present, Milady?" I asked her to have Mrs. Brown, the housekeeper, summon the rest of the above-stairs party to the sitting room— should they not already be there— and attend that room herself, awaiting orders. I also requested that Mary then assemble at least a few strong electric torches and bring them to the sitting room. She bustled off to execute my commissions, clearly speculating as fast as Professor Lawless and I.

Mary always was a quick girl. Had her station been different I'm sure she would have done well at school and perhaps even some further training. I am not sad to report that even Oxford University, which my poor sons attended before their country called them to their doom, is now granting degrees to the more pragmatic sex. Naturally, I do not agree with the old-fashioned like Major Bly on the issue. And I am sure, with only a little persuasion, that had Sir John survived, he would have concurred with my view. He usually did, after all. The secret of a long—but not long enough—and happy marriage is congeniality of disposition between the partners, is it not?

Before Lawless's troubling discovery, we had both located the volumes we desired, but abandoned them carelessly on the table—along with a new novel about the Great War someone else left earlier—and exited the Library. The young, lanky, sloped-shouldered antiquary assisted me, at my suggestion, in checking the polished marble between the library and the Office door with some care. As we found one or two traces of the sort I expected—I will not insult the reader's intelligence by specifying what they resembled—we then proceeded directly round the corner and between the entrance hall and the foot of the stairs and passed the dining room. We then entered the place I had appointed for our little rendezvous.

It did not take long for Brown to assemble the party.

Miss Leigh came from her office-sitting room, I assumed. I had heard the tap-tap of the stiletto-healed patent leather shoes she wears to better show off her seemly calves starting down the staircase as we reached the sitting room door. She appeared genuinely concerned and asked if there was news of Charles immediately. Of course if what I suspected was true, her concern could equally mask a more sinister interest in any discovery, or merely worry over her employer being missing.

Mr. Hood, Charles' American business associate, and Major Bly, Charles' friend and companion, appeared from the games room, or as the former preferred to put it, the pool hall. The Major was complaining, in the over-loud voice of the somewhat hard of hearing, at the interruption to their entertainment and demanding instant enlightenment as to why I had taken the liberty of issuing commands. His usual dig that I was, after all, a mere charitable guest, was trotted out. He made me sound as if I were classed with the importuning stray traveler, forcing myself upon the household, stranded by the storm. I snubbed him with a few choice words, reminding him that he claimed to be an officer and, therefore, technically, a gentleman.

Mr. Hood seemed merely curious and alert. The Major was flushed. While his diameter is about half his fair height and he is prone to sweating like the proverbial pig upon significant exertion, he is still surprisingly strong and active for one of his age, girth, and eating habits. He also makes (one can only assume) inadvertent rude noises he either can't hear or ignores with unpleasant frequency, presumably due to his amazing eating capacity. His clothes were not well-kept either, though of respectable quality, tending to have many food stains remaining after inexpert and half-hearted attempts at removal only made matters worse. He had changed his tweeds to brown today, I noted; the first time in my three-day enforced stay. And already his tie and shirt bore stains, probably long-standing. He managed to look crumpled and slightly soiled. His flustered, red-faced state, resulted from my exercise of authority in his—shall we say one-time soul-mate's?—house, not exertion. That kind of thing—developed all too readily at all-male boarding schools with inadequate supervision—was why I insisted on my dear late sons, John and Ian, being educated privately.

Or could Hood's watchful coolness, or the Major's bluster, be from some more sinister cause?

Brown arrived, I assumed from either the kitchen or her office near the back stairs, given the time of day. She also bore a frown on her visage, and like her replacement in my successor's natural affections, Leigh, made bold to ask if there was any news.

Again, there was no clear indication of her motivation: a killer – should Charles indeed prove dead -- seeking information on what has been found out about her crime, or the natural curiosity and concern of the bereaved friend and dependent.

Now that they were all assembled, I started by explaining why I had summoned them. Leigh exclaimed in apparent alarm at news of the blood stains. I recounted my further investigations accompanied by the good Professor. Of course, he was not above my suspicions. It would be natural for him, frequenting the library, to be sought out by his victim there; and also for him to discover the stain with an unimpeachable witness, if I may flatter myself, on terms of social intimacy with the Chief Constable and his dear wife, present. As for motivation, he could have fallen for Miss Leigh and either been eliminating a rival or avenging her seduction.

As the servants had found no trace of Charles Mortlake outside the Manor or in, there were, as I said earlier, only two places where he might be easily concealed. He had ordered the servants to stay out of the secret passages. The evidence of the blood in the hall implied he had been struck down somehow in the library dragged across the room, through the brief section of the inner hall between it and his Office, and, one assumes, hidden in the secret passage leading off it.

Mary appeared with the electric torches just as I was proposing that I examine the Office and passage entrance, accompanied by at least the three male members of the upstairs party. I doubted the body I expected to discover would be far inside the passage. Charles was a fit, tall man of fair weight. I assumed the murderer would drag him as short a distance as possible. While Miss Leigh was a slight young woman, she had been a VAD nurse in France during the War. And nurses do learn how to move patients. Eyeing her surreptitiously, I concluded even she could not be excluded from suspicion.

Any of the servants—except perhaps Georges or Jeffries or Brown—seemed preposterous as suspects. Unless of course Charles had abused them; after all he had at least three lovers from what I could surmise, and all present in the household at once, too!

If I did not owe him a debt, and want badly to indulge an old woman's wish to maintain access to my old home, I would, needless to say, have had nothing further to do with Charles Mortlake once I had learned of his rakish tendencies. It did put me in a bit of an invidious position, seeming to endorse him to the county by my frequent presence. This made me uncomfortable, but fortunately he showed little inclination to join the set.

In the end the whole party accompanied me to the Office. I warned them not to touch anything. Once there I scanned the floor, carpeted with a red decorative motif on green. I was suspicious of one or two spots as stains of the same nature as in the library and hall, and suggested the others avoid treading on them.

I approached the corner of the room with a torch in one hand and my handkerchief in the other. I was quite familiar with the mechanism; John and Ian had often played in the passages—and got disgracefully dirty doing so—as children, but their father persisted in letting them, maintaining that it was a family tradition. He had done so himself at their age; he regularly inspected them to ensure they were still sound—don't spoil the fun. So I acquiesced. I had myself gone looking for the miscreants in the passages, when they couldn't be found elsewhere. I reached out to the carved pear in the decorated paneling with my left hand and turned it. The mechanism engaged and a section of the wall slid back, now well-oiled and relatively silent; in the old days it had issued creaks and groans, much to the boys' delight.

My torch was hardly necessary, but I pressed it on nonetheless to get a clearer look at the corpse. For corpse it clearly was. Mortlake's lifeless form lay on its back, the knees pushed up against the torso. The crumpled trouser legs suggested to me that the killer had pushed the cadaver in after dragging it by the ankles.

The electric light revealed that he was still in evening wear. It also showed a red, round puncture wound right between the eyes. There didn't seem to be much blood. Or an exit wound. We concluded he had been shot by a pistol of some sort, probably one of low caliber. I insisted we leave him *in situ* for the police, whenever they could get here, unless decay started to become significant before then.

I closed the entrance by reversing the pear after we had looked about and under the body for a weapon. The Major had exclaimed that Charles had kept a suitable gun in his desk drawer. He looked for it and it was missing. The box of bullets kept in a separate draw was missing some of its contents. Only the Major admitted to knowing of the gun and its whereabouts, but other inmates, servants, or guests might well know. Miss Leigh, Professor Lawless, and Brown had heard of its existence, but not precisely where it was kept.

All the guests and I imagine most if not all the staff knew how the passages operated; you cannot really keep much from them and they naturally tell each other about the kitchen table and so on. I myself sealed the door to the passage, and locked and sealed the Office door with paper and glue supplied by Mary and assisted by Professor Lawless. I asked Brown to have Georges and Jeffries search the other passage and the rest of this one, from the kitchen end, which came out in the scullery, for the gun. After that they were to seal the concealed door in the scullery. Gladys and Mary were to check the seals at hourly intervals during the day.

The party, except Mary, who went off to convey instructions and replace the unused glue and paper, withdrew to the sitting room. Brown soon returned with Mary, who sees to the locking up at night, as I had directed.

I ascertained that Mary finished her final rounds about eleven, drawing curtains and banking fires where necessary, and ensuring windows and outside doors where secured for the night. The Major and Charles Mortlake were smoking and taking scotch in the Office. Nothing unusual there. The Professor and Mr. Hood where making their way up the main marble staircase, discussing their late game of billiards. Mrs. Brown, the housekeeper, and the servants were already upstairs, except Cook, dear Mrs. Stout.

The "Mrs." was a courtesy title due her rank and well-earned, as is frequently the case with that most essential of servants in large households. She had been unable to sleep and was making herself some hot milk when Mary went up the back stairs to the attic, which leads off the complex of rooms that make up the kitchen. I made a mental note to consult her privately later, just in case.

Miss Leigh and Mrs. Brown, the former technically his private secretary, were both rumored to be Mortlake's present and/or former mistresses.

As I have already intimated, I had reasons to believe there was once a David and Jonathan thing between Mortlake and the Major. I believe the physical aspect of the relationship was over, but how can one be sure? They certainly spent enough time together in the Office, about the grounds, and the estate. They might still share more than a taste for each other's company, for all I knew. But I think that on Mortlake's side at least, the unnatural part of their friendship had lost all appeal.

Adding to the mix of passions—old and recent, real and potential—I suspected Professor Lawless of having a developing affection for Miss Leigh, which may have been beginning to be reciprocated. Further, it wouldn't astonish me if the sensually greedy Mortlake had his eye on Lawless as a possible unnatural conquest ripe for the picking, and more to his taste than his fat, older friend.

Mr. Hood associate with Charles had something to do with nightclubs, I believe. As far as I was aware he at least had no sexual entanglements on the premises. He was also bald on top, constantly chomped on unlit

Havana cigars, and while fit was rather short and somewhat ugly. Though otherwise he was perfectly fine, if not exactly from the top-drawer, not that such things matter so much in foreigners, especially Americans.

That was how our investigations stood till well after lunch.

I did manage to get a private word with Cook in the afternoon. She did have something interesting to add, which solidified my suspicions. She thought she heard some loud talking from the inner hall as she was about to take her milk up to bed, about eleven-fifteen, she thought.

It must have been very loud indeed to penetrate both baize-lined doors. She thought it sounded like Mr. Charles' voice, but she couldn't be sure. She even went through the passage and poked her head out. She thought the heavy library oak door was just closing and that it cut off quieter conversation as it did so. She believed it was Mr. Charles still speaking. But as to whom he had been speaking, she was unable to testify. This solidified my suspicions.

There was one more odd—one might more aptly say theatrical—event before we handed the matter over to the police. Agnes found what the Major testified was Charles' missing pistol, complete with a spent cartridge, under Professor Lawless's pillow when turning down his bed and retrieving his pajamas.

Only Major Bly admitted to knowing where the gun was located. As he spent so much time in the Office in his bosom friend's company, it hardly would have been plausible to maintain his ignorance. Even one of his limited reasoning powers—I shudder for the poor men formerly under his command; too many of them were probably killed in action incompetently-led I suspect, as all too often happened—had the wit to see.

While I have said to be fair that even we ladies could not be exempt from suspicion, it would have been extremely difficult, nearly impossible, for any of us to have dragged him so far. Mr. Hood had no apparent motive, having concluded his business with Charles on mutually satisfactory terms and not being part of the household, a neighbor like myself, or otherwise an intimate. Professor Lawless, while friendly with Charles, seemed to like him for his library more than his person and any attraction for Miss Leigh had not progressed far.

I had long suspected Stephen Bly was developing an unsuitable, jealous possessiveness as these intense friendships between a man in his declining years and one somewhat younger often do. The increasing time and attentions Charles paid to Professor Lawless, over the renovations at first and then in leisure since, had aroused him to a bitter fury. From what I had observed he was already considerably put out, not to put too much emphasis on it, over the new, comely mistress distracting his best friend from himself. I too was a target of his jealous hostility to other friendships, even of a purely platonic nature. Lawless was too much.

He may also have feared a change in the provisions of the will to his detriment, as I believe he and Brown had been generously provided for.

One must not overlook the obvious; he was the last person seen alive with the dead man. He probably got Charles to accompany him to the library on the excuse of settling a dispute over the contents of the war novel that had been left on the table. The library was chosen in one juvenile attempt to associate Professor Lawless with the murder, as was the laughable ploy of placing the murder weapon clumsily under Lawless's pillow!

A real criminal even in a panic could do far better than that. Why not simply wipe the gun of fingerprints after unloading it and replace it and the ammunition in the drawers from which they had come?

—Letitia Parrot

Leigh's Web

Over morning tea in bed, I usually enjoy my chocolate digestive and think over what the day will bring. Typically a few letters and telephone calls to make for Charles, perhaps some filing and typing up his notes on some project or another. Mostly he deals with the estate manager in person, so I rarely have to call or correspond on that for him. I'm primarily involved with his private affairs and liaising a bit with his business secretary at the bank in London—mailing things off to her, screening his mail and answering begging letters, that sort of thing. It doesn't take me all day by a long chalk.

Not at all like the endless days at the casualty station near the front. When there was a battle on we'd work round the clock dealing with the most beastly things in a sort of numb practicality. We did the best we could with the doctors and orderlies and sisters, but often it wasn't enough, or the soldier would be maimed for life in some way—soul-destroying. I used to smoke a lot, even if people at home would think it fast. I used to dream of home and normality as some sort of unreal place. At times it seemed there had never been a period before the madness. I sort of drifted after the war at home, but found it dull.

Then I met Charles and he offered me this job when he moved down here. I'd taken typing and shorthand for something to do; some of my friends were doing it. Father thought he'd be able to get me a job in the Ministry of Works, where he's a clerk, and that would keep me out of mischief until Mr. Right came along.

Well, Charles wasn't Mr. Right. Of course, when he offered me the job I was a bit naive, despite the experience at the front. I thought it was a Godsend to save me from being under Father's eye all day. Not that I don't love Father. But to be under his watch from morning to night practically, six days a week and a good deal on Sundays was not exactly my idea of a jolly prospect.

I didn't know then that Charles, while he did want a secretary, also wanted my virtue. He made it clear from the start he had no intention of marrying, but that he'd see me well situated if we parted. I felt a bit like a bee caught in Charles's luxurious web. Not that I really had the energy or determination to break free -- at least not quite yet. But I knew that eventually, break free I must.

I resisted of course, but when you're thrown together with a handsomely distinguished, fit older man, who's filthy rich besides, and knows how to win a girl over, I'm afraid my mother's Victorian homilies weren't adequate protection for my maidenly virtue. It all seems so different after that hellish war with the amputations, the bellies torn open by machine guns, the gas—you just want to forget. And Charles helped me forget. I didn't love him or feel he was Mr. Right. I feel a bit shop soiled, but not hopelessly ruined. But when I'm ready, I still hope Mr. Right might come along despite my lapses. Charles and I have been fairly discreet, though you can't hide it from the servants and hence the village. I've had looks. But I don't think the grapevine will extend back to London. Charles rarely entertains—perhaps I should say entertained—people from town, except perhaps a few business associates and even if they knew, they'd hardly broadcast it to East Sheen where my friends and family mostly live. Of course the Major, his former commander and more or less permanent guest would likely know, and Lady Parrot—or Mrs. Parrot, as Letitia preferred it now that the baronetcy is extinguished.

I doubt Professor Lawless is really Mr. Right, but his attentions have certainly reminded that me there are other fish in the sea besides Charles. He is well set-up and sweet in a naive fashion, if rather poor. I don't think he's yet cottoned on to Charles and I. But if he does, I don't think he'd approve at all and there'd be a ruckus, so I hope to keep the dear man in the dark. He took me for a ride and a picnic on his motorcycle and it was rather fun. I rode in the sidecar. He'd also cajoled me once into the disused but immaculate ballroom and we'd danced to his hummed version of "Blue Danube." He proved a fine dancer—better than me I'm afraid—very light on his dainty feet, surprisingly small for one of his height. If it's one thing Patrick's fascinated with besides manuscripts, historical architecture, and Tudors and Stuarts, it's that "infernal machine," as the old fusspot of a Major calls it. If he doesn't have his nose in a book or his head down writing, he'll be out in the garage tinkering with it, loosening things with his spanner so he can clean this or that, putting in new parts or repairing the old, and talking shop with Jeffries about engines and such.

Charles has begun to notice and is watching me, hence I'm watching myself. It's nice to have someone nearer my own age—he's about seven years older than me—to talk to. And I shan't stay with Charles forever.

But that morning Agnes, the chambermaid, delivered stunning news with my tea and biscuit. Mary had found Charles dead near his desk in his Office. The french windows were open and letting in the storm that had us trapped here. The Aubusson carpet by the window was soaked. For some reason this detail seemed significant to her; I suppose as the servants will have to mop it up.

She said his head had been bashed in. There wouldn't be any more days here with Charles, nor anymore surreptitious nighttime meetings either. That in itself took getting used to, much less murder.

She also told me that Letitia had given instructions for the window to be closed—with a gloved or clean cloth-covered hand—and the door was to be closed and locked. With the phones out and us cut off from the mainland by the storm, there was little we could do. I imagined a tramp marooned with us, surprised by Charles, and reacting violently—for there was the window. And surely it couldn't be one of us, could it? I felt a delicious frisson of fear run up my spine.

I hoped the police wouldn't fix on Jeffries. I rather liked the gruff ex-serviceman and felt sure he wasn't a murderer. But then how do you tell a killer from the rest? I glanced at the latest Peter Wimsey book on my nightstand, and felt like I had stepped into one of Miss Sayers' stories. Only would anyone play Lord Peter?

It seemed Letitia, in her practical, civilized fashion had decreed we would examine the crime scene only after breakfast.

At breakfast, I felt there was a certain constraint on conversation and I noticed Professor Lawless didn't eat very much and looked grave. He had been a Lieutenant in the war but had mainly been a paper-pusher, or so he claimed. With my practical nursing experiences, corpses in general didn't bother me, though someone you've been so close to was a bit of a different proposition. Still I ate my usual toast and marmalade without a queasy tummy. I noticed the Major scoffed his generous repast as usual. Letitia and Charles's American associate, Mr. Hood, ate sparingly but not abnormally so. I noticed Brown's hand was shaking as she helped Mary serve. She was Charles's former mistress in London. But she'd let herself go a bit, and her looks had faded, poor woman. Unlike me, I think, he let her assume they would marry eventually. It must be very difficult for her, but she didn't show me any particular displeasure, except being icily formal. She hid her East End accent well mostly, but sometimes when she got mad at the servants she sounded like a fishwife right out of Billingsgate Market. No "h"s to be heard and the complete Cockney dialect.

After breakfast we went to the office, Brown and Mary included. The old Major tried to take charge. He typically did in Charles's absence. Letitia ignored him and no one else paid much attention. Besides, Letitia had the keys to the office making quite a bulge in her right hand jacket pocket. She'd had Brown and Mary collect them. Even Brown generally obeys her. She seems more jealous of the Major than of me—he spends more time with Charles than either of us. I can't see the basis of the friendship myself, but I assume it's one of these wartime things mere women aren't meant to understand, even those of us who were near the front too.

Outside the Office door Letitia warned us not to touch or move anything. I almost felt like saying that we read detective books too, but restrained myself. I'm not up to Letitia's caliber. Come to think of it, I think the Major only reads war-like adventure stories, and while I know Patrick Lawless did read Chesterton, Christie, Doyle, and so forth, I had no idea about Hood, Brown, or Mary. Though Hood looked the sort who might be mixed up with the mob at home and might know American police firsthand. Especially as he runs speak-easies and the Americans have something rather idealistic called Prohibition on, or so I read in the papers. Touchingly naive of them, really. I believe Hood comes from Chicago.

Letitia unlocked and opened the door with a handkerchief-covered hand, stepped inside and we all followed. She asked me—as our closest thing to a medical professional on hand—to look at the wound. I crouched down by the body and examined it. Charles was lying on his front with his back to the french window, which had been open, letting the rain gusts soak the blue velvet curtains. Fortunately as the room was cold, I had on a thick red jumper over my yellow blouse and red skirt. I concentrated on the skull. It looked a bit like some cases I'd seen where a trench had collapsed and the beams had caught some chap on the head, except the area involved seemed smaller. There wasn't much blood, but while the room was cold, it wasn't cold enough to prevent the flies starting at the wound. I shuddered a little but got a grip on myself and informed the others of the obvious: trauma from a blunt instrument. Then I straightened up, glad to put a little more distance between myself and the corpse, as I forced myself to think of him. I'd seen many before, but few I knew well.

"So someone bashed his brains in," said Hood around his usual unlit cigar. "Would this do the job?" he asked me, removing the damp tobacco roll from his mouth briefly and pointing with it at a heavy metal lighter on the desk.

Letitia got out her handkerchief again, approached the desk, picked up the heavy cylinder and examined it minutely through her pince-nez. "I cannot see any traces of blood, hair, or skin, though it could have been wiped clean," she announced. Then she brought it back to the body; we both crouched down and compared it to the wound. The others looked down at us. I think Patrick was somewhat embarrassed at the ladies dealing with such things, for he seemed uncomfortable. Sweet, don't you think? Perhaps, I thought, he might be Mr. Right after all. One could do worse.

"No," I said slowly, "I think it was something wider and flatter." Letitia nodded her head decisively in agreement. We got up and she returned the lighter to its place. We went through the same performance with candlesticks, with like result. Then the Major drew our attention to the fact that a deep drawer in the desk was only partly closed, and opened it with his handkerchief to reveal a battered, empty cash box. The Major, puffing himself up with self-importance, confirmed that it was where Charles kept some ready cash for small local tradesmen's accounts, servant's wages, and so forth. I confirmed this and added that he motored over to Devizeston and drew a hundred pounds or so for it and his incidental expenses from the bank once every few weeks. Larger accounts he paid by cheque. He gave out the wages personally so all the staff was aware of its location. He also gave Brown the cash housekeeping money from it.

The Major uttered something indignant about vagabonds. Or he may have said gypsies. I wasn't really paying him much attention—people don't—until Letitia asked him if anything else was disturbed. He calmed down a little, though I noticed his fists were balled, and he'd taken on an alarming reddish color. He examined the desktop and opened the drawer—Letitia was unable to catch him in time to prevent him leaving fingerprints. But I think he made pretty free with Charles's desk anyway, so it probably didn't matter. He said he didn't really think so and expressed the opinion that it was either an outsider seizing the chance when Charles opened the window to take a breath of air, or perhaps one of the servants. I noticed Mary looking daggers at his back for this, and I couldn't blame her.

Letitia next drew our attention to the carpet. There didn't seem to be any real stain anywhere on the carpet from footprints, even near the open window. She didn't confine herself to the vicinity of the body or the path between it and the doors, but all over. All she found was a slight smudge of dirt near the entrance to the so-called secret passage. Of course everyone in the district knew of it. Some probably even knew which rooms it connected, but only Charles or his guests—and Brown and the restoration workers he had down from London—probably knew precisely how the mechanisms were activated. Some of the servants might know too.

Admittedly, even if there had been an intruder, there was a path of grass outside between the two flower beds on either side, but shoes do get mucky when the ground is sodden. She and I stuck our heads out too. There wasn't anything in the flowerbeds as far as we could see. If someone had stood outside either of the other windows trying to shelter while waiting for Charles to go to bed so he could break in, he'd left no footmarks. Letitia popped her head out the window on the shorter wall and couldn't see any in the beds there either. But he could have stood on the sodden turf. Letitia stepped out and took a few steps. Once she returned you could see her path. But how long would they have lasted was the question? She wiped her feet and on the sodden mat near the door, and it did seem to leave a greenish discoloration.

Letitia closed the french window again —she'd closed the one on the other wall once she withdrew her head, of course. She suggested we retire to the library and get everyone's movements of the night before straight. She was last out, locked the door behind her and pocketed the key, saying the police would want things as undisturbed as possible. The Major, muttering about high-handed females wearing the trousers, had removed his essential pipe, magazines, and other chattels under Letitia's considering eye.

Lady Parrot—or perhaps I should say Sherlock, with me as Dr. Watson? —interrogated Mary first as she was responsible for locking up, turning off lights and so on at night. She started her rounds about quarter to ten and finished twenty to thirty minutes later after having checked all the ground-floor windows and doors. In the morning she reversed the order of her rounds, opening curtains, unlocking appropriate doors and windows, and laying fires where they were wanted. Some nights a request for something from Charles or someone else might delay her. But the previous evening she reckoned she finished in about twenty-five minutes, about eleven-fifteen by the kitchen clock. She always started with the ballroom (rarely used), and worked her way round to finish in the scullery, pantry, and kitchen.

Mr. Hood was just leaving the games room with Patrick as she went in just before eleven. She recalled them wishing her goodnight. As Letitia had retired about ten, Patrick was dragged off reluctantly by the "pool" fanatic American for a game just before, and Charles and the Major had taken themselves off to the Office about nine-thirty. I went up about ten minutes or so later and read some of my Peter Wimsey novel in bed before I went to sleep at about eleven-fifteen. Brown reported going up after asking Charles if there were any further instructions for the staff, about ten.

The Major, who was present, confirmed this and Letitia had seen her following her up the main stairs. Brown had a bed/sitting room like me on the first floor, though I believe it was smaller; the fine gradations of status: secretary/current mistress superior quarters to housekeeper/former mistress. Though for all I know, Charles may have used her intimate services still occasionally for old times' sake or on a whim. I wouldn't put it past him. I doubt he had any concept of monogamy even serially, nor would he even if he were to marry.

The Major reported saying goodnight to Charles and leaving the Office about half-eleven.

There was no one in the kitchen and related back premises. She didn't check Brown's cubbyhole of an office, as its walls were all interior and its only exit was to the passage between the kitchen and the inner hall opposite the dining room. She remembered it was dark as usual under the door. Not one to burn the midnight oil perfecting the household accounts, our Brown!

Mary and Brown were dismissed to their duties.

Later in the morning, however, we were all in the sitting room and Letitia indicated that I was to follow her, without making it generally known. I made some excuse and left the room a few minutes after she had supposedly gone off to her room to write—whether letters or an account of our investigations was left vague.

I found her in front of the stair by the dining room in low-voiced colloquy with Mary. Once I came up to them Mary led us along to and through the two green baize doors into the kitchen. Mrs. Brown was apparently in her office with the door closed as the light was on, and apparently didn't notice anything unusual—Letitia had enjoined me to silence until we were safely in Mrs.

Stout's kitchen, so we did not have to deal with her curiosity.

In the kitchen she received a reciprocated warm greeting full of the familiarity between a skilled and faithful servant to her long-time mistress from Mrs. Stout, and a shy muttered greeting from Agnes, who was peeling potatoes for some luncheon concoction. We had to share a cup of tea with her, prepared by Agnes and with Mary and even Agnes, permitted by the kitchen's queen to partake. We had quite a delicious slice of Angel cake to complete the elevenses. Over the snack, Letitia delivered her skillful brand of authoritative reassurance. As always I was fascinated by her technique. I could never do it half so well, but there again I was not nor never would be gentry, much less the Manor's Chatelaine in its Edwardian late summer. Though in reality I was getting to be a fair little actress and mimic during my employment at the Manor, I still felt more comfortable with the servants than the toffs.

Cook also related at Letitia's request an exciting development for my benefit. Jeffries had reported over breakfast that he woke during the night and thought someone might have been in the garage below his quarters, which was left unlocked. By the time he pulled on his trousers, stuck his feet in his boots, grabbed a poker and descended however, the intruder, if any, had departed. Nothing appeared out of place or missing as far as he could tell, so he concluded he was dreaming, until learning of the "muddy mat" (whatever that meant) and the murder. He recalled one other detail. There was water on the flag-stoned floor and what might have been wet footprints, but he thought at the time that they were his from his last check on the generator, housed in an adjacent drafty outbuilding about eleven. They seem to be taking a long time to dry, but things did with the storm and all. So he went back to bed, reassured. Cook and Mary had decided to have Agnes tell Lady Parrot of this "quite-like" with her morning tea and news of the killing.

After this surprising development, Letitia borrowed an electric torch from Cook, fetched from a cupboard in which I glimpsed emergency candles and bandages and the other accouterments of a First Aid kit. Mary then led us into the scullery. Mornings she reversed her evening clockwise progress, proceeding from the kitchen quarters to the ballroom. She related how she had found mud that hadn't been there last night on the bristle doormat by the door to the walled kitchen garden. It was only then that I realized the import of Cook's reference to "the muddy mat" in telling Jeffries' tale. It had still been wet, as had the area between it and the nearby coat pegs to some degree where the Mackintosh Gladys used in inclement weather hung. This too was found to be slightly wet. A kitchen towel was missing and presumably had been used to inexpertly dry and clean up the floor in vicinity, and perhaps shoes. And yet the door was properly bolted.

Gladys would normally have been assigned to clean up the mess, but she hadn't finished her more urgent morning duties before Mary raised the alarm about Charles. Cook and Mary then put their heads together and had the foresight to re-bolt the door and decreed the mud should remain in place. Gladys was told to use the other scullery door to retrieve herbs, the one Jeffries usually came through for his meals, as it was outside the kitchen garden's walls and opened directly onto the stable yard.

I only recalled when Letitia pointed it out that this scullery door was very close to the entrance to the secret passage connecting the kitchen quarters and the Office. Patrick, the expert, had personally made a point of showing me all the entrances, with Charles's permission, and telling me more than I really wanted to know about them and their one-time use as priest-holes. I had not, however, ventured inside, despite his urging, but merely peered doubtfully in.

Letitia pushed on a carved section of beam that ran from floor to ceiling, and the restored mechanism smoothly opened the entrance. She put on the torch and shone it slowly over the dusty floor. The passage was deep with a film of dust. There were older footprints, now partly filled in by new accumulations and barely visible in the electric light. But there were also fresh footprints of a smaller man's shoe by the shape and size, Letitia opined, going one way only: away from us. Letitia then reversed the mechanism and closed the door and asked Mary to reseal the door right away.

She then suggested we brave the weather and visit Jeffries' lair. With that we concluded our investigation more or less. A few days later, the police were very pleased with Letitia for having the case laid out so well for them. Her friend, the Chief Constable, came personally to oversee the arrest and documentation of the evidence.

Sadly, it seemed Patrick had learned of Charles and I and in a fit of jealousy and outrage, had determined to make him pay for taking advantage of my position. He was even more old-fashioned in his attitudes than I had imagined. Perhaps it was his fascination with the Tudor, civil war, and Stuart periods. He took the heavy spanner—or wrench as Mr. Hood put it—from his motorcycle maintenance tool kit inside. After the servants and all but Charles were in bed, he sneaked down to the kitchen in old clothes, entered the passage in the scullery, closing the door behind him. He then surprised Charles in the Office, probably putting him at ease by pretending to have a new theory he just had to check out before sleep would come. Then he took the spanner out of his pocket when Charles's back was turned and killed him. He left by the french window—leaving it open to suggest a robbery—after cleaning his spanner as best he could on a rag he brought from the garage supply. He forced the cash box and later retrieved Agnes's Mackintosh in the passage before restoring it to its peg in the scullery on his retreat . He'd then returned the spanner to its proper place, waking Jeffries, but leaving soon enough to avoid detection. Then he'd returned via the scullery door he'd unbolted. After taking his shoes off, he got a kitchen towel to clean them and the floor. There were traces of blood on his spanner, his soiled clothes were found in his closet (which Agnes searched on Letitia's orders), as was the kitchen towel. The money was in the jacket pocket. His small feet I'd noted while we danced had given him away too, as had his known-fondness for me and for tinkering with the motorcycle. It was really quite sad. The press coverage of the case revealed me as a loose woman too. I had been well and truly caught in Charles's web.

—Grace Leigh

Brown's Case

Me, I first heard about it from Georges, Charlie's French "valet".

The storm that kept the mainland isolated from our lovely selves, still threw buckets of rain against the windows practically non-stop! A lively house party we're not, least if you believe me. The widow Lady Parrot who sold this drafty pile to Charles; the old windbag of a major who lives with us; Professor Lawless, who could talk your ear off if 'e gets going on history; little Miss Leigh, Charlie's new squeeze for delicate occasions, technical-like his "personal secretary"; and the sinister, sexy American Mr. Hood, who's doing some business with me Charlie. I could fancy him, despite 'is face. Baldy toughs turn me on. But Charlie would give me 'ell for making up to someone else, despite 'is declining interest in me body. Possessive he is.

Since the War Captain Charlie Mortlake's been taken on more of the la-di-da airs of the toffs, he has. Not that he weren't always one, with 'is family money, but before the War he liked 'is bit of fun and plenty of cuddle with Music Hall *artistes* like me. That's how I first met 'im. I had an act on the circuit. We met backstage in Cheltenham. The Halls had a good class of clientele then, we did. And I was good looking in a busty sort of way. Charlie especially liked me bosoms.

Any'ow he picked me up and we started by going to dance palaces and some of them high class night clubs. Often used to end up in me sack, did Champagne Charlie as some of the girls called 'im. I wasn't the first, and I knew there'd not be much hope of me being last neither, but he bought me plenty of fancy clothes and meals and trinkets.

Took such a shine to me, 'e did, that he made me 'is lady "house keeper" when he set up a place of his own in the West End separate from his folks. They didn't know anything about me personal relationship with Charlie. They just knew he was a caution for sowing 'is wild oats and assumed he'd get over it and settle down. I didn't have that much to do really, the maids and cook did the real work. I just told 'em what to do, and had a talking to them when they let things slide. I was really there to keep Charlie entertained at night and in bed. We still went around to the clubs and the Halls. He was tireless in bed. Many a time I'd 'ave liked to knock off after the first time or two. I'd even think I'd got my wish. Then soon as I was asleep it seemed, he'd shake me awake and go at it again. Did make a girl sore sometimes, but I knew what side me bread was buttered on, and I never complained. Though he could be a bit rough sometimes. I just put on makeup to disguise anything showing and soldiered on.

Speaking of soldiering, Charlie got patriotic, he did, at the start of the Great War. He was ten or fifteen years older than me, though still a fine looking man, and with his folks rolling in it, he could have easily opted out, or got a cushy paper shuffling "military" job to avoid the White Feather crowd who shamed many a man to join up and die like an animal in them mud fields between them there trenches. But he went full out for a commission. And by and large what Charlie wanted he got, though his parents would have preferred the paper pushing for their only son and heir, they didn't feel right standing in his way.

So Charlie went to war. He was wounded a few times, but nothing serious. He kept up the house in the City and kept me on for his home leave. He did well too. And I don't think it was just the Major being his mate to say the least. The Major didn't look too bad back then and wasn't fat like now. Charlie used to have him stay when they were both on leave. A time or two he had me in bed with the Major and him in his big four-poster. Didn't much enjoy that. The Major seems to like being spanked. And Charlie liked to oblige. 'E was a bit rougher with me too, and I was getting tired of it, to tell you the truth. Natural fun 'tween a man and a woman is one thing. I don't like being a spoil-sport, but I didn't want to be mixed up with that stuff they liked. No threesomes. Cost me a tooth or two when I told Charlie. But I was still young then and had me looks. And perhaps he was really attached to me, or he liked keeping control of 'is toys. Either way he kept me on and used me like before the War. Only he played rough more often. It stopped being much fun for me as you can guess.

After the War, the Major more or less started living with Charlie as a companion. He had a place of 'is own at first, a cottage in Kent somewhere. But you'd not know it for the time he spent there. Charlie and he were thick as thieves all hours.

I think it was the Major, who put the idea in his head to buy this godforsaken place and play Lord of the Manor.

The idea of violence started exciting Charlie. Like I said he liked the rough stuff before the War. I got the feeling the War gave him the same lift like. Oh he doesn't let on he still sleeps with me as well as the new middle class "secretary" bird he seduced. Don't think he's been rough with her much. Haven't been any signs, except maybe just recently. She's sometimes had a lot of makeup on and she don't usual wear none. He's been keeping that for me and his other old pals. The Major with his loony investments relies on him to keep him ahead of the Baillifs. Charlie knows we're trapped well and truly. Promises us both annuities if we're still with him when he dies. Good bet for me; maybe not so much for the old Major. But I reckon Major Bly never grew up and can't see he'll likely die before Charlie. Maybe Charlie has little Miss Leigh caught now too. Maybe she'd be afraid to go back to her folks in East Sheen, a fallen woman in substance if not in name! Not that since the War a lot of the girls are doing it without benefit of clergy as they say. I suspect Charlie's as tired of the Major as of me. The old geezer's putting on weight like billy-oh and my bottom's getting as big as me bosom and neither's firm anymore!

I also suspect Charlie boy wants to pick up Professor Lawless. 'E's treating him very nice like he does before seducing someone. Not sure if he's tried it on yet, or if toffy nosed bloke will stand for it. But in me time in the Music Hall I used to see a lot of it amongst lads down from Oxbridge, so maybe Charlie has a chance. He has an eye for vulnerability, he does!

Enough reminiscing! Georges, the frog valet, knocked on me door just as I was finished dressing after me bath. I have a private bath *en suite* as the Frenchies say, like Charlie, Leigh and the Major. Charlie spent a load of money getting this dump comfy.

I asked Georges what it's about. He said Charlie ain't slept in his bed or changed from his evening duds. I said maybe 'e's slept on the sofa in the Office? He sometimes stays up all night, does Charlie. Monsieur Georges said no, he'd asked Mary. She's the parlour maid and opens all the curtains, lays the fires, unlocks any doors and windows that need it, and does the reverse about eleven at night. Not a hide nor hair of him seen, she tells Monsieur, who kind of fancies her despite her horse face and starch. Though he told me she'd found the french window in the Orangerie open and the wind blowing and rain blowing in onto that marble floor so she had to mop up. She swears it was shut last night, so maybe he went for a tramp. But Charlie hardly goes near the Orangerie so why didn't 'e go out from 'is Office or somewhere else he uses?

Maybe he's gone for a walk, I says, like to clear his head, if he's been up all night. Might have taken his latchkey. I don't think she bolts the big front door. Not much crime around these parts, not like London no how.

I told Georges to put Jeffries looking about the gardens and walks. Help him yourself if your so concerned, I added. He took himself off.

I wasn't as confident about it as I made it seem. I thought I'd let the old Dragon, Lady Parrot, know about it. She prefers to use Mrs. as the inheritable knighthood died off like the dodo with her hubby. Seems her boys were killed in the War and there was no one else to inherit. All the servants, except Monsieur Georges and Jeffries — the chauffeur-mechanic — were hangovers from her days, all from the village or near about. They worship the ground she steps on and constantly say "milady" this and "milady" that and "Lady" the other so often, I picked up the habit. She can be a bit of an old tartar, a bit like the Dowager Duchess parts in some shows I was in as an *artiste*. For all that she knows what's what and notices more than you'd think.

I went to her room to consult her. The Chamber Maid, Agnes, had already had retailed the gossip when she brought the morning tea. She didn't seem surprised, though concerned. Suggested that Monsieur Georges should help Jeffries search the grounds and expressed the hope he hadn't ventured too near the cliffs bordering the headland the grounds were on. "The winds there can be so strong during a storm that if you are caught by a gust in the wrong direction it can actually overbalance you. And if one was walking the path along the cliff..." She spoke more to herself than to me, thinking aloud like. "Well I certainly would advise against it in the strongest of terms under these conditions to anyone who asked me. You may recall my warning to Charles about it?" she said.

"Yes, ma'am, I believe I do," I said slowly, feeling alarmed more than reassured. I recalled that the Orangerie door was closest to the cliff path. That corner the house was southwest-facing. In good weather it got the sun; in bad it got the worst of the winds. "You don't really think ma'am that Charlie — Mr. Charles has fallen over the cliff!"

"Very likely not," she admitted, "but I believe he had been drinking heavily when I encountered him by the stairs near midnight. Not truly drunk but near it. I deliberately stayed up until the Major retired to talk out that err ... little matter we spoke of yesterday."

"Yes ma'am" It hadn't been such a little matter. Charlie'd got soused and tried to feel Agnes up. She went to the dowager and the old lady had Mary summon me to her room for a council of war. She told me all the inside servants, except maybe Georges, were ready to leave and such behaviour fully justified it. She explained that I must know this was hardly a respectable house as it was and they'd almost left when they'd figured out about me and little Leigh and Charlie. They didn't suspect anything with the Major or else, she couldn't have restrained them. She agreed with me Charlie had designs on Lawless. She had counseled them to stay as long as Charlie's escapades were in private and didn't extend to one of their number.

She herself would have supported an earlier exodus, she explained, except out of sentimental attachment to access to her old home and gratitude to Charles for taking the place off her hands at a good price. She could easily find the servants decent places. Except perhaps Gladys, she said, and she could manage to employ her if necessary. Gladys was slow as they say.

"Once Charles realized what I wanted to talk to him about, we were near the Orangerie and so I suggested we go in there in case someone was near enough the top of the stairs to overhear.

"It was there I told him that if any such incident was repeated I would no longer use my influence with the servants to restraint their departure. As it was I felt I'd have to find a place for Agnes. And if it happened again I would no longer keep quiet about his shocking behaviour. He took it better than I expected, especially as he was inebriated. I left him there after he agreed to not interfere with the servants again."

This didn't seem like Charlie, not when he'd been drinking. He'd usually "belt" an interfering dame as the doughboys used to say. I'd plenty of bruises since the war to show it. And I suspect little Leigh was starting to get the treatment sometimes. There again he knew the Lady weren't in his power. Plus she was friendly with anyone who was anyone in Devizesshire and knew quite a few people in London besides. His goings on with the Major at least could be a matter for the coppers or a scandal, of course. Maybe he was afraid of her. Yes, that could've been it.

And if she'd left him there it explained why 'e used the Orangerie door.

Once I'd left her ladyship, I passed on her order to Georges, who went along with it. My head was whirling. I couldn't stop thinking about it as I went down stairs, through the baize door, consulted with Cook over the day's menus, and then went to me office. Maybe Charlie had really been more drunk than she thought and did fall off the ruddy cliff. Could've stormed out the nearest door to walk off his fury and had an accident. Maybe he broke an ankle or hit his head and was lying out there somewhere in the wet.

I couldn't settle to nothing. I decided to take a look at the Orangerie meself. And maybe outside too. Pity Mary cleared up. I grabbed a Mac from the pegs near the scullery door and told Cook what I was about while I was at it.

Then with the raincoat over me arm, I passed through the inner baize door and practically collided with Mary going the other way. I stopped her and asked some questions about the Orangerie.

"Well," says she, "There was water all over the floor near the french door. The doormat was soaked. After I'd closed the door, I draped it over the edge of one of the beds to dry out some. Then I went for the mop and some rags from the broom closet." This was under the back stair. "Funny thing though, there weren't any rags. But I could swear there was plenty yesterday. Maybe Agnes or Gladys had a need for them. Anyway I took the mop and bucket and cleaned up. Put me back a good twenty minutes, it did."

"Was there anything else but water on the floor?" I asked.

"Some dirt and leaves and twigs. Likely blown by the wind. Nothing else I remember."

I thanked her, went through the hall and entered the Orangerie. As I closed the door behind me, I noticed there was a slot empty in the tool rack along the wall. And a trowel was only half in its place, as if it'd been put back in haste. I was passing the raised plant beds when I noticed one near the french window. About the base of a rubber tree the earth was loose. Like someone — Lady Parrot likely as she mostly saw to things in there even though she lives across the causeway when not stranded — had been turning it over with that trowel for some reason. Didn't look like the rest of the soil. It also looked wetter. I also noticed there was sap oozing from a rubber plant where a leaf looked like being cut off, though it was crusting over scab-like. A bit like coagulating blood only the wrong colour. Somehow that idea disturbed me with Charlie being missing. It was making me all fanciful. Suddenly I was sure Charlie was dead. I don't know why. It gave me the shivers. But I pulled meself together and walked towards them glass doors.

When I reached them, I pulled on the Mac and tied the rain cap under me chin. I opened the french window and stepped out. Closing it behind me was quite a pull against the wind, but the storm wasn't as bad as it'd been so I hoped if Charlie were injured we could get a doctor to him soon. The rain came down in buckets, but not lashing in your face no more. The wind was steady off the sea, not gusting any which way.

As I turned away from the door, I saw the rose bed to left had been dug up a bit. I wondered if there were badgers or something about after insects or worms or some such. Maybe moles? I wasn't paying much attention. I can't tell you why it stuck in my head. Shock I guess. You just focus on little things.

The paths were covered with gravel and pretty well packed down. There were a few small puddles here and there where footfalls had a few hollows. In one or two patches a rivulet of rain had washed aside the surface. I've seen it happen before with these storms. The gardeners have to check the paths add more gravel from a wheelbarrow and use a roller to make it good afterwards. It happens in the same places mostly. In one place it was muddy, but the rain was slowing now and the water flow had lessened. I noticed a single tire imprint, something like a wheelbarrow. Maybe Jeffries had used one since the storm began, though he usually left that work to the jobbing gardeners from the village. And they hadn't been able to come since the storm hit.

I met Jeffries near where the path started to go along the cliff's edge. He was standing by the edge and looking at a bush. Some branches and leaves were torn off. Like someone had tried to hold on, but hadn't succeeded. I looked at the ground and saw Charlie's gold lighter under the bush. As if it had fallen out of 'is dinner jacket pocket.

Me and Jeffries looked at one another. If Charlie had gone over there his body would have hit the rocks. I've heard the current is something fierce. I remember Lady Parrot telling folks that even if a body by some miracle survived the fall, unless it had been wedged in the rocks it would be taken out to sea. It might be weeks or months, but it would eventually wash up somewhere along the coast nearby bloated and much worse for wear. Not always. A shark or something might take a fancy to it when it was fresh meat and not leave enough, she'd added.

I thought of Charlie being a shark's breakfast, or washing up unrecognizable on some slab of rock. Maybe it was for the best. He was getting pretty testy and violent. But I remembered the good times and began to blubber. Jeffries awkwardly put 'is arm about me shoulder and took me back to the house. Usually I'd have not allowed familiarity from the servants, but Jeffries is a bit different. We'd been together at the London house just after the War, I fancied 'im, and besides I was too shocked to care.

I pulled meself together, changed me wet duds and reported the finds to Lady Parrot and the rest of the party at breakfast. They were suitably shocked.

Later in the day Lady Parrot was back in the Orangerie gardening, it seems, 'cause she made a fuss about the pruning knife being missing. Had anyone seen it, she asked, at luncheon. I couldn't care less meself at a time like this. There again gardening was 'er passion and who knows what was going on behind that stiff upper lip. Old ladies don't like their habits disturbed. Least me aunts and mom don't. Not that the lady's that old, probably only sixty, I'd say, and 'earty for it.

Charlie's body was washed up two weeks later. Crabs had been at the face and neck something horrible they said at the inquest, but 'is dentist was able to tell. I'll say one thing for old Champagne Charlie, 'e kept 'is word about the annuity, so I don't 'ave to find no work. The Major, nor Leigh neither.

Meself, I was uneasy like about Charlie's death all along. 'Twas only later like, I begun to put two and two together. I think he were killed.

Lady Parrot, she was the last to see 'im alive. Something don't sound quite right about her account of her little talk with Charlie-boy about Agnes. It didn't sound like 'im, taking it like a lamb, least not when 'e was soused. 'E always had a foul temper when he was crossed then, specially by a dame. He'd've yelled at 'er like the devil hisself, maybe even pushed 'er around, forgetting like how important she is down in this here part of the sticks.

And if he'd really frightened 'er, she may've grabbed that pruning knife to defend herself. That'd really get 'im going. Charlie, he could never stand being stood up to by a woman, 'specially when tipsy. She'd'ave to use the knife or take a horrid beating — believe me I know me Charlie!

I suspect 'e fell on the plant bed near that rubber plant. Maybe she got him in the neck or some vital spot and 'e up and died on her. That'd explain the broken leaf. I think most of the blood spilled on the earth there, and she covered it up with dirt from the flower bed outside. That'd explain the raked up look of the earth in the bed and the digging outside.

It'd also make sense of the barrow wheel mark on the path to the cliff, when the gardeners hadn't been around for days. There's nothing much for them to do near the cliff no how. No beds or nothing like. Just some trees and bushes and some grass, which they don't scythe like the lawn near the house. I think she cleaned up, got 'im in a wheel barrow from the gardening shed and wheeled him to the cliff and rolled him over.

But why? It'd have been self-defence. She'd not even be charged more than likely, being a friend of the Chief Constable and all the local toffs. She'd be believed. And the servants would back her no matter what...

It makes me wonder if she didn't have help disposing of the body. Even Jeffries and Monsieur G. got to like her. I sort of did meself. But I think she probably did it herself. She wouldn't endanger others if she could help it. And for her age she's very fit, not that she's more than fifteen or twenty years older than me. Especial if all she had to do was roll 'im off the bed into the barrow and get him in proper like. I think it'd be a stretch, but she's got gumption and stamina.

She'll have torn the branch and planted the lighter to make it look like 'e fell while walking and tried to save hisself by catching at the bush. Then she'll have put the wheelbarrow away. What blood the rain didn't wash off wouldn't show. I had seen the gardeners using them barrows. They're dirty and rusty and ain't been cleaned in years. Bloodstains would look like rust and wear off soon, especial if she rubbed some more earth from the rose bed over it. Likely she used the barrow to take the dirt inside.

She had cleaned up any blood inside. She knows where everything like rags and mops is kept. Then she'd leave the door open to suggest someone went out, and Bob's your uncle, it seems like "Accidental Death" like the Coroner's jury found.

I've been thinking hard. She likely covered it up 'cause it would be in all the papers and be a scandal like. And Agnes would 'ave to tell about the groping. In places like this it might be a big deal, shameful like for her. Maybe hurt 'er chances of getting a husband. You never can tell in the sticks. They're funny like. Not sensible like Londoners where they don't care if a girl's been round a bit as long as she's been discreet and not in the family way or nothing. In town a master hugging a maid and stroking her like, would be "bad form" like the toffs say on 'is part, but nothing against 'er. Especially if she made a fuss and left over it.

I don't miss the rough stuff. Not one bit. But when 'e wanted to, Charlie could be charming, like he were a prince in a fairy tale and me a princess. He was like that a lot at first. Like I say it was mainly the War that brought out the devil in him.

I'm glad to be back in London. I have no proof. No one would listen to me, a woman they think of as a tramp down there. Anyway, like I say, I think it was self-defence knowing me Charlie. And I don't blame her for it. Sometimes after a beating, I felt like topping 'im meself.

So long, Champagne Charlie! I miss the good times.

— Hettie Brown

Lawless's Turn

I was cataloguing books in the library. Lady Parrot came in and started rooting around. Apparently she could not find the volume she was looking for.

"Can I help?" I offered, feeling that the sooner she found what she wanted, the sooner I would be left in peace.

"Not unless you know where the Shakespeare Folio is. I want to look up something."

This was tiresome. She would blame me for its absence, though in some sense I couldn't help it. "I'm afraid it's in London with several of the other rarer items. When I drew Charles' attention to some of the things he had, one felt the insurers would insist on it."

"What other items are in London?" she said. I wasn't sure if she was just interested, or realizing she should have kept them or sold them herself and not let them go with the property. I understand she had been forced to sell off most of the plate and the good pictures before Charles purchased the place and most chattels in it. She hadn't yet got to the books. They'd probably been the last to go as she was a reader, knew the collection well, and was fond of it. She may not have even realized the value of the choicer pieces, poor dear! Though in most things you couldn't get anything past her, the library collection was so much a part of the house to her that she may not have even considered its monetary potential. Besides the renovated lodge where she now resided, while spacious for herself and her maid and cook, could not have adequately housed the whole collection. Still, she could have kept or sold the Folio.

"Well, let me think. Quite a few things really," I gestured indicating ten or twelve empty spaces. "The first of Johnson's Dictionary and of Boswell, the Pepys, the

Pope, the Milton, the Blake, the Wordsworth, and perhaps half a dozen or so others. I could copy you out the list."

"Is Charles intending to sell them?" she asked, a martial gleam appearing in her eye.

"Oh no! Not at all!" I improvised, not wanting to cause premature trouble. Besides, they hadn't been sold yet. Things were still in the pricing and consideration stage, proceeding cautiously. "It's just the insurers fussing. And rightly so, dear Letitia, rightly so! You had some quite rare and sought after works here. Some are only of scholarly interest, like the Reverend Doctor Pennwith's *History of Devizesshire and Surrounding Parts*—early eighteenth century, very useful to me in my researches, a real gem, but of modest financial value."

"Oh good," said she, apparently reassured. One could never quite tell what was going on behind that stiff upper-lipped countenance.

"I've persuaded Grace Leigh to go for a walk before we change for supper. She's been cooped up in this house too much with the storm. I'm quite in need of some exercise too. Want to come along?" I said with an appearance of indifference. I'd of course rather have Grace to myself.

"No, I think not," said the dowager Lady Parrot, "I'll leave you young people to your private business." With this Parthian shot she left the room. So she had noticed our attachment despite precautions. Perhaps it was inevitable with an experienced matron. But I believed Charles was still in the dark. And the Major too, or else Charles would know one way or another from that old fool, whether my suspicions of the nature of their relationship were true or not. So-called "public" schools and the military do seem prone to bring out such dual tastes. I attended a state grammar school myself.

Truth be told, Grace had fallen for me pretty hard, and like any youngish swain, I wanted to maintain her devotion.

Besides, she could type. Very useful to an academic without private means. Being appointed to the Hanshaw Chair in Early Modern History was quite a feather in my cap for one so young, but its financial benefits were pretty thin. Genteel poverty really. That's why all this consulting work with Charles in between terms has been so useful.

And of course without it I wouldn't have met—how shall I put it?—my soul-mate. Yes that's *le mot juste*. The work had been useful to my research for my latest book too. And Grace and I had plans for our outing, of course, besides some routine ambulatory exercise. There were of course a number of outbuildings. I hoped to finalize things, especially with this new development.

I had long suspected Charles of ungentlemanly conduct towards one in Grace's difficult position. But only in recent weeks had we become on such terms that I learned that not only was that true, but that Charles had started abusing her in non-sexual ways. Not seriously so far. He was always contrite, even claimed accident, but then I hear it always starts that way with that sort. And then there is Brown's attitude towards Grace; almost sympathy perhaps? Strange for a former mistress for the latest one, unless this behavior in not the first instance.

Naturally, I longed to confront him directly. But financial prudence led us to more careful plans. We had married quietly, when she last visited her parents in East Sheen. She had prepared the way in her letters, and they were pleased. If necessary, she would send a regretful letter of resignation, on the excuse of parental pressure to join her father's office on her next trip to town. But we had some things to be tidied up first. Then we could embark on our honeymoon and announce Professor and Mrs. Lawless's wedded bliss in the *Times*. Fortunately her parents felt an announcement in the *Barnes and Mortlake Herald* was all that was needed.

I would like to complete as much work as possible before the final step in our plans reached fruition, but it seemed we would have to regularize the situation a little earlier than expected.

Our "walk" proved very satisfactory indeed. Grace is a skillful young lady. Somehow I suspect, but have refrained from asking, that Mortlake is not her first experience. Probably some opportunities arose during her nursing activities in the War. That situation lent itself to intense emotional flings. Even I was not immune, though of course a decade older than my intended and far better educated. I was working on my doctoral dissertation at the time. It was annoying to interrupt it, but difficult to avoid, so I took a post in the military intelligence bureaucracy. Later, forces conspired to put me in the thick of it for a while -- interrogating German prisoners and so forth. Interesting work really, but a tiresome delay in one's career plans.

The evening passed off smoothly enough. Lady Parrot made a passing reference to the valuations, but Charles was of course aware of that, having authorized it. No harm done.

I even managed to snatch a few words alone with Grace before the American, Mr. Hood, dragged me off to the billiard table as was his want. He seemed to have no other ideas for recreation, except reading dime novels. Life in Chicago with Scarface and his boys running things was fantastic enough, he said. "You don't want to get real distracted at the wrong minute, or you could wind up dead." I felt he might make a very good murder suspect himself, if Charles met an untimely demise. He certainly had mob associations, though he claimed he only paid protection money, as he called it, for his "speakeasies." I had learned his nightclubs operated with Charles as the silent partner in such a way that he would own them outright should Charles die. The authorities might find that suggestive.

Towards ten-thirty I begged off from yet another game and went off to read. He had taught me pool, as he called it, a bit different from billiards. I'd become adept at the latter when billeted with fellow officers at a French chateau when I was near the front.

I was suitably startled when Agnes brought me the news of Charles' demise to my bedroom along with my morning tea. She found it quite disturbing, but it also titillated the poor country girl. She was obviously torn between alarm and morbid curiosity; the understandable fear of a murderer's presence—whatever that party's intentions were towards the servants—and wanting all the details. She was full of suppressed speculation, dreaming of being talked up, interviewed, and tipped by the *Daily Screech*, no doubt.

Mary, the Parlour Maid, found him in the sitting room sprawled across the Chesterfield with his head bashed in. Mary was opening the curtains and preparing the fires and so on. It appears the sitting room's french window was open and also the one in Charles' Office. Perhaps he was killed there, but it would seem to be a lot of trouble on the killer's part to take him to the sitting room.

A nineteenth-century Parrot with money had a positive mania for putting french windows in every ground-floor room, except of course the servants' areas. So inappropriate for the period of the house, and quite spoiling the facade, but what can one expect from the raw gentry?

But I digress, the open windows superficially suggested an intruder. Or more likely was merely meant to suggest one to the less rigorously educated (the police and the servants, one expects) and twits like Major Bly. One wonders how many of his orders legally killed needlessly in the War?

It was a pity for our killer that our location in a late Tudor Manor house on a storm-isolated promontory makes it a little less plausible, probably even to the police. Still it was no doubt worth his—or her?—effort. It might even give the police a convenient out from rigorously investigating people with influential contacts.

Letitia "Sherlock" Parrot had decreed the locking of the doors and collective investigation after breakfast. The way the servants and even the Brown woman run to her whenever something goes wrong, you'd think Parrot was the font of all wisdom. Quite civilized of her, though I hope everyone has a strong stomach. I'd seen my share of corpses at the front, as had Grace. And the Major, of course, must have inspected the carnage he and the higher-up idiots on the other side had wrought once it was safe. He also (or so he says with endless repetition) saw action in the Boer War, and there were plenty of bodies on view.

After the aforesaid breakfast, the house party led by Sherlock and Brown and Mary, proceeded to view the apparent scene of the crime first. We entered the sitting room. It was indeed Charles sprawled face-up over the chintz-covered Chesterfield—modern and quite inappropriate to the place but a concession to comfort rather than the period antiques I recommended. The side of his neck was discoloured as if struck with some force. The top of his head was caved in just above the forehead.

"Looks like the blighter first felled my old comrade by the blow to the neck and then finished him off! Some blackguard of a robber no doubt. A vagrant must have been hiding in the outbuildings, saw a chance to get some food and perhaps cash, and been caught in the act. I'll see he hangs if it's the last thing I do! Oh Charles . . ." said the Major punctuating the last declaration with what he would doubtlessly consider a stifled "unmanly" sob.

His analysis of the sequence of blows, at least, made sense. Did it explain that the shirttails were partly out, the front of his trousers were unbuttoned, his tie was missing, and his belt was undone? Perhaps he had taken the tie off in his Office and heard the proverbial noise when in the WC, which was under the stairs, with its entrance facing the dining room? Perhaps that would sound plausible to the police.

I looked at the Major coolly and considered the possibilities. I quite liked him as a police scapegoat, not out of vulgar prejudice (likely to work on the police, I suspect, if all of his relations with Charles were revealed). After all, he was usually the last one downstairs, or so I understood, other than his bosom friend Charles. Lady Parrot stared at him also before pronouncing.

"Just possible Major, I grant, if he was using the facilities and heard a noise made by an intruder." She paused before delivering her alternative explanation, perhaps choosing her words with care. "But if you were in that situation, wouldn't you fasten your trousers before investigating? After all, it could be one of the guests or a servant on a legitimate errand.

"No, to put it delicately, his state of undress suggests that he was under the impression that his attacker had amorous intentions toward him. There might be a slim possibility that he was so inebriated that he thought himself in the bedroom or water closet and was starting to undress, but it seems improbable unless the servants have found him sleeping it off downstairs before. Mary?" She turned to the homely but efficient maid with an eyebrow raised.

"No, Milady. None of us have found him sleeping or undressed or nothing down here, unless someone's keeping secrets from me. And I'm the one most likely to find him," Mary said.

"Charles could handle more Scotch than any officer I have known. He always made it back to quarters, even on the rare occasions when he was a bit wobbly on his pins," said the Major.

"In that case, I think the drunken stupor possibility more remote than your burglar hypothesis, Major's,"— Bly practically puffed up at this tepid statement of support for his theory—, "or the alternative. That he knew his killer and hoped or expected amorous interaction with her. Or him."

"Him!" bellowed the Major, going beet-red in the face. "Let me tell you, Milady, that Charles was a man's man. Unnatural encounters were completely foreign to his tastes. An utterly outrageous suggestion!"

"My dear Major, let us be rational and civil. You may believe or know the truth about the range of Charles's sexual activities better than I, whether or not you choose to reveal them publicly. But the police, when we once again have access to them, will not rule out such possibilities, I assure you. I know the Chief Constable well. He is a man of wide experience and sense. Nor does he employ fools as senior officers."

It didn't pass me by that the Major's bluster was likely more aimed at protecting his own reputation than that of his friend. And by maintaining his supposed honor, and concealing his possible physical relationship with Charles Mortlake, he would also reduce his ranking as a suspect. Besides, given Charles's apparently simultaneous use of Brown, my bride, and possibly Bly, I wondered if even a comely housebreaker either sex could not get him interested. He seemed to like the frisson of danger. I was not blind to his attempts to add me to those in his lecherous coils. I studiously pretended incomprehension. I was not a "public school" old boy, thank God!

"In any case," said Parrot, as if dismissing the tantrum of a naughty boy from her mind, "we can confine our attentions to two possibilities: Charles believed he was to be amorously involved with his assailant, or he was surprised at a disadvantage by someone, whether or not an intruder. Did he often remove his tie in the Office after supper, Major?" asked Lady Parrot.

"Yes indeed. He said it felt like a noose and took his off whenever etiquette permitted."

"That explains that then. Does anyone see anything of note here?"

"Yes ma'am," replied Mary after we all looked about. "The small throw that's usually draped over the back of the settee is missing. The one you embroidered with a view of the sea on it."

"So it is. Thank you, Mary."

"Anyone else?"

No one responded.

"Well then, I shall take paper and glue from the writing desk over there and paste a seal over the entrance to the secret passage linking this sitting room and the Orangerie. Mrs. Brown, will you see to it that the Orangerie entrance is also sealed? Write "sealed" over where the door would open and sign your name. Please also see that the scullery end of the other passage from the Office is also sealed. I will see to the Office end." Brown went off. "Now we will lock this room and I shall keep the key. Mary collected the spares for me earlier."

The window had already been secured. The carpet by it was wet but showed no signs of mud. There were a few leaves, but they were probably deposited there by the gusts accompanying the storm. I noticed that the tempest was slackening off. Perhaps the police could be contacted soon. We all obediently trooped out, the door was locked, and we walked en mass past the doors of the dining room, the entrance hall, and my library domain to Charles' Office.

"Sherlock" Parrot unfastened the door and proceeded in. The french window had been closed earlier. The carpet immediately in front of it was in about the same shape as that in the sitting room. No suspicious muddy footprints for us to speculate over and preserve for the authorities. The only other oddity Mary noticed in the morning was that the door to the inner hall, usually closed, had been open, and the electric standard lamps—one by Charles' desk and the other between the guest armchair and the settee—were alight.

It was the Major who drew our attention to the not-quite closed state of the bottom desk drawer. This he told us was where Charles kept his moneybox with cash for personal and household expenses, drawing perhaps a hundred pounds or two a month from his account at a Devizeston bank branch as needed.

On closer examination the drawer had been levered open and the wood about the lock split in the process. The cash box had also been forced open, perhaps with the poker, and was empty.

"Major," asked Sherlock once these facts had been ascertained, "do you have an idea how much money was in this box."

"I believe it must have been over two hundred. Probably closer to three. Charles cashed a check when we went into town just before Mr. Hood arrived. The wages and accounts are due this week. He paid the wages for the Home Farm laborers that way too, as well as the servants. He only gave cheques to Mrs. Brown and Goodson, the estate manager who also oversees the Home Farm and has his quarters there. Upstanding young chap; was a subaltern in the Regiment towards the end of the war. Charles likes—liked—to keep a lot of cash on hand, just in case he saw some antiques or art or something that appealed to him. Always said people felt safer with cash, and he often got better prices with it."

"With this development, Major, I suggest you get some torches and your service revolver and we inspect the passage to the scullery along with Professor Lawless. Perhaps Miss Leigh and Mr. Hood might station themselves in the scullery while we do so. Arm yourself with a poker or some such, just in case an intruder is hiding in the passage and we flush him out. I don't expect it. But if Charles knew him or even if he was a total stranger, he might have known about the passages. I'm sure most of the village does and some may know how to open them. It, but it never hurts to make sure."

"No need to get my gun," said the Major. "Charles keeps one loaded in the top drawer." He opened the drawer, withdrew a revolver, and put it in the pocket of his fawn brown-flecked tweed jacket.

"Then perhaps Mary, will you assemble electric torches from the emergency supplies?" The maid went off to do this, Hood and my wife went off with her. Hood taking the poker as ordered.

While we waited, Parrot asked the Major if anything else struck him as out of place in the Office. The Major looked about the room carefully, but the only thing he noticed was that the heavy polished-marble lighter Charles kept on his desk, was not in its usual place, but on the blotter. Parrot examined it—I half expected her to produce a magnifying glass, but alas she was not so equipped—holding it with a handkerchief. The Major and I also came close to see.

"Wiped clean very recently," the lady detective concluded, without benefit of magnification. "Note the scrap of white cotton caught in the metal fitting near the top. And I think that is a hair. These rusty marks also on the end may be blood.

"Good show, Major!" she said. "I think you've found the murder weapon." She put it down carefully in the approximate position it had lain and put her hanky away.

About then Mary returned with Mrs. Brown, both carried large torches. Parrot, Bly and I each took one. Parrot suggested Brown and Mary remain in the Office, armed with fire tongs and coal shovel, but cautioned them to avoid touching anything else, particularly the lighter and anything about the desk. I don't think she seriously entertained the possibility of an intruder concealing himself in the passage. I suspected she was looking for something else.

Parrot led the way—deflecting the Major's argument that as a military man and the one with the revolver he should lead the party, by equipping herself with one of Charles' stout walking sticks to serve as a cudgel, and handing another to me. She briefed us that we should pay particular attention to the state of the dust on the passage floor, as no one, as far as she could ascertain, had recently used it. Unless Charles had, and he was in no shape to tell us. Bly thought not. Of course, if the murderer was amongst the house party, he or she or possibly they may not have been telling the truth.

Thus it wound up that Parrot turned the carved pear in the paneling that opening the concealed entrance and was first to step through once the panel moved out of the way. We left it open. The Major was next, then I. For some reason—it could plausibly be the possibility of an armed murderer at my back or in front of me—I was distinctly nervous, although I undoubtedly knew the passage better than any of them.

Lady Parrot soon drew our attention to the absence of dust in a swathe to the right side of the passage along the inner wall. She suggested the murderer had likely used the passage for some reason currently unknown and used something—the missing throw from the sitting room she suggested? — to erase his tracks, and therefore clues, including his or her shoe prints. We had traversed perhaps half the passage when the pristine dust appeared in her torchlight as far as it reached. It wasn't long after the widening of the passage that had served as refuge for Catholic priests during the Morthead family's brief tenure of the Manor they had built ended with their alleged involvement in the Gunpowder Plot. The government of James I/VI had declared the property forfeit on the squire and his son's conviction and sold it at a handsome price to the first Parrot to reside there, who also purchased his baronetcy from the canny Scot monarch.

Lady Parrot argued persuasively that there was no need to search further. Inspecting the dust at the other end and the two ends of the sitting room-Orangerie passage would settle whether the remainder of this and the other passage needed searching. She rather thought not.

Hence we retraced our steps. Once we mere men had started past the priest's cell with its wooden bench for a bed and bucket for relieving oneself, the Major realized that Lady Parrot was not following him. We went back to investigate. She was shining her light into the bucket as we arrived.

We asked her what she was doing. She said she was looking for what the culprit had hidden, as if it was obvious. "There had to be a reason why he or she came along here and then turned back. I doubt—for ease of speech let us say "he"—went for a stroll just after killing someone. He clearly didn't use the passage to come upon Charles from the kitchen at any rate. It is just possible he hid here, waiting on the bench, and came out later to confront Charles or rifle his desk for cash. That would rule him out as one of the house party or the inside servants, as we were all seen after Charles and the Major retired to the Office. But I rather think a surprised robber-turned-killer wouldn't think of concealing his shoeprints in the dust. Hence I am wondering if the theft was not a mere diversion. If so the money and the rug must be concealed somewhere. Unless the intruder went out and threw them into the sea. Of this we have seen no sign. He turned back soon after here. It occurred to me that as well as carefully examining the walls and ceiling of the passage generally, the bucket, bench, or elsewhere in this cell might be where something is concealed. I shall now check the bench. There is nothing in or taped to the bucket. Perhaps you gentlemen will shine your torches systematically over the walls, floor, and ceiling."

"Very good, Letitia!" said the Major who started to search as directed as did I.

As we examined the passage, she leant down and shone her torch on the underside of the bench. She soon interrupted our efforts once more.

"The throw is certainly here. It is folded with precision and taped to the underside of the bench." She removed her kid gloves from the right-hand pocket of her tweed jacket and put them on. Being nearest, I kneeled down and shone my torch on the rug. "The tape may hold finger prints," she cautioned. "Please allow me to ease it off unless you also have gloves. Shine the light as I direct you." Thus put in my place as a mere male, I complied while the old dragon performed this operation. Once she had the throw free, she straightened up, still kneeling. She was beginning to make me uncomfortable, but at least I was able to straighten up too and relieve kinks in my back. She shook out the folds of the rug. Nothing was revealed. She leaned down again and so did I. Our torches revealed another small bundle tapped securely to the back of the underside. The lady retrieved it—this time lying down—and then stiffly got to her feet, and triumphantly revealed her find to us.

"Now we have located both the throw and the money from the cash box." She held up and then pocketed a sizeable wad of Treasury notes. The idea of a stranger or outsider began to look more remote. The Major was somewhat deflated, and I, as a potential suspect, didn't feel too gratified. We made our way back to the Office.

There were no new developments until after supper. The dust at the kitchen end of the passage seemed undisturbed as did that at either end of the other passageway. I had not used it for weeks myself, since the last time I was down. The ends of each passage were resealed.

We were all gathered, a rather gloomy party, in the library, the next most comfortable room after the sitting room and office, which were locked for obvious reasons with the keys in Lady Parrot's custody. Brown and Mary were serving out after dinner tea and coffee when Agnes put her head round the door and nodded to the "lady detective," as they call them in the cheaper sort of American novel. She excused herself and went out of the room, assuring us she would return shortly.

A few minutes later she came back in, carrying something wet rolled up in a towel, sat down, and commenced to explain the mystery.

"I took the liberty to have Agnes search for something I thought might be concealed in one of our rooms. I included my own." She soon dealt with the Major's indignant protests that he had not been consulted. "This was found in one of the old chamber pots under someone's bed. It was soaking in bloody water." As she said this she unrolled the towel, revealing the top part of a wet crumpled pair of men's pajamas and a number of men's handkerchiefs. None of these items were monogrammed or labeled, she revealed. Then she dropped her bombshell.

"How do you explain their presence under your bed, Miss Leigh?"

My Grace looked stunned, her face reddened, the hands with which she put down the cup and saucer shook but a little, but she rallied, sat up straight-backed at the front of her chair and said,

"Why, the Major saw the light under my door late last night and knocked. The poor man said he had had a severe nosebleed and asked me what to do about it. I told him to change his top and give me the pajamas and hankies and I would soak them in cold water. He came back a few moments later with the top and hankies. I drew some cold water from the bathroom next door with my jug from the washstand, and poured it into the chamber pot, thinking it would be less in the way than in the sink. It's important to soak blood stains quickly in cold water – not hot -- you know, or it sets." She was remarkably calm and convincing.

The Major blustered, categorically denied her claims, saying he didn't own a pair of pajamas that color and his handkerchiefs were monogrammed. The last Agnes corroborated and said she didn't recall such a pair amongst the Major's wash.

Unfortunately, my love's performance just bought me time. For indeed Lady Parrot had found me out. I did it for the money, of course, both from the sale of the rare books I had pretended to send for appraisal, and from Grace's annuity in Mortlake's will. I also felt revolted at Charles' sexual pursuit of me and outraged at his assaults on and affair with my wife. I couldn't let that pass. The wages of sin are death—even the Good Book says it. Charles had certainly done enough sin to merit execution. Ironically, it is I who will be executed. Poe has one of his characters in a macabre tale say something like "A wrong is unredressed if retribution overtakes the redressor. One must not only punish, but punish with impunity." Apparently I failed at the impunity part. They have the goods on me for sure. Grace should escape. She's sticking to her story, that she told the truth except the identity of the supposed nosebleed sufferer. And once our true status was revealed, what would seem more natural than going to one's wife with such a problem? They can't prove she's lying. I wish her well and think she'll get her annuity.

—Patrick Lawless

Cook's Look

"It wasn't till I turned back from the front door and headed for this one that I noticed something under the love seat." Mary, the parlor maid, indicated the one just to our left as we stood looking through the doorway into the entrance hall.

She forced herself to cross the threshold. I followed her to just in front of the love seat, six or seven feet away. "Then I realized it was a gentleman in evening dress on his side with his face towards the room with his legs drawn up against his chest." And so he was. I stared, fascinated and repelled at the same time. It was the Master, sure enough. His position was sort of like a baby or a little child. His face was plain to see if shadowed, almost like normal, except for the round hole just between those roving gray eyes. It was surprising how little blood there was about the hole, though there was some.

Then I noticed that tucked between his arm and his body, near his hand, was a gun. I assumed it was the one that killed him. I pointed it out to Mary, saying he must have killed himself.

"But why would the Master blow his brains out?" I asked Mary, not really expecting an answer, but reply she did.

"Why would he kill himself curled up like that, under the loveseat and in here? And he's not been behaving odd-like lately, for him anyway. Just as normal, I'd say."

"You may have something there!" I conceded. Mary's shrewd, she is. "And there's those open drawers in his Office and them feathers here and there, you told me about on the way here. It don't add up to me, Mary. If he killed himself, I'm the Queen of England!"

"What do we do now? Wake the Major, or Mrs. Brown?"

"Certainly not that old fool of a Major! Have some sense, Mary dear! Mrs. Brown I suppose, we *should* tell. But I think we'll see what Lady Parrot thinks first."

"You're right there! Lady always knows what to do!" said Mary sounding happier. We have a lot of faith in Lady P., we do, in the servant's hall.

"Right then," I said. "Let's go tell her."

That wasn't exactly the beginning, so I'd better go back a little.

The murder happened during an enforced house party while a fierce storm blew itself out and isolated Morthead Manor from the mainland.

Being the senior servant hereabouts—at least female, and Monsieur Georges, Mr. Mortlake's valet as a foreigner, hardly counts—you'd think I'd be in the thick of anything that takes place at Morthead Manor, with so few junior servants nowadays. But slaving away over a hot stove all day and keeping the house going from daylight to evening, I don't have time for peering and prying amongst the gentry. So I hear about all the goings-on from the inside servants, Mrs. Brown the Housekeeper, and Jeffries, the chauffeur/handyman. Mostly I don't get to see them a lot.

This was one time, though, when I was in the thick of things.

Esther Stout's me name. That's Mrs. Stout to you, unless you're friend, family, or Lady Parrot! Or I answer to Cook. I've not been married, but "Mrs." I am by tradition of office.

Before telling more about the murder, I'd better tell you a little about the household.

We have a so-called "lady" housekeeper, "Mrs." Brown, who's no more married than me. She's a former Music Hall *artiste*. That's where Mr. Mortlake, the Master, picked her up, we understand. Agnes, the chambermaid, has seen her souvenirs on the walls of her bedsitting room—posters and photos and such. Hettie Brown, she is. Screeches like a Cockney fishwife when anything goes wrong. Never lifts a finger otherwise. Just gives orders. She talks posh to the upstairs party, but it's as phony as her peroxide-blonde hair. Didn't take us long to figure out she's the Master's long time mistress, though now he's gone and seduced his young "personal secretary," Miss Leigh, her days may be numbered.

Not that there's much else to be said against Grace Leigh, the secretary. It's more Mr. Charles' fault than hers, I expect. She was one of them VAD nurses at the front during the War, and I do hear that unsettled a lot of young folk and that there were a lot of goings-on with all them men and only a few women about. Not natural or healthy. The Great War's got a lot to answer for.

The maids and me wouldn't have stayed at the Manor a minute but Lady Parrot, our old mistress, told us it was all right as long as Mr. Charles kept things quiet and didn't take liberties. I worked for Milady since I were a girl. I'm from some miles away, nearer Devizeston, the county town. The maids were born and bred in the village, Morthead Minor, across the causeway from the Manor or on the estates. I started, like young Gladys, as kitchen maid, low as you can get. But unlike that poor girl, I got a head on me shoulders and old Cook and Milady took a shine to me. I learned to cook proper for a gentleman's table and succeeded Mrs. Jackson when Sir John pensioned her off just before the Great War.

The time I'm thinking on, I heard the news first. It was about eleven, I was just about ready to turn out them electric lights Mr. Charles installed when Mary came a knocking, frantic like, at me door. She was out of breath from running up the back stairs.

Once she told me what she'd seen, I had to see for meself. It just didn't seem possible. I pulled me bones out of bed, put on me dressing gown, went downstairs with her, through the kitchen and across the inner hall to the opposite corner of the ground floor. The lights were still on. As we neared the corner room, the Office, I could see the lights were on there too 'cause the door was open. But it was in the entrance hall next door that Mary said she'd found him. We stopped outside between the Office and the door from the front hall while Mary told me how she had come upon Mr. Mortlake.

"I was on me rounds locking up, starting from the ballroom as usual. I'd just done the Office," Mary said. "It was like the Master stepped out for a minute." We turned and looked over the Office. "Just like now." I saw the chair was pushed back from Mr. Mortlake's desk. There was a whiskey glass to the right of the blotter, papers out, and the standard lamps were on. "I thought maybe he'd gone to the cloakroom or to fetch something. I've never know him go to bed before me. He always finishes his whisky too. The glass is always empty when I collect it in the morning. There was Major's drained by the couch, so I thought he'd gone up."

I noticed one odd thing about the Office. There were a few feathers here and there under the furniture where someone in the room wouldn't see them. Like a pillow or a cushion had a hole in the cover and had been puffed up or something. I noticed the desk drawers on the right of where the Master sat were wide open too. He kept his gun in the top one with his keys, except when he was out. The lower one, usually locked, had the strongbox where he kept money for bills and wages and such. He doled them out to us last Friday of the month. He was a smooth one, always a smile on his face and a compliment about me cooking. If I didn't know better he seemed a very nice gentleman. And perhaps he was, except with the ladies, which was a big blot. But he had charm. I'll give him that.

"So I went on to the reception hall, turning on the lights as I went in." Mary suited words to actions and led me across the inner hall to that door, standing open too. She'd already told me it had been closed as usual, with the lights off inside when she entered. Mary stopped by the doorway and we looked in while she talked. She was reluctant to go back in. But her colour was better and she weren't shaking no more, so I felt she had enough of a grip on herself to go on.

"It all looked so normal. Just like earlier when I'd drawn the curtains on either side of the door." And it did too, with chairs along the walls here and there for callers to wait on while Mary saw if whoever they asked for was in. "I walked across and checked the windows and doors."

The reception hall's not much used except when guests or Miss Leigh or Professor Lawless are arriving or leaving. Sometimes the Master and the Major leave the car outside that door for Mr. Jeffries to put away or have it brought 'round when they're in a hurry. But mostly it's only used for the rare caller like the Vicar and his lady wife. I daresay on a normal day no one goes into it but Mary to dust, draw curtains, mop the parquet floor, and so on. The resident gentry, or those aping them, come and go through the french windows old Sir James had a downright mania for.

Where was I? Next came the part I started with when we were looking at him and decided to tell Lady Parrot.

So we went upstairs, taking the liberty of using the gentry's stairs to save me legs, nobody being around, excepting Captain Mortlake, and he was in no condition to object.

As we approached Lady L.'s door—not the master bedchamber like in the old days, but the green room— we saw light under it. She was a great one for reading in bed. We knocked quietly—nothing wrong with Lady's hearing. She said "Come in!"

When she saw Mary and me, she knew something odd was afoot and had us sit down while we told our story, asking questions when she found something a bit unclear or wanted more detail, like. She felt the same way we did, that there was something fishy about the business and decided we'd better all go down and poke about before telling anyone else. So she got on her red silk dressing gown and her carpet slippers and we all went downstairs.

First Mary went over how she'd discovered the Office empty and then the body. Lady L. had her walk through the route. She checked the Office, being careful to leave no fingerprints, and found the source of the feathers. The Major uses a big cushion, almost pillow-size, on the settee. Lady carefully lifted it up with dove-gray kid gloves she'd brought down for "handling possible evidence," as she put it. On one side of it there were black marks like it was peppered with coal dust, but ingrained like and a burnt area around a hole. On the other side was a bigger round hole but not so noticeable 'cause it didn't have them marks and wasn't burnt. That was the side that was out when Lady picked it up careful-like, and put it back the way it was. A few more feathers dropped out while we looked at it, despite Lady's care.

Looking about the room, she poked about the fire which was still going and found a few feathers amongst the fine gray-white ash beneath the grate.

"It seems someone shot the gun you saw, or another one, through the pillow, so it didn't make as much noise. Then they cleaned up most of the feathers and put them on the fire. Fortunately, my dear Esther," she sometimes uses me Christian name, does Milady, "you were sharp-eyed enough to see the few he or she had missed and alert me. I must say, it is odd. If trying to make a murder look like a suicide, I would think even an idiot would do a better job. For instance, leave him slumped over the desk. Press his fingers on the gun after it had been used and leave it on the desk. I think he probably was at the desk; some whisky has been spilled and mopped up hastily and the glass refilled; I believe that will be the explanation for these marks on the desk near it. The liquor would have evaporated, but there seems to be a residue and it may have even damaged the finish . . . ." Lady bent to examine the desk closely. She lifted the papers. "I believe this blotter's been changed too. Likely the one here had some blood on it if he slumped forward. You can see there's no ink or writing impressions on this one as there would be if it had been used." She started to examine the papers. "Ah! This letter from a tenant farmer is missing the second page. Charles had probably been reading it. And slumped forward after being thrown back against the chair.... No hole in the chair back. Probably means no exit wound. Fortunate for the killer—less messy. Might mean a small caliber weapon or it could be that the thick pillow slowed a more powerful bullet sufficiently so it couldn't make it through the skull I suppose . . . " Lady always did like a mystery novel. She's also friendly with the Chief Constable and he tells her a lot. I could tell she liked playing Sherlock Holmes. The storm cut off the telephone as well as flooding the causeway, so we couldn't tell the police right away.

Lady looked over at the fire. "The blotter and the missing page will have gone on the fire. There doesn't seem to be any trace of them I'm afraid, unless the police can find some charred fragment in the ash .... " She walked 'round the desk and stood in front of it and then backed up till she reached the Major's chair. "Yes, if the wound is as you describe it, it might have been done from anywhere in this area. The killer would have to be a good shot though, and quick, especially with the impediment of the cushion. I suspect from the charring pattern the barrel was pushed right into it."

She walked back around the desk and looked in the open top drawer. The usually-locked bottom one was open too. She asked us to come closer. Once we was there, she said, "Note the absence of Charles' revolver. I only saw it once but I believe it was one of the heavy Webleys officers were issued in the Great War. I think Major Bly has referred to one too. You will remember, both of you, the boys setting up a target near the cliff and doing practice with theirs while on home leave before going over that last time ...."

She had a bittersweet smile on her face. Both the young masters had been killed in the same battle. Sir John was never the same after he got that telegram.

"I don't see anything else amiss in this drawer. The key ring is here." She went on briskly, putting memories firmly aside. It was just as she said, neat as a pin. Closing the top drawer, we looked in the lower one. The cashbox was behind the files as usual, but open. It wasn't damaged when Lady L. examined it. There was little money in it. Only about twenty-one pounds and change. Lady counted it with her gloves and put it back the way it had been. That may be a lot to me or you, but Mr. Charles usually had hundreds in there, and it was petty change to him with his bank and all. I told Lady so.

"Interesting. Also inconsistent. Why try to make it look as if someone had bungled an attempt to make it look like suicide? And why remove the money? Perhaps to confuse us and the police?" She turned to me and asked, "Mrs. Stout, was the key on the ring in the other drawer?"

"No, Ma'am. He kept it and the drawer key on his watch chain. Kept both drawers locked when he was not using the room I understand."

"So that means if money was removed it was after he was killed, unless he voluntarily gave it over, or at gunpoint. But who? Odd. Do either of you know were the Major keeps his revolver?"

"Agnes says he keeps it in his bedside table drawer. Major warned her not to touch it or the drawer. Told her it's loaded, though he said the safety's on. He said he kept it handy in case of burglars in the night."

"Is there a lock on that drawer?"

"No, Milady," said Mary, who had been a chambermaid in her time. It's the same furniture as the old days, just refinished."

"I think we're about finished in here. Except we should search the room, especially the floor, for the cartridge. I'll take charge of Mr. Mortlake's keys so we can lock the Office. Oh, we'd better paste some paper across the entrance to the secret passage and verify the windows are still locked." The Lady placed the Master's keys in her dressing-gown pocket, found paste and paper in the desk, and sealed the passage, saying how we'd at least know if someone snuck in that way to try to clean up. I checked the french windows while Mary looked all over for the spent cartridge. All this didn't take long. We didn't find a cartridge. Once done, we went to the entrance hall to see the corpse with Lady.

Lady Parrot seemed quite revived by the situation. She made it feel like a practical problem like catering or organizing a fete. It sort of helped take me mind off murder being done in the house. In the hall Milady first examined the body.

"You notice that a feather is adhering to his shirt front. There is definitely no exit wound," said Lady after bending down, peering through her pince-nez, and pointing at his hair. I hadn't noticed the feather meself, but it was there sure enough. Lady then crouched down and held open his dinner jacket wide. It was unbuttoned. Now we could all see what was underneath. "Note that there is no key on the gold watch chain."

Then she picked up the gun in her gloved hand and straightened up. "One wouldn't want to disturb finger marks." She sniffed at the hole in the barrel. "Odd, there doesn't seem to be any odour. I doubt it would have entirely dissipated so rapidly. He surely died in the past couple of hours. He and the Major departed the sitting room after coffee about nine-thirty, just before I went up. Did you see either of them after that, Mary?"

"I saw the Major heading for the stairs at about ten-thirty. I was just taking the tray back from the sitting room to the kitchen for Gladys to wash up in the morning. I noted the time on the hall clock particular because it was so early for him."

"Was anyone else downstairs then?"

"The American was playing billiards. I heard balls hitting each other through the door. I didn't hear voices, so I assumed he was alone. I didn't see him. Nobody else, Milady."

"Thank you, Mary. Most helpful. I assume the games room was empty when you came back and checked the windows? When would that be?"

"Yes, ma'am. Likely about a quarter or ten to eleven ma'am."

"Excellent!" said Lady L., returning her attention to the gun. "A Webley revolver certainly." She took a firmer grip and pushed something and the part with the bullets came out. "Interesting. Ian showed me how they worked. One bullet missing. So either our murderer removed a bullet, or this weapon has been used. How peculiar. I think I see a pattern. A Webley would make a bigger hole I think. The killer wants deliberately to confuse the authorities. I wonder if the Major, assuming he is innocent, would know if this was Charles' revolver? Most likely. Men treat guns as toys and show them to their friends." She put the bullet container thing back in place, crouched down, and replaced the gun.

"One more task here for tonight, I think. Let us look for the cartridge!" What a sight we must have been: two older women, one a Lady, walking about the room staring at the floor. Mary got down on her hands and knees and looked under the furniture. Lady looked round the body even, but no casing. Finally we left the room and Lady locked the door. I saw from the hall clock that it was past midnight now.

Lady suggested we all go to the kitchen to prepare cocoa or hot milk for us all, after completing the lock-up with Mary.

Over hot drinks, we made plans. Lady decided with the storm raging, there was no rush to tell everyone. She made sure Mary had an alarm clock and asked me if I needed to borrow hers. Mary has one and Gladys wakes me up in the morning after she's washed up the evening things and made a pot of tea. Then she brings me cup, wakes me, and my day starts. Mary and Agnes would be about their duties too.

Lady L. decided Agnes and Mary should search all the upstairs rooms in use—including her own—while the party was at breakfast. They served themselves from chaffing dishes. Mrs. Brown ate her breakfast with the gentry. Lady wanted a private chat with Agnes before she delivered tea to anyone else next morning. We were to be quiet about the murder to the other servants until it was generally known. She said there was no need to put Gladys in a fret too early, she'd only break more dishes than usual. Lady knows our Gladys!

We discussed possible motives while drinking cocoa. Some should have shocked Mary and me, us both being good respectable, Christian spinsters, but the old saw about no secrets from the servants is true. What one of us doesn't see, another see signs of, or overhears being discussed.

Brown's, Major Bly's, and Miss Leigh's motives could be money. It was widely understood Mr. Charles had left them provided for in his will. They might also be jealous of the attentions he was paying to one or both of the others. Or Lady suggested two or three of them conspiring, like!

Mr. Hood, being in the nightclub business with the Master, perhaps he'd benefit if the Master died? Or if he'd been cooking the books and Mr. Mortlake found out? Milady said his home town, Chicago, is run by a crook called Al Capone! Seems people in Mr. Hood's business need "protection" from gangsters, it being illegal to drink in America! Could he be one of them gangsters himself?

We all know Professor Lawless shows signs of being sweet on Miss Leigh. He could be outraged by her relationship with the Master and be jealous or wanted to marry her with the money she'd inherit. Still, he seems a respectable young man from what I've seen and heard of him. Could him and Miss Leigh be in it together?

When Agnes brought Lady L. her tea in the morning, she was put in the know and given orders. She was to pay attention to the reaction of each person to the news and anything they said and to report back to Lady after she'd taken tea to all of them. One of them, Milady felt, probably already knew. Milady also told Agnes to say the Master's been found dead in the reception hall with a gun to hand, and that Lady Parrot's looked over the situation and felt it needless to wake everyone, especially as the police couldn't be contacted right away.

Milady also had Agnes ask the Major to meet her at eight-thirty to view the scene and discuss what was best to be done. She wanted to hear what he said about them guns. All were at breakfast soon after nine when it was put out.

It all went like MiLady planned. I wasn't there with the Major and Lady L. in the room with the corpse, but Mary was and told me about it. Mary said he seemed shaken at his friend's death. Lady made it like she was taking him into her confidence; at least about the night before and her conclusions it was murder. Mary said murder, not suicide, seemed to buck him up a bit.

He said he'd gone up early 'cause he had an upset tummy, just after half-ten. He'd had the nerve to blame his stomach on me buttered lobsters from lunch! Undercooked, he said! They were as sweet a bit of work as ever came out of this here kitchen! He's just greedy, he is. Always eats too much. That's all there was to it. He admitted he'd had a minor disagreement with Charles. Said he'd blame himself for parting in a huff, like. Could their "disagreement" have led to murder?

Lady L. asked him if shooting the revolver through a pillow would slow a Webley bullet enough to prevent it exiting the head.

He assured her that it wouldn't. Said them Webleys pack a big punch and use big bullets. He added that he doubted it was a Webley revolver did it. The hole seemed small for it, he said. He claimed he'd shot Huns and mutineers with his up close so he knew what they'd do to a head!

Of course he could have been trying to divert suspicion. But we remembered Lady couldn't smell smoke or whatever it is you smell.

Lady L. asked him if he could tell the gun was Mr. Charles'. He squinted down at it over his specs like a peering Walrus, Mary told me. He looked puzzled, and then said it wasn't. It were his! He could tell from the marks on the handle. He was mad someone had stolen his gun, or so he said, and was trying to throw suspicion on him for killing his best friend. Mary said he was convincing, but it could be acting all the same. Swore he'd get the killer hanged and all.

Then Lady showed him the Office.

Lady Parrot asked him when was the last time he saw his gun?

He said he kept it in the back of his night table drawer, cleaned it once a week, and did target practice with Mr. Charles once a month. Thought he'd seen it within a day or two.

Mary told me all six of the upstairs party were at the breakfast table by five past nine according to the hall clock. Mr. Hood was last to come down. Then she went up to help Agnes search, tidy, and make the beds. Lady had them wear the white cotton gloves they use for cleaning the silver. Their efforts didn't come up empty.

It was just before the house party finished -- towards ten -- that Mary made it down the stairs and entered the dining room. She handed Lady L. a large brown paper bag. Mary whispered in her ear about what they'd found and where. Lady L. thanked her and then whispered some instructions.

She then announced there'd been developments about "our host's untimely demise", Mary told me, and asked them to bear with her for a while

Before then, only the Major and Lady knew officially that it was likely murder. Lady L. got up and walked around the table, pausing to whisper something to three people, first to the Major, next to Professor Lawless, and last to the American gentleman.

Then she resumed her seat and started her show-and-tell.

First she explained that she'd ordered a search of all the bedrooms, her own included, and that Mary had just handed her items which might be "pertinent to the murder of Mr. Charles Mortlake."

At least one of the party appeared startled. Miss Leigh dropped her napkin. Professor Lawless, stone-faced and tense, picked it up for her. Mrs. Brown screeched out something about her Charlie being murdered, went pale, and looked fit to faint, but pulled herself together and started blubbering instead. Those who had been whispered to seemed less than surprised.

One by one Lady Parrot pulled out of the bag: four smaller boxes; one small and cylindrical brown paper package tied with string; and another parcel that looked to have cloth inside. She put them all in front of her on the table. All eyes were on them. It was ever so quiet, Mary said.

Then Lady P. told them that she and the Major had looked things over in the Office and entrance hall and decided the master were shot between the eyes in the Office, the gun being held up close to a cushion to muffle the noise. For some reason the corpse was taken from the Office, pushed under the loveseat to the left of the door nearest the Office with a Webley service revolver by his hand. She said when she was summoned to the scene last night, the body was still relatively warm, but there was no whiff of gunshot from the muzzle. The master's Webley was missing from his top desk drawer, which was open. His cashbox was also open and held much less than usual. The Major has identified the gun by the body as his Webley, usually kept by his bed in case of intruders.

Mary told me Lady then said that she was familiar with Webleys through her late sons. They fire a large bullet, and as the Major put it, "pack a heavy punch." The Major has used his Webley to shoot the enemy and even has experience with similar wounds. She said she and Major Bly were of the opinion that even when fired through a pillow, a Webley's bullet would go through the head. This one hadn't, and there'd be a larger hole too. So they'd got the idea the murderer were trying to confuse things and throw suspicion on innocent folks. Laying false trails, like. That's why they had Aggie and Mary search the bedchambers.

Next she told them a bullet was missing from the Major's revolver and they suspected the killer put it back in the Major's box of cartridges. She held up an unfired bullet, a big thing for a handgun, Mary says. Being a country lass, she knows about guns.

She pulled a pair of kid gloves from her pocket and put them on afore starting to open one of the smaller boxes. You could cut the tension with one of me carving knives, Mary said. When the paper was undone, MiLady put a large intact bullet on the table. Then she told them about us not finding the spent cartridge in the Office or hall, explaining it was thrown out as a gun fires, automatic-like. Opening a second box, Lady pulled out a cartridge and said 'twas probably put in Mrs. Brown's bedroom wastepaper basket by the killer. When Lady Letitia put it by the Webley bullet, it was obviously smaller, Mary said.

The other Webley was found in Professor Lawless's suitcase, as Lady told them. Lawless's eyebrows shot up, but he said nothing, Mary told us. Milady opened the largest box and put the master's Webley on the table by the bullet and cartridge.

Next she opened another package and put a small four-inch handgun on the table. Mary found it in Miss Leigh's desk drawer, like Lady told them. Miss Grace said she'd never seen it before.

Then she asked the Major if the Derringer—which is what she called it, Mary said—could have killed the Master if fired through the pillow. Maybe, but it would have to be very close to his head, he thought. He said if that were the weapon, Mr. Charles would have had to be unconscious or distracted somehow.

When Lady Parrot opened the small cylindrical package, it was a wad of Treasury notes and two keys. Agnes found them in Mrs. Brown's desk. Lady told them they would be the desk and cashbox keys, which were missing from Master's watch chain and the money from the cashbox. Mrs. Brown also said she had no idea how they got there, her accent slipping to pure Cockney. She were real afraid and used the Lord's name.

Lady P. turned to the last package, opened the string, and pulled back the paper. A man's dress shirt was revealed. Milady held it up for inspection. "Please note that it bears the label of Martins' Taylors, Oxford, and was found in the Professor's closet with dirty clothes. It also has two lower buttons missing at the front, its seams were strained at the shoulders, and there was blood on one cuff.

Then Lady P. told them she now knew enough to decide who killed Mr. Charles.

Here's how Lady explained it to me later, over tea in the kitchen. The Major and Professor Lawless weren't quick enough to overpower Hood before he got the gun out of the holster under his arm, the actual murder weapon it proved. Fortunate it were that Lady had told Mary to stand behind him and keep the Port decanter to hand and brain him if that happened. "Ever so exciting," Mary said it was, saving the day like that.

"The false clues," said Lady Parrot, "especially the cartridge and the shirt could only have been planted after the killing, when all but the killer and Mary were in their rooms. Thus they were placed in the morning after people had left their rooms, probably after they had gone down for breakfast, to minimize chance of detection. Only Agnes would have been left upstairs and he knew she generally didn't start making up the rooms till nine. Mr. Hood was the last one down, throwing suspicion on him. He also had no clue found in his room—also suspicious. A Derringer is an American weapon. Guns are easy to get in Chicago—mob-run, you know! If the killer wore the Professor's shirt while killing the Master, he must have been both wider at the shoulder and thicker at the waist than Lawless, straining the seams and popping the buttons. The Major was too big to fit Lawless's shirt at all. Mrs. Brown's generous bosom and padding elsewhere would have probably ruled her out. Miss Leigh, if anything, would have strained the chest, not the shoulders, nor the waist! So it must have been Hood.

—Esther Stout

Major Bly's Peril

One of the servants seemed to be having hysterics, or so I assumed from the sound she was making. I was trying to relax by doing the crossword in the last issue of the *Times* we had received—two days old now—before the storm cut us off from the village. I was on 25 Down: "Noun. Damages mad fruit case, 3 and 7." Servants pick awkward moments to make a fuss! So tiresome.

Who am I, you say?

Major Stephen Bly, Army, retired. I've seen action from the Boer War to the Great one. I decided to deal with this lack of consideration for the peace of one's betters in the ranks. I got up a bit slowly. My knees are a trifle stiff and with the easy living at my old subordinate and best friend Charles Mortlake's (Captain, retired) Devizesshire place, Morthead Manor, I'm putting on a little weight about the midriff. But I can still move smartly once the old gears are engaged. Charles had gone out of the Office to see to something or other a while back—when I was on 10 Across, I think. That was a tricky one, I can tell you. At least for a plain military chap. He'd been working on the accounts. I wondered where he'd got to and assumed we'd have the pleasure of abating the nuisance together.

Once I opened the door and went through into the marble-floored inner hall, I could make out that some woman, Mary the parlor maid I thought from the voice, was yelling something like "Help! Murder!" I wondered what bee had got in her bonnet to make her scream such nonsense! After all, murders hardly happen in well-run gentleman banker's establishments like the Manor, but rather in the East End, labourers' cottages, or on ill-frequented roads late at night. She's usually a quiet, polite, efficient spinster too, even if she has a face like a horse and won't see forty again.

As I passed the stairway I caught a glimpse of one of Miss Leigh's shapely legs clattering down the steps. So it seemed the noise had penetrated Charles' secretary's office on the first floor. I could hardly blame Charles for making the young lady his new mistress, the old devil. Once I was passed the stair, I could see the unusual spectacle of Mary out of countenance. She was standing in front of the dining room door nearest the kitchen quarters with her mouth open making the repetitive racket. Absurdly, she was still firmly holding the handles of a tray full of what looked like the chaffing dishes that keep our breakfasts warm. I inferred that she must have been going to put them away when she went raving mad, or found someone murdered. I hoped the former. The open door she was partly blocking was the one behind the grand stair. Odd that Charles hadn't had one made directly opposite the kitchen, he'd had so many builders about.

Perhaps that pretentious puppy Lawless had felt it was not "authentic." He was a minor Oxford Fellow Charles employed about the renovations and was currently cataloguing the library collection. He was making soulful eyes at the curvaceous Leigh woman. Not that I blamed him, but it could cause uncomfortable complications.

From the direction of the kitchen I saw Mrs. Brown the housekeeper—and Charles' older mistress (supposedly former, but I have my doubts)—presumably on a similar mission to my own, followed by Cook. Brown dressed in black. She ate breakfast with the gentry. Her usual lacy cuffs seemed a dark color, not their typical white.

From beyond her I saw the Lawless lad with Lady Parrot, my *bête-noir* and the former chatelaine of this pile, catching him up. The lady and I cordially dislike one another and let no appropriate opportunity pass to get the better of each other. I assumed Lawless had been in the library and the Parrot woman in the Orangerie. Completing the party, I saw the shady American, Hood, Charles's partner in a string of fashionable nightclubs, appear behind Lady Parrot. He likely came from the games room, or "pool hall" as he referred to it. He had made it his own haunt while the gale isolated us from the mainland and enforcedly prolonged his stay.

Brown beat me to Mary and told her to stop yelling and put down the tray. Mary put the chaffing dish on an occasional table. Brown then dashed into the room. Then she started screaming hysterically too. "It's me Charlie!" When I got to the doorway and looked in, she had thrown herself across the back of what looked like Charles— from what little of him her ample form did not block from view. Charles, if it were indeed he, was sprawled across the dining room table, face down. Brown had him in a bear hug and was keening, tears flowing down her cheeks.

If it were one of the cheap Music Hall acts she used to appear in, it would be a convincing performance of the grief-struck wife or lover. Knowing Cockney Hettie's grasping, practical nature, I suspected she was thoroughly enjoying the opportunity afforded by whatever had befallen Charles to reenact some performance from her days of youth and good looks.

Then I noticed there was a good deal of dark liquid on the well-polished teak tabletop. It looked like blood, which in fact it was. It seemed to have come from Charlie.

"Hettie Brown!" I commanded, "Enough of your theatrics! This is a police matter, not the stage!"

That blew the wind out of her sails and the wailing stopped at least. She stood upright, a petulant, combative look on her face that I recalled from when I first met her during the War at Charles' London place. "Who gave you the right to tell me what to do, Stevie! No one's got the right but Charlie here and someone—very likely you, I might add—gone and killed 'im! Stabbed 'im in the back and cut 'is throat with that there razor! It's yours, ain't it?" She gestured at something out of my sight, hidden by Charles' corpse. "You always were jealous of me and Charlie, weren't you?" I noticed that her dress-front and her sleeves where now drenched in blood, and ignored her childish loss of control and absurd, distasteful accusations. People who accuse others of jealousy, in my experience, are usually seeing the mote in the other's eye! I was indifferent to Charles' mistresses, though Grace Leigh still had her looks and was a superior, middle-class sort, not from the gutter like Hettie.

Now that she was no longer in my way, I could see the truth of her purely factual statement. There was indeed a long, bone knife handle sticking out of his back and it did look like his throat was cut. From the handle, the weapon looked like the carving knife from the sideboard where Mary was presumably intending to stow the chaffing dishes when she discovered the body. I gingerly stepped nearer. There was indeed an open cutthroat razor similar to the one I use, though I don't know how Hettie would know, as I'd got a new one since we left London with an ivory handle, a present from Charles when I damaged the blade of my faithful old wood-handled one. Hettie hadn't done a scrape of physical housekeeping work since we came down here. She must have been snooping.

I must admit I was a bit shaken, between the little guttersnipe's performance and seeing Charles like that. We were indeed very close; the best of friends; naturally her insult was groundless and I ignored it like the officer and gentleman I am. I felt a bit stunned and froze for a minute. I noticed Hettie's tears had turned off as fast as they had begun.

Then the room became rather crowded with people pushing past me."

Leigh offered a shriek when she saw the body and artfully collapsed weeping into young Lawless's arms. Lawless seemed very pleased to be lending her a shoulder to cry on. I glanced out the door and saw Cook outside peering in, her arm around Mary, comforting her.

Hood stood against the wall to the right of the door as I faced it, propping it up, arms crossed across his chest, face watchful, interested, alert, perhaps even amused? I found him a rather sinister, shady character and felt Charles unwise to finance his night clubs, but the older and perhaps wiser head was ignored. It seemed in Chicago where he got into the business, anyone has to pay a group of gangsters he refers to as "Capone's boys," "a percentage of the action" as a cost of running a "speakeasy," as the Americans apparently called their now-illegal drinking clubs.

The Gorgon—one of my pet names for *dear* Letitia Parrot—at once took it upon herself to warn us not to touch anything and chastised Brown for interfering with the crime scene. Faced with the authority of generations of "benevolent" domestic tyrants, the Brown creature reverted to her "lady housekeeper" role, complete with exaggeratedly posh accent. "Sorry, ma'am. I am afraid I lost control. It won't happen again."

The Gorgon looked her up and down like a doubtful specimen of fish. "Well then I suggest you go upstairs and change your clothes. Your dress, especially the arm, is now soaked in blood. Mrs. Stout, perhaps you and Mary could go with her and bring all the clothes to me when she's done. The police will want to examine them. Allow no measures to remove the blood to be taken. Send Agnes to me."

"Yes, Milady!" affirmed Cook, a steely, pleased look in her eye. I suspect the servants liked Hettie's performance even less than her main audience, to which she was usually polite, and the good lady enjoyed an opportunity to see her put in her place. Mary revived a bit and seemed pleased too.

I saw a rebellious look in Hettie Brown's eye and she started to protest. The thunderous look on Lady Parrot's hound-like face and a steady Medusa-like glare through her pince-nez, cowed even our guttersnipe and she went peacefully with her escort out of sight, presumably up the main stair to her rooms.

"Now," started the Gorgon, "as the mainland of the county is temporarily isolated from us, we must postpone our duty to notify the authorities. First I suggest we fix in our minds the scene before us so we can render an accurate account to those authorities eventually. No doubt my friend Major MacKean, the Chief Constable, will come round and take charge as soon as we can notify the constable in the village. The Colonel and Mrs. MacKean live only three miles from Morthead Minor. We must preserve the evidence. As the storm is bound to abate by tomorrow, if I still have my weather bump, I think it best to lock the door and leave everything as it is. We shall have to eat on card-tables in the sitting room or perhaps the ballroom. That might be more convenient for the staff. I will arrange matters with Cook later."

"I agree as far as it goes," I stuck my oar in. "Though it does seem hard to leave poor Charles lying there in his own blood. But surely we should also each account for where we were when we heard the commotion?"

"Yes, Major. Very astute of you. But first things first. We can do that in the sitting room later." Thus, cavalierly, was a gentleman routed.

"Very well, Lady Parrot," I said with what good grace I could muster. I used the title to irritate her. Since the baronetcy was extinct, she felt her courtesy handle might as well be too. Hence she preferred "Mrs. Parrot" or Letitia to the well-acquainted.

It really is a man's place to take charge in these sorts of circumstances. I thoroughly disapprove of these pushy modern flapper women. It's bad enough with the young ones who look at you like some fossil, but from one's relative contemporaries!

"Now," continued the last Parrot of her breed, and that only by marriage, "let us examine the room. Perhaps Professor Lawless, you can take Miss Leigh to the sitting room and give her some medicinal brandy, as she seems to be a bit shocked. Mr. Hood and Major Bly, if you would oblige me by aiding in the examination of this room and noting details. Three witnesses are always better than one."

She proceeded to approach the corpse. "The throat seems to have been cut quite efficiently. And the razor blade does seem covered in blood. But there again from the amount of blood that would pulse out from the carotid it would whether it or the carving knife were used. Both would be sharp enough; the cutthroat perhaps easier. Mr. Hood, would you open that drawer in the sideboard so we can ascertain without removing it that this indeed is the carving knife. Please use your handkerchief to not confuse finger marks."

Hood did this. We all took a look and saw various utensils, including the carving fork, but no sign of the knife. "Well, the carving knife is certainly not where it is meant to be. And as I recall it was not used this morning at breakfast so it isn't being washed up. So we must conclude that the knife in Charles's back is the one from the sideboard." She looked more closely. "I recognize that slight chip in the horn handle. I think that's conclusive. Would you close the drawer—" She broke off as if something had caught her attention. She had glanced back at the drawer. "There's some piece of jewelry amongst the cutlery. How odd. The servants don't wear any and Brown doesn't do any of the manual tasks." She went over to take a closer look. "It's a diamond earring. Similar to the one Miss Leigh was wearing at breakfast yesterday morning. I believe she said Charles had just given them to her and he wanted to see them on. Not very appropriate as a present for a young secretary nor for daytime wear, but I cannot recall her coming near the open drawer. Perhaps she got out an extra serving spoon?"

"No, it couldn't have been during that breakfast," said Hood. "I complimented her on them just as we left the room. She had both on then."

"How odd," the Gorgon replied. "Will you use your trusty hanky to close the drawer again?" He complied and we turned our attentions to the table. Blood was all over it, pooled near Charles's neck and outstretched arm. Some was slowly dripping over the table's edge.

I've seen a lot of dead men and dismembered body parts, but that was on the field of honour where men become hardened to it. This was my dearest friend and constant companion for many years now, during and since the War. I am not ashamed to say that it was hard to keep a stiff upper lip and a dry eye, but manly to the last, I managed it.

A razor very like mine lay open in that pool of blood near his head. "Is that your razor, Major?" asked Parrot in her blunt, unbecomingly mannish fashion.

I looked carefully at it. "It is either mine or Charles's. When I broke the blade of my wood-handled one shortly after we moved here, he gave me one with an ivory handle of the same sort he used. Unless Mr. Hood, Professor Lawless, Jeffries, or Georges have a similar type, which I doubt as it is inlaid with silver in a distinctive pattern, it's one of the two." Both she and I glanced at Hood, who shook his head. "Though I fail to see how Brown recognized it as mine and not Charles's. As far as I know, she hasn't been in my room since we came here, much less rooting through my tackle. I haven't seen her doing a lick of housework since Charles moved down here. She used to in London, and likely knew what my old razor looked like and Charles'. So logically she'd think it was his."

"She may simply be a snoop," suggested the Gorgon, "it wouldn't surprise me in the least. Especially about people she is jealous of, I'd suspect, like you and Miss Leigh, no doubt."

"True. But it could also mean she knows because used it herself to frame me. Charles was catching onto some new tricks of hers and wasn't pleased about it . . . Of course I would say that if I was guilty, wouldn't I? But it's true, I swear, on my honor as an officer and a gentleman!"

"Very good, Major. It's not really my place to judge of course. Now let's all look about the room for anything else suggestive." We did so, examining the table and the carpeting, including under and around it. All we bagged were three handkerchiefs, two men's and one woman's. All near or under one of the chairs Charles's had collapsed between onto the table when attacked. One bore the monogram SB, I'm afraid, and the other PL. The lady's was a plain white affair with a lacy border. "These appear to be yours and Professor Lawless's. Do you agree, Major?"

I did.

"Do you know how yours got here?" Parrot asked.

"No."

"Do you carry one only, or a spare as well?"

"Usually one in my trouser pocket in case I take the jacket off—I keep the other one there in the inside pocket."

"Will you check to see if they are both there and produce them before us if so?"

It didn't really sound like a request. I produced one crumples one from my trouser pocket and a fresh one from my sports jacket.

"Thank you, Major."

"I believe the lady's hanky is of the sort Miss Leigh uses, probably bought at Woolworth's or some such," Parrot remarked. "For what, if anything, they are worth we'd better put them back on the floor and lock the doors." She had Agnes retrieve the keys earlier and had them in the pocket of her tweed jacket.

We went out of the room and she secured the doors.

The three of us stood between the stair and dining room. Hood leant negligently, his shoulders against the door of the cloakroom under the stairs. He'd got out one of his cigars and clamped it, unlit, between his teeth in a characteristic pose. Parrot had her back to the door she had just locked, while I had mine faced in the direction of the reception hall.

Parrot asked, "Major, when and where did you last see Charles Mortlake alive?"

"In the Office," I answered, "probably about thirty minutes ago, though it seems an age!"

"When he left the Office, what explanation did he give?"

"He said he wanted to have a word with someone. As best I recall he didn't mention the name. I assumed it would be Leigh, or Brown more likely, as he sounded decidedly put out and he'd been poring over an accounts ledger. I was doing the *Times'* crossword and wasn't paying close attention. He said something about being back soon and I said right-oh or some such. I never dreamed it would be our last exchange!"

"Naturally not, Major, assuming as we must your innocence. For present purposes, at least."

At about this time Cook and Mary returned complete with Brown's clothing wrapped up in newspaper and string. Parrot gladly received the parcel. Made sure through questioning that it contained all the clothing Brown had been wearing, unlocked the dining room door and placed it on the sideboard, before rejoining us and relocking the door. Brown was reported to be having a bath and "furious mad, ma'am," as Cook reported with satisfaction. She thanked the servants and dismissed them for now, suggesting that Mary, though she seemed quite recovered, have some sweet tea and something to eat. Cook agreed and bore her henchwoman off to her domain.

"Oh, by the way Mr. Hood, what were your movements in the past hour?" asked Parrot.

Hood took the cigar out of his mouth with his right hand. "Now let me see. Since breakfast—I think that was about an hour and a half ago if I'm not mistaken," he said, glancing at his wristwatch, "—I went up to my room to get something. Used the john. Then for over an hour I've been shooting pool in what you folks call the games room. I was there when I heard the to-do and came to investigate, like everyone else."

"Thank you. Did anyone see you in that time?"

Hood rubbed the bridge of his nose with his left forefinger. "I think I passed the Professor when I came out of the john and took a look in at Miss Leigh in that office of hers. She may have seen me. I think I saw Mary downstairs on my way to the billiard hall. That's pretty much it. No one came in."

"Thank you," said Parrot. "We'll first proceed to your room, Major, to see whether your razor is in place, then check on Charles's, and lastly I suggest we take a quick look at the Office, before repairing to the sitting room."

We fell in with her plan as if mesmerized. I was preoccupied by the peril I faced. With my razor perhaps being used to murder Charles, someone was obviously trying to get me hanged despite, I swear, my innocence. Of course if I were a scoundrel, I would probably protest my innocence without blinking an eye after swearing on a stack of Bibles. Whether the police believed me was the crucial point. I can't say things were looking too good.

We climbed the stairs, my heart full of the gloomy conviction that someone—likely Brown in a fit of jealous pique—had killed Charles and tried to incriminate me. The lady's handkerchief and the earring in the drawer might support this idea, as would Lawless's kerchief. Brown would be jealous of Charles's new lady love, and I dare say also of Lawless, as Charles has been lavishing attention on the Professor lately. And who knows how that woman's twisted mind works, and what depths of evil might result!

It was as I feared. I opened my razor case—quite an elaborate affair with matching ivory-handled brushes and so forth—and the razor's slot in the brown velvet lining was empty. We proceeded to Charles's rooms. Parrot rang for Georges. The other servants had naturally informed him of his master's death, and he was pale but had control of himself like the good batman he had been. After we explained our mission, he led us into Charles' bath, opened the deep mirror-doored cabinet over the sink, lifted a case the spitting image of mine onto the edge of the washstand, and opened it. Charles' set was not, as I anticipated gloomily, complete. Its razor was also missing. Which was the one that had done the deed? Where was the other?

Lady Parrot was unperturbed. After a moment's thought, she ordered Georges to summon Agnes and Mary and make a thorough search of the house party's rooms, including her own and Mrs. Brown's, and the offices of Mrs. Brown and Miss Leigh.

After she had dismissed him, she commented, "Not that it makes much difference where the second razor is. I suspect it will be found in one of the three with clues already to their name. Or perhaps a fourth to further confuse what should be a quite simple matter, if only someone unimpeachable saw something. I must check with Cook and Mary later I think. And Georges and Agnes. I very much doubt it will be found in association with the true killer. Unless he or she is more clever than I think."

Was it my imagination or did she look at both Hood and I speculatively? Especially me. I knew we exchanged barbs regularly and she had no great opinion of my understanding or mental acuity, but did she truly think me capable of murder? I believe she blamed the whole officer class, especially commanding officers, for the extreme loss of life in the Great War, including her sons. Even though I was but a lowly Major of infantry, I suspect some of her low opinion of the intellect of staff officers and heroes as Kitchener, Haig, and Marshal Foch rubbed off on me.

We went downstairs and reached the Office. The door was open just as I had left it, the fire burning in the grate. It had been such a happy retreat for both Charles and I. Memories of collegial work, discussion of our wartime successes, estate business, and more flooded back. I could barely bring myself to enter it knowing all that was irrevocably past! Alas for happier days!

Parrot made a beeline for Charles' desk, Hood and I were pulled like satellites in her forceful wake. She commented that the ledger Charles had been examining was the household accounts. It had been left to one side of the blotter. On the blotter was a handwritten letter addressed to the senior partner of Charles's main solicitors in London. In Charles's hand it read:

Dear Netherhill:

Please go ahead with the new will I discussed with you earlier in the week by phone. Even if the party makes restitution, the betrayal makes me disinclined to benefit the person we discussed as a major beneficiary any longer. Substitute the minor benefit we discussed.

Yours Truly,
Captain Charles Mortlake, Esquire

"Is Charles' writing familiar to you Mr. Hood?"

He replied in the affirmative that it was and he had no doubt that either this was his hand or a brilliant forgery. I concurred, put out that she had not asked me. I was also quite surprised that Charles was contemplating altering his Will without mentioning it to me. He was usually quite open about its contents, at least regarding Brown, Leigh, and I. It disturbed me. What if Charles was changing his disposition to me? That would pretty well cook my goose, and make me hard up to boot, a retired Major with few private means. My elder brother inherited the land. I went in for the military and my younger brother, being more bookish, took orders. When she died recently, mater left us equal shares in what little she had to leave in her own right. It was helpful, but not a living.

Parrot looked about the room some more but found nothing to interest her, playing detective as she was. She felt these documents should be left undisturbed until the police arrived and hence locked the door. I barely remembered to retrieve my pipe and the *Times*. We proceeded to join Lawless and Miss Leigh in the sitting room.

We found them a picture of unconcern. Two cooing doves. Lawless actually had his arm about her shoulders and she was resting her head against his shoulder, a smile on her face at something he had said. You would not think she had just lost a lover and employer, and he a benefactor! These young people are so selfish. No sense of decorum. Admittedly he removed his arm and she sat up straight and blushed as soon as we entered, but really! No mourning in that quarter, I could see. I wondered if that earring and those kerchiefs were plants, as Parrot seemed to think.

"Sorry to be so long Professor, Miss Leigh!" said the Parrot, giving what she probably thinks of as a gracious smile, but reminds me more of hound about to bay. "We made a few puzzling discoveries." She proceeded to describe them. Neither admitted knowledge of how their property got there. Both checked—Lawless his trouser pocket; Leigh her sleeve—and produced handkerchiefs, both wet, I assume with Leigh's earlier tears. Leigh claimed she had no idea when the earring went missing, but she remembered putting both in her jewelry box the night before. She had on faux-pearl earrings today.

Just then Brown flew in, wearing the spitting image of the dress she had ruined and a furious expression on her face. "The servants are searching my rooms! I'd like to know who gave you the right to give orders round 'ere, Milady high and mightiness! Yesterday's goods! If it weren't for Charlie buying this rotten dump you'd be in queer street, you old bag!"

Parrot ignored her ranting. "I have no right but a moral one. My aim is to find facts for the police to work with to identify and convict the culprit. I am assuming you wish your—employer's killer to be brought to book like a reasonable human being. Perhaps I am mistaken?" That took the wind out of Brown's sails. She gave an incoherent rambling self-justification, which trailed off into mumbled, insincere, apologies. No need to record it here.

Parrot deigned to brief her on developments.

"Might I ask where the three of you were when Mary raised the alarm and for the hour before? The blood, I note, had not really started to clot. The Major says Charles left the library about half an hour before to see someone unspecified."

"I was in the library working on the catalogue Charles wants. Wanted," said Lawless. "I went there right after breakfast and was still there when I heard the yelling."

"Thank you Professor! And you, Miss Leigh?"

"Well, after tidying up after breakfast in the bathroom and my room, I went down and got my instructions from Charles. He wanted some letters to the bank and some associates typed. They were replies to letters received the day before yesterday." That was when the storm hit in the afternoon, trapping Hood, who had been going to leave the next day, and Parrot who had come over for tea and stayed too long afterwards in the Orangerie to get back across the causeway to the

Lodge. "Charles had written in the margins how to respond. The Major was there, weren't you, Major?" I nodded. "Then I went upstairs and started to work on the letters. I'd just about run out of things to do and was about to take them down to Charles to sign when I heard someone calling—I always leave my door open and it is near the head of the stairs—and ran down the stairs."

Parrot thanked her. She looked significantly at the sulky Brown, eyebrow raised.

"If you really 'ave to know I went to the kitchen to talk to the cook about today's menus after breakfast. Then I was mostly in me office,"—this was a cubbyhole beyond the baize door that used to be the butler's pantry; a passage way in front of it leads into the kitchen through another swinging door—"though I may have come out once or twice. Charlie's murder has me in a tizzy!"

So ended the above-stairs portion of the investigation. Parrot alone interviewed the servants later and kept the results to herself until the police came the next day.

I was right. It was Brown. Charles had caught her pilfering regular sums from the supposed tradesmen's accounts—he'd found out she took a "commission." She'd tried that once before in London and he'd warned her if it happened again there'd be no annuity for her in his will, despite their relationship. It seemed he meant to leave her a thousand pounds instead. He had hinted at his discovery and told her he would speak with her about it this morning. When informed of his resolve, she was prepared, complete with my razor—which it later came out she used first—the kerchiefs, and the earring. She was unaware that Charles had actually talked with his solicitor over the telephone about it. She also hadn't realized Cook as well as I had noticed her suddenly darkened wristbands. She threw herself on the corpse, as Parrot had suspected, to make it unclear when she got the blood on her dress. She hadn't dared go up either stair to change in case someone saw her full on.

The one thing she had forgotten was to bring a change of clothes down with her. Otherwise, but for the telephone call to his solicitor and Cook's sharp eye, I, an innocent man, might have been hanged.

—Major Stephen Bly, Devizesshire Foot, retired

A Hanging Offence

After breakfast, I freshened up in the downstairs cloakroom and decided to put in some more work gardening in the Orangerie, despite a stiff back and sore shoulders and arms. The result of prior gardening, in a sense. One must expect these things at my age, even though I am pretty fit from so much gardening. I might as well make my storm-enforced stay in my old home productive. Besides, I find gardening soothing. Pruning back, cutting off deadheads, weeding are all fulfilling in their quiet way. It's a pity that people aren't more like garden plants, but there again that would make us more like God, I suppose!

"Letitia, the devil makes work for idle hands," as Mother was all too fond of admonishing. She could be quite tiresome really, always full of proverbs, adages, clichés, bromides, or maxims, whatever you choose to call them; I sometimes wonder if anything else ever passed between the dear old thing's lips. Were they the sole subject of her inner thoughts? A frightening idea! But it takes all kinds to make a world, as she would be all too ready to say! All her actions required endorsement by some saying. Not an overly bright woman and decidedly mundane, but good-hearted, practical, and well-meaning for all that.

Thank God I took after Father! She was a Saunders of the Devizes branch. Father was a country squire, a Debenham of the Clifton Debenhams, but had been to Cambridge. Not just for the social contacts like too many gentry either. He took a First in Modern History. He always regretted being the only son. Otherwise I'm sure he'd have made a brilliant career in the Civil Service. His tutor had the Treasury or the Foreign Service in mind for him. But it would have broken his father's heart. Grandfather was a rather stupid man with a bovine countenance, who thought little about anything except the estate, hunting, and livestock. His mother had all the intellect in that family -- the mirror image of my own.

Acting on my worthy resolution, I rounded the stairs from the cloakroom and proceeded to the Orangerie. I had slipped in at about ten-thirty on my way to bed the previous evening to retrieve a tweed jacket I had taken off there and forgotten. So I checked that the french windows were bolted and, meeting Mary in the inner hall about to start her lock-up rounds, told her that I had seen to the garden room. As there are no curtains, she doesn't go in there in the morning except later to take a duster and mop over the marble, but that was well after breakfast.

I entered the room and came face to face with Charles Mortlake himself, the relatively new Master of Morthead Manor.

After Sir John Parrot, my husband, died, there were no heirs as our boys died in the War and there were no collaterals lurking about. The hereditary knighthood was thus extinguished. Hence, I prefer to be called Mrs. Parrot now, though I am still entitled to the honorific "Lady." The property was badly in need of repairs and death duties took most of the modest living that remained after wartime taxation. So the estate and mortgages landed in my lap.

Fortunately Charles Mortlake, a rich, darkly handsome financier nearing fifty, paid me a good price, immaculately renovated and modernized the place, and let me retain the Lodge. My new home is just across the causeway on the narrow isthmus separating the main grounds on the large Headland from the village of Morthead Minor. I cleared enough to renovate and modernize it into a cozy little haven for two maids and myself, with enough left for a comfortable income for my modest needs. I am occupying myself with creating a lovely, if rather miniature garden refuge at the Lodge. I see it as a memorial to my husband and sons, as is the fortunate material rejuvenation of the Manor. The morals of its new owner—with a "former" mistress as housekeeper and a newly seduced, confused young woman of reasonable if middle-class family, as personal secretary and mistress—leave a lot to be desired. Not to mention a close friendship with an older former comrade—I suspect that of being rather too close to be natural, if you can take a hint. Still one must take the rough with the smooth, as Mother would doubtless say, choosing not to see any sign of debauchery. As long as he didn't frighten the horses, as some Lady wittily put it, by going for the servants, I would hold my tongue. Were anything untoward to happen, I would get them new situations with my various friends about the county. The "servant problem" being what it is, that should not be difficult, though I would prefer my former servants to remain caring for the old place while they can do so in all decency. Charles's behaviour towards me has been on the whole generous and impeccable. I can drop in at any time and work about in the Orangerie or gardens or look something up in my "old friends" in the library. I am not sure what will happen to the Manor if Charles dies, but there again that is likely to be after my time, as I am over a decade his senior. Sir John was twelve years older than I and died of a broken heart really. The boys, you know.

Unfortunately at that moment Charles was not his usual suave, composed self. In fact he wasn't at all. I mean he was hanging by the neck, his feet almost touching the floor, from a noose made from the bell pull-rope just in front of the raised beds. His eyeballs were bulging, his mouth was open, and his tongue protruded like some Maori god or warrior. The eyeballs were flecked with burst blood vessels. The air, usually a pleasant mixture of earth, flowers, and other plant odors, included the scent of urine. His trouser-front seemed soiled.

It seemed our host had departed this world. He had put in electric bells and disconnected the old mechanical system, but left the pulls for some reason. Aesthetic, I suppose, or perhaps an odd sense of humor picturing frustrated guests pulling them and not noticing the nearby buttons. I suspect he had a touch of the sadist in him in a discreet way. He may have hoped that my friendship would prove useful with the county set, the village, and the estate workers. If he felt I would be saddened at seeing someone else ruling the roost in my old home, he saw no sign of it and got no pleasure in that direction. Generally I was not unhappy with my lot in life. I have always been a realist and accepted the inevitable practically. Perhaps there is something of Mother in me after all. Father was a bit more a dreamer, though an intellectual one.

My legendary sangfroid was almost thrown for a loop by encountering Charles's remains. I did, however, manage to keep from yelling "Help! Murder!" or some such foolishness. Besides, it looked rather like our host had left us voluntarily. Yes, I noted, the wire from the old bell system still partly attached to the rope had been pulled down and securely attached to the stout wooden tool rack along the wall by the door. The rope had been slung over an ornate satyr head at the top of one of the wrought iron columns that supported the iron structure holding the glass roof up. Charles may have prepared this, then stood on the marble edge of the raised bed behind him, put the noose about his head, and stepped off to meet his maker. Yes, it looked as if it could have been that way. Charles didn't seem the type, but he had seemed unusually bored lately, perhaps a sign of some deeper malady.

Instead of yelling my head off, I restrained myself and walked—I think steadily enough, though I must admit to being somewhat discomposed—to the Office to inform the Major. He was already, I knew, deeply perturbed at the unused state Charles's bed was found in this morning. Silly, as he was invariably the last up and the french window in his Office was left open, despite Mary's checking it was bolted at about 10:45. He reputedly never slept well since the War and only took to his bed when quite exhausted. Usually between midnight and two, I am told. The Major had insisted that Jeffries, the chauffeur and handyman, search the grounds. The storm still isolated us from the village. The telephone lines were down, otherwise I am sure he would have called in the authorities, so great had been his unease over breakfast. We had tried to calm him to no avail.

I found him pacing the floor, his thin hair disordered as if he had been passing a hand through it, his wire rimmed glasses hung from their chain.

"Major," I said, gaining his attention.

"It's Charles, isn't it? Please tell me first if he is all right! Where has Jeffries found him? Why didn't he report to me?"

"Please stay calm, Stephen. Perhaps you should sit down. I'll pour us both a brandy. I certainly need one after finding him."

He crumpled into the nearest chair. "Confound it woman! You have a tongue in your head!" I noticed that, tiresome as ever, poor Stephen was turning a violent shade of red. "Tell me!" he bellowed. He had paused, looming over my seated form on the Chesterfield, making strangling-like motions in the air near to my head with his semi-clenched, outstretched hands, in a manner I found most objectionable. Such behavior towards an elderly widow lady is ill mannered. "Where and how is he?!"

Really! What behavior for a self-described gentleman! Addressing me like some domestic tyrant would a lackey, or an imbecile. Where was his stiff upper lip? I decided breaking it to him gently was not feasible.

Ignoring his ranting with commendable sangfroid—if I don't say it, who will, after all? —I decided to be blunt.

"I am afraid I found him. At this moment he is hanging by the neck from a noose in the Orangerie just in front of the raised edge of the bed. Quite dead, I'm afraid. It looks like he may have taken his own life. Not pretty. So sad."

His color changed from red to white with amazing rapidity. He had barely turned around and moved to my left before almost collapsing onto the settee, just missing me. When the bouncing subsided, I regained my feet and got those brandies from the liquor cabinet, taking the key from the top drawer of Charles's former desk. After downing a snifter in one gulp, like a cormorant swallowing a fish, the Major calmed down and said in a voice chastened with shock, "I do not believe Charles would take his own life. He had everything to live for! Money, friends, plenty of attention from the fairer sex...."

"Perhaps he was hiding something from you? Or was a secret melancholic?" I suggested.

"I don't believe it and you won't change my mind!" he said in that mulish tone I knew too well. He was a trifle flushed. "He was interested in the estate. Our times together going about them were happy. His broader business ventures, including this nightclub partnership with Hood," he said, scowling with distaste for my ape-like, reticent American fellow guest—personally, I found Hood intriguing in a risqué kind of way, "and the bank are in fine fettle. I tell you, it cannot be suicide!"

"Well, let us leave that to the coroner and the police to determine. Cook assures me the storm is calming down and the village will no longer be isolated by tomorrow at latest. We just need to leave things as they are."

"No!" he bellowed, slapping his knees forcefully. His color again became alarming and a vein swelled at his temple. "We must look into this at once, do you hear, Letitia! I am not going to let you take charge of this in your usual oh-so-superior way. And yes, I know the Chief Constable is a bosom pal of yours!"

I saw no alternative other than to humor him. "Very well, Stephen, I will not interfere, but I do think it best to leave the scene undisturbed for the police to examine. I have noticed Charles seemed rather more bored than usual lately. Perhaps it was more serious than that. . ."

"That was just the storm and being out of touch. He never likes being cut off from the bank or any of his business interests! He was perfectly happy. Don't start any talk about depression. It's poppycock! Charles lived life to the fullest like a man. Always did. Always would. And a real man doesn't take his life! I must go to him." With this he stopped haranguing me, jerked to his feet, stifled a sob, and dashed out the door. I reluctantly followed, after buzzing for Mary, at a leisurely pace. Mary met me in the hall, I told her the Master had been found dead in the Orangerie, perhaps having taken his own life, and asked her to alert the other members of the enforced house party.

Soon we all—the Major, Patrick Lawless, Grace Leigh, Mrs. Brown, Mr. Hood, and I were assembled at the doorway, crowding the space in front of Charles. Brown, the lady house keeper, was blubbering. Leigh went white and needed Lawless's supporting arm. I noticed she was wearing heavy makeup, unusual for her, except just lately. I wondered if Charles had been getting violent with her. I hear he had a nasty temper when inebriated.

Brown habitually wore makeup almost plastered on, so one couldn't tell with her by look. But she did seem sore at times, which led one to speculate if Charles's "manly" side included battering mistresses. There had been that deplorable incident after he pinched Agnes' bottom, she slapped him, and he retaliated. But I should not bring that up here. Hettie Brown was loudly sobbing, the tears making little runnels in the pancake.

I'd thought Grace Leigh, as a former front-line VAD nurse, would display more composure before a body. After all, she probably saw hundreds—thousands perhaps—during the slaughter they now call the War to End All Wars. Men are so naive and expect everyone else to accept their silly nostrums. Statesmen worst of all. But there again this was somewhat different from a dead man brought into a casualty station.

I wondered if those two children, Lawless and Leigh might make a match of it. The Professor seemed to be quite taken with her. I wonder if he knew about her relationship with Charles, and if he did, what his reaction had been when he realized. If so and Charles's were knocking her about, what would he do?

When the Major saw Brown, he ordered her to stop shedding crocodile tears, get Georges, and send Gladys for Jeffries if he wasn't back. Georges was Charles's French valet, and Jeffries was the Charles's former batman. Charles ended the War unscathed, and as a Captain in the Major's infantry battalion, unlike my boys. Gladys was the kitchen maid, lowest in the servant "ranks," as I'm sure Stephen Bly would put it!

Against my advice, he had Jeffries and Georges get the body down and have him carried upstairs to his bedchamber. My old servants later told me that, once there, he had them undress the body and bathe the nappy smell from him. He had them put Charles in another suit. His evening dress the Major had them set aside for the police. Once Charles was decent again—if a corpse can be "decent"! — the Major practically frog-marched Grace upstairs to examine the body. Lawless, protesting ineffectually on her behalf, came to support her, and the rest of us followed out of curiosity.

"Nurse, first look at his neck!" the Major ordered. "Do you see anything peculiar about the marks?"

"Well, there do seem to be two overlapping ligature marks," said Leigh, frowning. "Also some abrasions, like fingernail scratches perhaps. He may have changed his mind, poor fellow, and tried to get his fingers under the rope, but failed."

"Now look at his fingers," he said, frowning at her unwelcome interpretation.

The hands were laid out on top of the sheet. She picked them up and examined the fingers carefully on both sides. "The fingers and thumbs seem bruised. Some of the nails seem torn, as if he was trying to save himself."

"Exactly. Now I want you to have a look at his backside. I'll pull the sheet back and, Georges, if you would please hold him up on his side so the party can look."

Once he was on his side, we all saw that much of his exposed skin was a purplish-red, like a bruise.

"Now what would that be? Was he beaten?"

"I'm not quite sure," said Grace Leigh, "but I think I've seen it before quite often. When a body lies in one position after death, the blood pools at the lowest place, and if it lies undisturbed for say half an hour it stays in place, even if it's moved. My God, that means Charles was moved after death!"

The implications of that began to sink in. It seemed inescapable now. If she were right, Charles was likely murdered. Or at least someone moved the body after death. How inconvenient. No easy verdict of suicide while temporarily deranged.

"I think he was garroted, not hanged," asserted the Major. "Then he was strung up to make it look like suicide."

"But where was he killed, then?" I asked, a bit stunned, but struggling to put on a good face like a decent gentlewoman.

"Remember the smell? A man often lets go of his bowels and bladder when he's killed. Unless the servants or any of us have noticed it anywhere else, I think it was right there in the Orangerie."

"Well, then, it was after ten-thirty or it may have been ten forty-five," I said firmly. "I went in then to get the jacket I'd left behind earlier." I hadn't needed it under the old car coat I use as a smock to protect my frock while gardening about the Manor. "I met Mary in the inner hall just starting her rounds. I told her I'd checked the french windows and they were bolted, so she didn't need to go in herself. She doesn't go in early in the morning, as there are no curtains. The plants need as much light as they can get, especially with winter coming on. The doors are left bolted unless someone goes out that way," I added by way of explanation.

"When did you last see him Major?" I asked.

"I went up early. Bit of a gippy tummy."

"As I understand it from Mary, Charles wasn't in the Office towards eleven, though his papers were still spread out, the lights were lit, and the door open, so she assumed he'd just stepped out or gone to retrieve something. She didn't see him on her rounds, so perhaps he went upstairs . . ." I trailed off as a memory struck me.

"What is it, Lady Parrot?" asked Professor Lawless.

"Well, I just recalled that there was a peculiar odor when I was in the Orangerie last evening, and it might have been the same smell, only weaker, but it had slipped my mind somehow. I didn't put on the lights. I know the room so well. I just reached my jacket from the hook by the door. And then I thought of the time and checked the bolt on the window. The light from the hall through the door was enough for that. He was definitely not hanging up there. But he could have been laid down on the beds or perhaps . . ."

"What is it?" the Major demanded.

"It just occurred to me that he could have been in the secret passage. The odour wasn't as strong, as clearly identifiable then, as it was this morning. Just a slight unpleasant air. Perhaps he was even killed there, or at least left in the passage for a time until the suicide could be more conveniently stage-managed overnight? Everyone is shown the secret passages as part of their initial grand tour. All the village knows about them too."

"The idea sounds plausible. Let us check it out immediately!" pronounced the Major and started for the door.

"It could have been one of the servants, or an intruder . . . Mary found the windows in the Office open this morning. That's why we assumed he might have gone for a breath of fresh air and slipped and got hurt after all," suggested Professor Lawless.

"Just possibly," the Major admitted, pausing near the doorway, "but we've been isolated by the storm for two days. A tramp would have to have been hiding in one of the outbuildings. And Jeffries is a good man. Sharp. Wouldn't shirk his rounds. Would have detected the incursion."

"The alternative would be that the killer opened the Office window to make it look like Charles went out and had not come back," I said.

"Very likely, although why would he want to delay the body being found?"

"Perhaps to give him, her, or them," I corrected, "more time to dispose of incriminating evidence?"

"Could be a sound idea. Perhaps they wanted to dispose of the garrote, if I'm right about that."

"Would considering who might know how to make one would help?" I suggested.

"Good. I'd know, of course. So would Jeffries and Georges. Did you see service, Hood?"

"I was a dough boy, yes. But I wasn't trained in making garrotes. I could kill a guy with a rope if I took it in my head it'd be a good idea. I didn't though."

"Neither did I, but we would say that, wouldn't we?"

"Lawless, did you answer your country's call?"

"I was a lieutenant and eventually a captain, yes, but with my degrees they assigned me to intelligence. I do believe I could strangle someone with a rope if I wanted too. After basic training I felt like strangling the drill instructor!" This drew a chorus of just-between-us laughs from the men present. Even Georges permitted himself a discreet smile. "But mostly it was desk work. I only got to the front on a few occasions when something hush-hush was going down. I am not sure of the details of making a formal garrote."

"Of course the ladies would not know," said the Major, ever naive.

"What is so difficult, at least theoretically, in getting behind someone you know, getting a cord round their neck, and putting with all your might?" I asked rhetorically. "My sons discussed such things on leave after training. I even practiced with their Webley revolvers by the cliff."

"I've seen the results and can imagine how it is done," offered Grace Leigh, in support of women's capabilities.

"Ah, but I don't think a woman alone could have strung up the body! Nor, if I don't miss my guess, would your friend the Chief Constable, Letitia!"

"But two women, or a woman and a man might, just playing Devil's advocate, of course," I put in.

I would imagine the most likely pairing in police minds would be Grace, a fairly strong young woman—I imagine from her nursing experiences—who gets an annuity in the will, and the smitten professor, especially if he knew of Charles hitting her. She might even have managed it herself.

It was hard to see an accomplice for Brown out of love or friendship. She wasn't very popular. Unless the Major was putting on an act? He also benefited in the will. Perhaps he was cleverer than I thought . . . There are, however, other motives. Perhaps as a partner of Charles, who might benefit by his death in various ways, Hood might make common interest with her. Brown also was meant to get an annuity if she was still in Charles's employ—an unfair condition she must feel after a long, and perhaps abusive, relationship. She must be relieved in a way that he's dead, as long as suspicion doesn't fix on her. The Major could have made common cause with her. They have known each over longer than anyone else, though I believe the relationship was more one of rivalry, or jealousy, over Charles's various attentions and, in his own somewhat twisted way, affections.

I? Perhaps I could have just done it myself. Gardening makes even an old woman stronger than mere males think. And being weaker means using your head to get around obstacles. Or I could have allied with one of the servants, particularly if Charles had actually assaulted her—not, I hasten to add, that I would involve anyone else if I contemplated such a, shall we say, weeding exercise.

The Major became impatient with endless speculation. He brusquely ordered Agnes to get some electric torches and bring them to the Orangerie and be damned quick about it. Presumably to check for signs the secret passage was used as a temporary depository for the body. We all dutifully trooped down the front stairs to the desecrated Orangerie in his wake. Now it was to be forever associated with the not quite savory Charles Mortlake's death. But even such associations can be cleansed by time. Especially with living, growing, breathing plants lovingly tended to refresh the spirit and the air, and work their healing magic.

After impatiently waiting all of three or four minutes for the torches, the Major led the party to the room's far corner. A passage connects the sitting room with the Orangerie. Demonstration of the mechanisms was one of the party tricks of the house. Professor Lawless had perhaps most extensively explored them recently, both to advise on the renovations and to pursue his historical interests in such passages and priest-holes for his upcoming scholarly tome. All the non-glass walls, as well as the facings of the beds and the floor, were of Italian marble. There was a sort of frieze going around the room just below glass-level in most places, but roughly at waist-height in the corner and the few other spots where solid wall reached up to the glass roof.

The Major fumbled trying to find the mechanism. I brushed past him. Counting from the corner, I twisted one of the lozenges to the left. Part of the wall moved out of the way. I stepped out of the others' line of sight and the Major and the Professor shone torches inside. Nothing but an impression in the dust of something lying there was visible from outside. The two gentlemen stepped in.

"Definite smell of—bodily products. Stronger than in the room!" the Major exclaimed excitedly. "And what's this!" he said as the torchlight shone on the steep stair that took the passage above window-height into the stone work of the ground-floor walls. "The blighter's gone and left his weapon here. A tough, braided rope. It's threaded in a loop. It would act just like a tourniquet if placed over someone's neck and turned 'round! A garrote indeed!" He went out of sight and retrieved the rope. I didn't waste my breath about not disturbing the evidence. He would have been too bull-headed to listen in any event.

And that was pretty much the evidence as the police found it the following day.

The killer was I, of course.

You may recall that I had sore shoulders and back? More nearly wrenched from hoisting that noxious weed of a man up to make it look like suicide. I didn't know about the pooling of the blood. It's not come up in the mysteries I've read, unfortunately, even if they are accurate, which one often doubts in too many cases.

You may also recall that I was the one who prevented Mary from entering the room on her rounds the previous night. Not that Charles had yet been hoisted. He was safe with the garrote about his neck in the passage entrance. But the smell was considerable. So simple a solution, it escaped attention. How could an assumed fragile old woman manage it? I felt fragile after it for weeks, I can tell you! Usually I am quite robust for a lady in her sixties. Men's odd assumptions, including policemen's, sometimes can be used to our advantage, can they not?

They never could put together a good enough case to make the murder stick on anyone, so in the end no one was charged, though pretty well everyone from Gladys on up was grilled. The Major, Brown, and Leigh got their legacies. Lawless got a bonus of income with Grace. I'm sure he did not regret that. There had been a recent incident where Charles had fondled Agnes, the pretty chambermaid. She handed in her notice of course. Though she got away, and consulted no one but her mother and I, the incident with Charles led to suspicion of one or other of her hulking brothers, poor fellows.

Even the police can overlook the obvious, especially as I am a friend of the Chief Constable's and have been more or less the mainstay of the village for a generation now, and friendly with the county set. I told Agnes I would take care of it. I think she suspects, but doesn't think worse of me for it. I got her an excellent position with Lady Postwhistle on the over side of Devizeston as parlor maid. No roving male eyes in that dowager's well-run establishment. I prevented Mary from checking the door, not because of the body, but because of the odor. Its presence would have tied me to the death. I wasn't totally sure of Mary's loyalty in such a case. And even friendly, youthful policemen looking upon me as an upper class grandmother figure might not overlook that pointer.

Charles had become like bindweed. You can't let that get hold, or else you'll never be done pulling it up. He had already sexually corrupted at least two people with his lure of security and gain if they endured his attentions and occasional distasteful games. Not that I'm accusing the Major of anything unnatural, mind. The exact state of relations between him and Charles is immaterial. I did feel for poor Brown's plight in an abusive situation. I don't believe a man has a right to knock his lady about. He seemed to be starting on Grace Leigh and I wasn't sure she could break free of his enveloping tendrils. Agnes was the last straw. If allowed to proceed, that would have created a scandal. And I could not have let my servants and their families—like my own really, now I had none of my blood left—suffer. Besides, I resented his inherited wealth. My John could have done without years of scrimping just to maintain appearances and given the boys a better education, as they weren't going to get a great deal more but responsibilities. And he went through the War without a scratch, mainly a staff officer and the Major's pet, I suspect. Though I believe he actually liked killing, from some things he said about service.

No, he was a weed and needed decisive action. Pulling out root and branch.

It was very difficult stringing him up. I had hoped the investigation would be superficial. I first dragged him out of the passage, propped him up against the edge of the plant bed, and then pulled and pushed the debris up bit by bit. Once I got him on the bed and propped him against a straight back chair, I got the noose about his head and tightened it, then removed the chair, before easing the hanging body forward. The bed was higher than his knees, so his feet didn't reach the floor. Covered the marks of the chair legs and so forth on the bed as best I could. I had caught him in his Office alone before Mary's rounds, and lured him over to the Orangerie on an excuse about storm leakage. Disposing of him was a distasteful necessity. Think of it as nipping a nasty weed problem in the bud.

—Letitia Parrot

Death on Green Baize

It was after tea, but quite a long time till supper. I was beavering away at the catalogue in the library, and I must admit was pretty bored by then. The door opened, and Hood, Charles's associate in a nightclub venture, came in.

"What are you still doing that stuff for? Come on! Let's have a game of pool. Don't be a killjoy. All work and no play's not a good motto. Especially if you're in my line of business!" He tried to affect a winning smile.

As the American had just shoveled his usual unlit Havana back between his "pearly whites," this produced an effect that might interest an anthropologist—or perhaps a phrenologist—given that his head bore only a thin tonsure of hair and his face resembled a mobster in a motion picture. I sopped my conscience with the thought that saying no to a possible mobster, or at least one who confessed business links to Chicago's Mr. Capone, might not be a good idea and said, "Right-ho! I've just about done my stint for the day. And as Grace is still stuck in her office . . ." I put the file cards in order. Left the books I'd done with to be returned to the shelf come morning, stood up, and shrugged into my jacket.

"Yeah, I wouldn't mind spending some heart-to-heart spooning with that dishy, red-headed, sweet-smelling armful myself. If Mortlake was one of Capone's lieutenants, she'd be his moll— or one of 'em. I'd sort of steer clear of that territory if I was you," Hood said, nudging me in the ribs. We exited the library and we turned right along the corridor toward the games room. He had taught me the rules of the American variant on billiards and often dragooned me into a game, since we were stranded here by this storm, which put the sea over the causeway to the mainland two days ago and made boat passage too treacherous. I didn't mind. Hood was an interesting study, had a sense of humor, and the mild diversion was welcome.

Besides, I was more or less obliged by politeness to entertain him. His host and mine—who I did a fair deal of consulting work for—Charles Mortlake, spent most of his time with his bosom bow, Major Stephen Bly. So as part of the genteel section of the paid help, the task of entertaining his business associate in nightclubs more or less devolved to me. While I wouldn't put it past Lady Parrot to know how to play billiards—her former Manor, after all, did have this room—she seemed far more interested in reading or gardening in the Orangerie than social activities, per se. As a dinner guest when the rough weather hit, she too was cut off from her new residence, the refurbished Lodge in the village across the causeway.

I led the way and so was first in, Hood close behind me. We were making small talk. First I and then my Trans-Atlantic companion trailed off abruptly as our eyes took in the scene. There were feathers everywhere on the carpeted floor, apparently from a cushion from one of the easy chairs in the corners. Some of them also lay on the flower patterned cream and red carpet between the table and the side door we had used.

It was not exactly what we expected. Especially of Charles. Finding him in *flagrante delicto* with a maid on the billiard table probably would not have surprised us by this point. Nor would it embarrass him in the least, I suspect. Where these matters are concerned he seemed to be listening to the "free love" Bloomsbury set, at least for himself. I had my doubts about his happiness if anyone like me trespassed upon his fun and games territory.

But our host was most definitely not in that condition. Oh, he was sprawled across the table all right. But he was fully dressed, unless you count the bloody bullet wounds in his white shirt-front framed by his unbuttoned, impeccably tailored (Saville Row, no doubt), Country Squire tweeds. He was on his back across the table, arms flung out, where he had apparently crumbled. If he wasn't dead already, he looked as if he soon would be without immediate surgical attention. I didn't like the quantity of blood. It suggested his attacker had got the heart or a major artery. It had spurted over the floor for quite a few feet, but seemed to be coming out in a slow ooze now.

No doubt about it, Hood wouldn't be playing his favorite game here anymore. The Green felt was soaked in blood. The American seemed almost as concerned about this desecration as our host's violent demise, muttering something about bastards who stage hits with no consideration. Nonetheless, Mortlake, as a probable body, was definitely not amusing. His eyes were wide open. He looked as shocked as I felt. Then I noticed yet another loud clap of thunder—it had been going on for the past hour or so—and a breeze, and realized the french windows opposite the main door were open, letting the rain in and making the thunder even louder. Perhaps the thunder had disguised the sound of the shot.

As she was the only medically trained person, I sent Hood for Grace, while I went for Major Bly and Lady Parrot. As I was next door to the Orangerie, I checked there first for the lady. Sure enough as she wasn't in the library, I found her there with her old-fashioned car coat on gardening. She was doubtless surprised at the news, but maintained her well-bred sangfroid and displayed nothing but practicality. She ascertained I had sent for former VAD nurse Leigh, started unbuttoning her coat, and suggested I go to inform the Major. She rang for the parlour maid, while we spoke and promised to arrive on the scene as soon as she had removed her coat, tidied up and sent for the first aid supplies. She was on a drop-in basis with our host and maintained the plant beds in the Orangerie immaculately for him.

I found the Major in the Office. He was pacing like an anxious, aging heavyweight and said he had been on the point of going to look for his pal, as Mr. Hood would say, when I appeared with the fell news, at which his face took on an alarmingly red hue. He assured me, in outraged tones, when I suggested he rest and let me get him some brandy, that: "I have no intention of lolling about downing his spirits when Charles needs me to take charge and track the blackguard down!"

Having delivered this melodramatic speech, he pushed past me through the doorway and waddled at a surprising speed for one of his girth and years past the grand stairway to the games room. I saw Lady Parrot would just beat him to it, and felt there was considerable doubt about who would "take charge," the military man or the former chatelaine. Grace looked smashing in a designer frock with a long string of cultured pearls (all courtesy of Charles), and her flapper hair as she click-clacked fetchingly down the stairs in high-heels from her secretarial office. Hood followed her. I saw Mary rounding the corner, also at a good clip, with a large white-painted box in her hands. Either the noise or Mary had alerted Mrs. Brown, Charles's once (and possibly current) mistress and housekeeper for as I walked towards the games room, she too rounded the corner hastily.

By the time I got there, all but Brown had entered the games room. Out of breath and in apparent distress from the tears running down her cheeks, Brown pushed past me into the room, proclaiming melodramatically:

"Oh no, me Charlie's dead! I'll knife the bastard who done it, sure as you're living, I will!" But I recalled cynically, she had once trotted the boards of both Music Hall and dramatic theater, and could have just been enjoying the opportunity to employ her talents, or even using them to cover guilt.

Grace had opened his shirt and was feeling for a pulse in the throat. Finding none, she pulled a pocket mirror out of her neat leather handbag—I had wondered why she'd been carrying it—and put it over Charles' mouth. After a moment she took it away and showed a mirrored surface with no mist.

"I'm afraid there's nothing to be done. He's dead," she said.

"Outrageous! An important financier and landowner like Charles shot in his own home!" bellowed the Major, close to tears. "If the police don't get at him first, I'll throttle the viper!" At that moment I believed he would. I then noticed the odor of urine and feces. It appeared our host had let go as he died. In my limited front-line experience during the War—as an academic with a knowledge of German, I was given a desk job in intelligence—this was quite common with casualties.

"Now that there is nothing to be done for him in this life, I ask you all to be careful not to trample potential evidence!" barked Lady Parrot. "Watch not to walk through the blood splatters. I believe they can give the experts information. Watch where you are stepping and avoid getting feathers on your shoes or clothing.

"Perhaps most of us should stay outside the doorways while the Major and I, assisted by Professor Lawless and Mr. Hood, look over the room. We cannot immediately summon the Police due to the inoperative condition of the telephone and the ongoing storm."

Everyone complied. I suspect the Major was included because he would not stand anything else. He might also have some knowledge of firearms, I suppose.

"Now let us each take a quarter of the room and look for further clues. I'll take the one near the side door, if I may. Major, perhaps you could take the one by the open window? Professor would you search the other one near me, and Mr. Hood, the one on the far side of the billiard table? Call out if you find anything possibly relevant, but please do not touch anything you find. Finger marks, you know."

We each went to our assigned areas and started examining floor and furniture carefully, including under the cushions and in the pockets of the easy chairs. Lady Parrot was first to find something. It was pushed or kicked under the leather armchair by the side door. A handgun—a German pistol by the look of it. After pulling on a pair of clean gardening gloves she drew out of her jacket pocket, she retrieved it. We remaining three searchers came over to take a look and the rest, except Mary and Grace who were already standing there, came round to the side door to get a better look.

"Now look here!" said Hood, when he got close enough to see details. "That's my heater! Someone's trying to frame me. I didn't kill Chuck. And if I had, I sure enough wouldn't drop my Luger at the scene and kick it under a chair for the cops to find. That pistol's my war souvenir. Got it off a dead Kraut. Do I look that stupid?"

Lady Parrot took this information calmly. "Where is it usually kept?" she asked.

"Locked in my suitcase on the floor of that big wardrobe upstairs. Not that there'd be much problem forcing the lock, or probably even finding a similar key or using a bobbypin. Those locks aren't any use against crooks, just honest snoops."

"Then after we finish here, perhaps we should go to your room and seek some sign that your luggage has been tampered with and verify this is indeed your revolver and not a similar one . . . How does one see the bullets . . . Ah, yes, thank you Mr. Hood. I'll do it, as you aren't wearing gloves, though the killer may well have, I suspect." She got the magazine out of the butt as directed. "There are five bullets here. How many more does it contain?"

"It holds eight nine-millimeter loads. It automatically spring-ejects the spent cartridges and loads another round. There's likely one ready to go, so be careful! The safety's not on." He explained how to put it on and Lady Parrot gladly did so.

"Was the magazine full?"

"I loaded eight in the butt before leaving the U.S. I've got a box of cartridges with me, but I haven't used any rounds or had to pull it. Nice change from Chicago."

"So am I correct in assuming that there was one 'ready to go' as you say, and seven in the magazine?"

"That's right."

"Which would match the two holes in Charles's remains." She smelled the end of the barrel, then gave the Major, Hood, and I a chance to do so. "It does smell like it has been fired recently, so I think we have the weapon, if not the shooter." This was likely aimed at Major Bly, who was eyeing Hood like he was contemplating precipitous action.

"Have you mentioned the gun during your sojourn here?"

"The Major and I got to taking about the War," he said diplomatically. The Major always talks of one war or another, mainly the Boer and Great wars. "It was over dinner. Chuck chipped in and I think Paddy here did too."

"I remember," I said. "And then you, the Major, and Charles got your hand guns and treated us to a discourse on the merits of the English Webley versus the German Luger in the sitting room over coffee. I believe both loading and firing mechanisms were explained, and I was left with the impression the Major kept his in his room, Charles's was in his Office, and Mr. Hood's was kept in his luggage. Any of us could have known," I concluded.

"While you held forth," said Lady Parrot. "I was looking through some bound back numbers of the *Complete Gardener* from the library. Such a fascinating publication. I must admit I barely paid attention to your most interesting demonstration. I recall thinking that perhaps it was unwise on general principles to broadcast the locations and workings of firearms in the house. Sir John was very strict on the point. All rifles and side arms were locked in the gun cabinet in the Office when not in use. Most unfortunate Charles didn't maintain a similar policy.

"Well, gentlemen, let us return to the search."

The Major found the next clue: a muddy footprint entering the room from the french window and what looked a streak where someone had wiped mud off on the carpet.

"A largish shoe size. Perhaps size-twelve at a guess. And a man's." All four of us looked at Hood's feet. They were on the small side. Perhaps an eight or even a seven. The Major, on the other hand, had big feet about that size. Mine were about average. None of the ladies or Brown had large feet.

"Outrageous! Someone's trying to imply I murdered my blood brother!" bellowed the flushed retired officer.

"Interesting, don't you think? Two clues so far. Both pointing rather heavy-handedly to particular individuals," remarked our preceptress.

Once we had finished the only other clues were two ladies' handkerchiefs. One had the initials HB embroidered amidst the lacy border. Henrietta Brown? Brown naturally denied involvement in outraged tones. But there again she would, wouldn't she? The other was initialed GL. Grace admitted ownership but was also baffled at its present location.

"No spent cartridges, how interesting. I wonder where they are?" said Lady Parrot once we had completed the search.

After locking the doors to the games room and taking custody of the keys, Lady Parrot led us up the front stairs, left along the gallery to the corridor with the men's rooms. I saw Agnes, the comely chamber maid, discreetly join Mary who whispered to her. No doubt revealing the state of play so far. The Major and Hood agreed to a search of their rooms. The lock of Hood's case was scratched, perhaps suggesting picking? But it hadn't been forced. We tested it—or rather Parrot of the gloves did—and it relocked automatically. When he opened it with the key, the contents were searched and no gun was found. With Agnes's and Mary's assistance, the rest of the room was searched and nothing more of interest was found, except that Hood reported several pairs of missing socks.

We then proceeded to the Major's room beside mine and next to Charles's two-room suite. A pair of muddy boots was found at the back under Charles's bed. "Someone with small feet can wear large shoes by layering on socks," said our oracle.

With grudging permission, Brown agreed to her bed and sitting room being searched, as well as her housekeeper's office. One cartridge of appropriately the right caliber was found beneath a load of newspapers in the kindling box by the bedroom fireplace. "I didn't put it there! I swear!" said Brown, a touch of hysteria in her voice. "I didn't kill Charlie! 'E were a bit rough, but he done right by me!"

"Quite possibly it is as you say, Mrs. Brown," soothed Lady Parrot.

Next Grace's bedsitter was searched. The other cartridge was found under the top layer of coal in the scuttle by the fireplace.

The case was taking on an *Alice in Wonderland* air to me.

Mary and Agnes were then ordered to search the other rooms. We all dutifully went with them, perhaps wondering if something had been planted in our rooms. Nothing more was uncovered in my room, Charles's, or Lady Parrot's. We went back downstairs, and Mrs. Brown's office was searched, with no further result.

Lady Parrot suggested we adjourn to the sitting room for further consideration and discussions and asked Mary to bring a pot of tea to help us in our deliberations. Only Hood openly said he'd prefer a stiff Scotch, though I privately agreed, and I thought Grace looked rather strained and pale, despite the heavy makeup she had on. Usually she wore little or none so you'd notice, though she did favor a soft perfume.

"You look like you could use some brandy," I said, and added politely, "perhaps you also, Mrs. Brown?"

"Oh me?" Grace replied. "No, I'll be fine. A nice cup of tea will put me to rights. Don't fret about me, Patrick dear." She smiled bravely at me as I stood by the arm of the settee where she sat. I wound up getting brandies for Brown, Hood and the Major, while I maintained solidarity with the tea party comprised of the two ladies and myself. The Major and Brown took tea as well as spirits. Mary was just passing their cups to them when Gladys, obviously discomposed at being sent into the gentry's quarters, hesitantly came through the door.

"Yes, Gladys, what news do you have for us?" said Lady Parrot kindly to the obviously tongue-tied, gawky kitchen maid. She was barely out of her teens, if that, with dark hair, an unfortunate lack of chin, and rabbit's teeth.

"Mrs. Stout's compliments, milady. She sent me to tell you, Mr. Jeffries found a load of shabby clothes and lots of socks in one of the outbuildings." Lady Parrot had asked earlier that a search be made of the outbuildings.

"Very good, Gladys. Where are the clothes and Mr. Jeffries?"

"Well, seeing it's raining cats and dogs still and pretty windy, Mr. Jeffries, he got a tarp and bundled the clothes in it to keep them from getting any wetter—some he do say are damp, though the roof of the building's sound. Least he says so. I never been in it meself, Ma'am."

"But where did he bring them too, Gladys? The kitchen?"

"No. Mrs. Stout told him to put them on the stone bench in the scullery where I put the clean clothes after I've put 'em through the mangle-like, afore I put 'em on the line, you'll know the one, Milady. He's waiting in the kitchen for you, in case you have any questions."

"Very good, Gladys. You've now made it quite clear. Please tell Cook and Jeffries we shall be along directly, as soon as we have finished our tea."

"Well, it sounds like my socks have been found," said Hood gloomily. "But I'll probably never get them back. The cops will want them for evidence in this crazy business."

"I believe they return most evidence eventually, Mr. Hood, certainly after the case has been wound up, but that could be quite a long time, even if there is an arrest and a trial," remarked Lady Parrot in her quiet, authoritative manner.

After we finished our tea, while Hood had another brandy, we all trooped dutifully behind our mistress past the dining room, through the outer baize door, past Mrs. Brown's cubbyhole office, and into the kitchen.

Mrs. Stout—who fit her name—and Jeffries got up from the table where she was dousing the chauffeur with tea and a slice of cake left over from tea time, and no doubt exchanging intelligence.

"Thank you so much for diligently searching in this dreadful weather, Jeffries!" began the self-nominated detective-in-chief.

"Anything I can do to help catch Captain Mortlake's killer, I'll be pleased to do, Ma'am," he replied firmly.

"You were the Captain's batman during the War, weren't you, Jeffries?"

"Yes, ma'am. For the final years of it." He was obviously pleased that she recalled this detail.

"Now where exactly did you find the clothing?"

"In that shed we don't use now. In the olden days the gardener done told me it was the piggery."

"I know the place you mean. Yes, it hasn't been used that way since my husband's great-grandfather's day, if I recall correctly. Is it fair to say it is perhaps the nearest ill-frequented outbuilding to the french windows on the games room-side of the house?"

"That'd be the west-side, near the south corner where the Orangerie is, Ma'am?"

"That is correct, Jeffries."

"Well then it is closest, I'd say. None of the sheds and such about there is used. Least in weather like this. The gardeners, they do use 'em for storage of dried manure or tools some times of year, but 'course they're not 'round with the storm on."

"And where were they in the former piggery?"

"Just in the middle of the floor door all dumped on the floor. Like someone was in a hurry to get out of them, I reckon."

"Very good Jeffries. Perhaps you would accompany us now to the scullery while we inspect the clothing."

And we like sheep followed our shepherd out of the room and into the scullery, whence one of the house's best features—from the standpoint of my research—the not-so-secret passage to Charles's Office started. However, we passed by the wall opposite the larder that concealed the entrance and proceeded to the stone sinks, complete with the promised mangle for wringing clothes fairly dry before being put on the clothesline.

By the stone counter beside this necessary apparatus, we stood around while Lady Parrot—gloves back on—examined the clothes. There were no undergarments, simply a large men's shirt, tweed jacket, and woolen trousers with a belt. All were quite worn and looked like they might have come from a rummage sale. There was a similarly worn tweed cloth cap, which didn't match the jacket. Besides these, there were eleven pairs of men's socks wadded up into balls as if hastily taken off, except two pair which were still folded up together. Lady Parrot suggested that someone with small feet had used layers of socks and the folded pairs in the toes to use Major Bly's boots, or alternatively the socks were meant to give that impression. The jacket, trousers, some of the socks, and the chest of the shirt were, to varying degrees, wet from the trickster-killer's passage through the rain, one assumed. The Lady made a rough inspection of the clothes, but, consulting her watch, proposed they be locked up in the library and examined with magnifying glass and better light, once we had dressed for supper. I help Lady deposit the clothes in the library and checked the french windows were bolted. No secret passage, or even a nice priest-hole, could be accessed from that room. Once we were outside, she relocked the door and pocketed the key. Then we followed the others upstairs to dress.

The Major, Lady Parrot, and I were first down. The Major was impatient to start our examination of the clothes and had secured a magnifying glass from Charles's Office. Lady Parrot unlocked the door. We put on the lights and proceeded.

Lady Parrot, with gloves once more, handled the actual examination. She found a few long auburn hairs on the lining of the cap and a couple more on the shoulders of the threadbare tweed blazer. These she put in an envelope, also retrieved from the Office by the Major at her request, sealed them in, wrote were and when we had found them, and had us each sign the flap as a seal.

She was almost finished with the cap when she noticed a faint smell and put the fabric closer to her nose. "Gentlemen, I believe I recognize this scent, but judge for yourselves." She held the scented cap-lining out to the Major first, then to me. We both detected a pleasant, flowery odor that was certainly familiar, but we couldn't quite place it.

Then Lady Parrot put down the cap and started examining the jacket. Then she sniffed the collar. "The same smell, I believe, gentlemen," she said and gave us each another whiff. It was definitely the same.

"I wonder if the clothes had been stored in a drawer with lavender," I said, still as stymied as the Major.

"I don't believe it is lavender. In any event such a method of storage would be unlikely for men's clothing," dismissed the Parrot. I could see her point. It also wasn't lavender, but something a bit more modern perhaps?

Grace, Brown, and Hood joined us at this point. Lady Parrot searched the jacket pockets and found a pair of black leather gloves. In contrast to the other clothing, they were well-used but in good condition. They were for fairly small hands, at least for a man. They clearly could not fit the Major or Hood, both of whom have large paws. At the Parrot's suggestion Brown, Grace, she, and I tried them. They didn't quite fit my petite hands. Grace struggled but did not seem able to get them on, though they looked big enough. Brown had surprisingly small hands. They were somewhat loose on Lady Parrot.

We found little more suggestive about the clothing. Here our investigations ended.

I was being willfully obtuse. I just didn't want to face the implications of finding Grace's very familiar perfume and hair on that cap and jacket. Brown got it first time, as I could tell when the Parrot had her take a whiff. The more, the better she said, as it will probably have faded by the time the police arrive. The strained look on Grace's face also told a tale. As Hood had said earlier, she was "a dishy, red-headed armful" and those auburn hairs matched the length of her bobbed locks. It had to be an insider, of course, to plant the misleading clues and to steal the Luger, the socks, and the boots. It turned out later she had picked the men's clothing up at a church sale in Devizeston, the county town, saying they were for a down and out ex-serviceman she knew in London. She had them and the boots and socks in a bag concealed behind the curtains. Then she lured Charles in for a quick "word." Pretending to get her lipstick out of her bag, she turned her back on him, pulled on the gloves, which fit perfectly, brought out the Luger, and shot him. The thunder made us think the shots were more of the same. Besides, those old doors are very thick, as are the internal walls, and the ceilings. Then she planted the gun and the hankies and scooped up the cartridge cases. Then she put the men's outfit on— socks, boots and all—and went out to get the boots muddy in the flowerbed to one side of the french windows. She made the prints and boot marks and then went across to dump the clothes and pick up the Wellington boots and Macintosh she'd left there. Her frock got rather crumpled. The shirt was just camouflage, she didn't actually wear it.

And she did it for money, for revenge, and for me. She wanted me, but not to be poor. She saw a chance to get the annuity in Charles's will. He had also started hitting her when she balked at his sexual demands, which were becoming increasingly odd and degrading. That was why she had to wear heavy makeup at times.

And if it hadn't been for her perfume and a few hairs, I might now be happily, unknowingly, married to a murderess! It makes me feel queasy when I think about it.

—Patrick Lawless

Death by Firelight

The Lodge,
Morthead Minor,
Devizesshire
May 18,193—

My Dear Theresa,

What an amusing question you posed in your last letter! I am quite taken with it.

The most extraordinary event I can think of that has happened to me in a now-long life? A good question, my dear Theresa. Upon due reflection I believe the one I'd pick happened while I was marooned for a couple of days at John's and my old home on the southwest coast, Morthead Manor down here in Devizesshire.

Though now your marriage has taken you far away to India, you will recall that you and your cousins, my boys, found adventures when a storm rendered the causeway impassable at my old home, more recently Charles Mortlake's country estate. In those days we had no electric light or telephone service so the inconvenience was mainly in being confined to the grounds. We couldn't receive the post and John couldn't go about estate business, nor could generations of Parrots before him. In that respect Morthead Manor was an inconvenient (if historic) residence, and also in the lack of modern conveniences like gaslight, running water, and later electricity and telephones, which Londoners take for granted in the big towns. But country houses, unless their owners where possessed of a large fortune, were not like that in the old days as you will remember from girlhood.

The events I have in mind happened on just such a storm-tossed marooning. I was a dinner guest of Charles Mortlake's at a small event to honour his American associate in a nightclub venture, Mr. Jack Hood of Chicago. Quite a character there, I can assure you—full of references to "Scarface's boys" and the lawlessness of his home city, which he took quite as natural!

The storm broke during coffee and as similar eventualities had left me stranded without clothing or other "kit", Charles had insisted a room be kept ready for me and that I keep enough clothes and personal effects there to weather the usual day or three in isolation.

The place was very different then from what you recall. Charles was a rich financier and had thoroughly restored and modernized the facilities, even getting electricity, water closets, and telephone installed at great expense. Such luxury! I took advantage of his installations and easing of the severe financial strictures after he bought the Manor to install the same facilities at my little Lodge. You won't recognize it, if you to come home on leave and take time for your promised visit. I should expect you will have to when the boys at least reach public school-age to settle them in, though I am sure there are excellent educators amongst our empire-builders in India. I personally deplore some of the all-too-frequent deviant effects of the great boarding schools, but I know Stuart will insist that the boys don't miss out on the connections a school like Harrow offered him.

But back to the extraordinary event you asked for.

It was the day after the storm broke, the mains electricity and telephone line had gone out, but we still had light, after a half-hour's darkness, as Charles had installed a generator that ran on gasoline after the first such incident during his tenure.

We were enjoying coffee and tea after supper in the sitting room. The party consisted of myself, Charles, Mr. Hood (an American business associate), Miss Leigh, Charles' secretary (and I suspected mistress), Professor

Lawless (who had been consulted on the restoration and was down to catalogue the library), Major Bly, (Charles's bosom friend and former Great War superior who practically lived there). There was also "Mrs." Brown—an odd, moody woman who served as housekeeper. She was a former stage and music hall entertainer, and as was pretty well-known Charles's "former" mistress who had some of her meals with the gentry. Mary had poured out and handed the cups around, waited to see if anyone wanted seconds, and then taken the tray off for Gladys to clean up.

As you can see, Charles even kept my old servants except Denton, whom he pensioned off, and Anne, who came with me. We do very nicely on our own with Jessie, a girl who comes in from the village to do the heavy chores, and Ben, Jackson's son, who helps out in the garden two mornings a week and can usually manage more to oblige.

I was immersed in bound back issues of *The Complete Gardener* from the library and so did not pay much attention to the conversation. I believe the Major was talking of war, or shooting, or the estate as usual with Charles, and the others occasionally made small talk amongst themselves or got a word in edge-wise. I'm afraid Charles never exactly took his duties as host very seriously, making no attempt to entertain his American guest, and taking the Major off with him to his office-cum-den by ten at the latest of an evening.

Suddenly someone—no one was quite sure who— overturned a flower vase. The water spilled around the base of a lamp on the same table. The cord must have been frayed. In any event it sparked, a noxious smell went up, and then all the electric lights went out. It seemed it had blown what they call the fuses all through the house, for when Professor Lawless made his way to the door by the light of the dying coal fire and opened it, we saw the inner hall too was affected. He suggested he should go in search of the fuse box.

"Oh, don't bother. Just sit down again. The servants will be preparing emergency electric torches, lanterns, and candles in the kitchen, and Gladys will be sent to summon Jeffries, if he isn't on the way already. Georges also knows what to do, and assuming neither breaks his neck heading down the stairs in the dark with just a torch to guide him, one or the other of them will have fixed the problem in under half an hour, I daresay. Just shut the door—there's a draught. That's the one thing the builders didn't totally fix. Oh, before you sit down, please take the plug from that lamp out of the wall socket, or else it might go again when they see to the fuses."

Making his way carefully in the dim, cozy firelight, Lawless traced the cord from the lamp to the wall somewhere in the shadowed, almost black regions away from the fire, for he quite disappeared from sight and presumably pulled it out as instructed. Then he took a seat not far from the plug so I could barely see his outline. I sat staring at the comforting sight of the coal fire burning in the grate as if mesmerized, thinking of my days at the Manor when lanterns and candles were the rule. I assumed everyone else was also staring into the fire—so compulsive, you know. I had naturally put my book aside on the settee beside me. There was ample seating and no one shared it, so I couldn't vouch for anyone's placement or presence for that matter. At some point I remember feeling a draft that came and went in a minute, but the door didn't open, of that I'm sure.

Then the door was flung open. I expected Mary carrying a tray of lights. Instead, a figure I could dimly see silhouetted at first in a deerstalker cap and an Inverness cape stood in the doorway. Then he raised a powerful electric torch. The figure swept the room with its light. The beam shone right in our eyes and dazzling me as it passed. I believe I saw the Major highlighted as it went by him, but otherwise I was so astonished I just stared at the pantomime figure. It—it was impossible to tell its sex—stopped when it found Charles. Then it swung down to light his chest in a yellow circle and two shots rang out. Charles crumpled. Someone started screaming, or perhaps it was more than one. The door slammed shut and we were returned to relative darkness.

All was confusion for several minutes. It took that long for me to restore order to our panicked group. Towards the end of that time I felt that draft briefly once more. Then I ordered Professor Lawless, who finally came near the fire again, to go and get lights from the kitchen. And I got Miss Leigh—to this day I'm not sure whether the screamer was she or Brown—who was a VAD nurse in France during the war to see what she could do for Charles.

When Lawless opened the door into the hall, we heard someone calling, "Help! Please help! It tied me up, it did!"

Going cautiously, I followed the Professor. I recognized the voice as Mary's. She was somewhere in the pitch-black inner hall, or so it seemed. Once we were there, the Professor started using his lighter so we could see something.

"Keep calling, Mary!" I commanded. "That way we can locate you!"

Finally we found her. She was not in the hall, but rather in the dining room, tied up with stout, wet cord to one of the chairs at the table. We managed to find the knots and untie her. Then we asked her what happened.

"I was on me way to the sitting room with a tray of torches and a kerosene lantern. It's on the table, though he took the lantern and blew it out once I was tied up. He was all dressed up in a big checked cape and hat like Sherlock Holmes. He had a gun pointed at me, and told me in a muffled squeaky voice to go into the dining room, or he'd shoot. I say "he," but with the squeaky voice I couldn't really tell if it were man or woman. Whoever they were they weren't that tall, I think, though what with the shadows and the great big cape and cap, I don't really know. He pressed the barrel of the gun into me back. With the hat and cape, I didn't notice if it was wearing trousers or a skirt or anything. The cape was so low and I was so scared. The gun seemed so big. He also had a woolly scarf round his face and neck and black gloves on. It was like something on the picture show in Devizes. Only there it's ever so-exciting, and this was horrible, it were!"

"Poor Mary, we are here and you're safe now dear," I said. "What happened next?"

"Once he had me tied up, he took the lantern from the tray and one of the better torches. He put out the lantern. Then the squeaky voice told me to keep quiet for ten minutes, or he'd be back to finish me. Then he went out of the room, leaving the door open. Some of the torch light spilled in for a bit, but then he put that out, and it went black. I heard a door being swung open and then the shots and the muffled screaming through the door. Me heart felt like it would burst it were beating so hard! I kept quiet for a bit—I don't really know how long. Seemed dreadful long, but were likely only a moment or two. Then I started yelling, figuring the thing with the gun were escaping, and you came, Milady, and God bless you for it!"

"That's a stout lass!" I said gripping her shoulder. "You behaved just as you should. Let's take you back to the sitting room with the lamp. Then we'll go to the kitchen to get the first aid box. Perhaps Professor Lawless will come with us and we can see what's being done about the lights."

Mary told us where to find the spare torches near by. Lawless retrieved them and handed one to me. I handed Mary the tray abandoned in the hall to give her something to do. And it worked, she stopped shaking, but the sooner I got her to Cook's attentions and good strong, hot tea, the better. In fact we could all use some, given the shock. I used the torchlight to examine the cord

I had rolled up and held in my left hand. I saw it was like the cord used for clotheslines. Was it the clothesline, I wondered? I made a note to have Gladys check. It certainly seemed wet enough. But first things first: treatment for shock before detective work. The sweet tea would do us all good.

Except probably Charles Mortlake, of course, who might have drank his last cup.

On this sad thought we made our way the short distance back across the inner hall towards the sitting room. When we got there, Leigh was trying to bandage Charles' chest with handkerchiefs for compresses and the gentlemen's shirts to hold them in place, assisted by the Major and Hood. The blood was flowing copiously and was seeping through the makeshift bandages. One suspected an artery had been hit near the heart. His breathing was rasping and shallow. Perhaps a lung had been penetrated. Brown was blubbering in a chair near the fire, looking on.

At least we brought light to bear upon the tragedy. I put the lamp down on an end table and lit it. Then we went on our mission to get proper bandages, though I feared anything short of a fully equipped hospital surgical theatre would likely prove useless. Just as we reached the kitchen by the wavering light of two torch beams— Mary carrying the tray behind me, Professor Lawless beside her—the proper lights came on. It seems Georges or Jeffries had succeeded.

We found Cook and Gladys, with lanterns and candles still lit, calmly congratulating the two men, who had both made their way in the dark to help—George by match-light down the back stairs; Jeffries by torchlight across the stable yard after checking the generator. The fuse box, it seemed, was in the scullery. All were unaware of the dramatic events that had occurred. The walls and doors are so thick. They were naturally aghast when told. Cook got Gladys to bring the kettle to boil, both for tea and in case of medical need. Jeffries and

Georges, both ex-servicemen, volunteered to search the house from top to bottom starting on the ground floor. I ordered them to go up the backstairs with the sadly disheveled and tired-looking, but game, Professor. His hair, usually slicked back, was disordered; his typically erect figure, slumped; his tie was askew. I told them to get the Major's Webley revolver from his nightstand first, just in case, and they went off to do so and start on the search armed.

With Gladys, the kitchen maid, importantly clutching the first aid kit to her flat bosom, I lead the way back to the fateful room. Alas, as I suspected, despite Grace Leigh and the gentlemen's efforts, we found that he was dead when we arrived. I stopped Gladys starting to blubber like Brown by giving her something to do. I told her to go back to the kitchen and bring tea and plenty of sugar to the library, and some cake or biscuits—whatever Cook had on hand.

"We can regroup and plan our strategy to catch the culprit there!"

"But we must be after him now!" insisted the alarmingly red Major.

"That's been taken care of. The Professor, Jeffries, and Georges are searching the house as we speak. I took the liberty, Major, of telling them to borrow your Webley first, as the culprit is, or was, armed."

This mollified him and we departed the room, leaving it to its deceased Master. I took the precaution of taking some paper and glue from the writing desk and pasting it across the entrance of the secret passage to the Orangerie. I also turned the key in the lock behind us in case there was any evidence. I felt we should regroup and get a chance to come to terms with things first.

Soon we were all seated about the long reading table in the library, with Mary passing 'round plates and ginger cake and raisin scones from the tea trolley. She had placed the silver tea service itself in front of me and I poured out, sugared the tea heavily, stirred, and passed the cups along regardless of personal preference. Shock after all needs treatment, sweet liquid being an elementary one.

I covertly surveyed the suspects—excepting myself of course—as they began variously to sip and nibble or gulp and wolf, as was their inclination; crisis often strips away formal mannerisms.

The Major still looked like a well-cooked lobster, but as his breathing was regular and he made regular threats to "see to the blighter" who did it himself if he got the chance, I presumed he was in no imminent danger of heart failure.

The Major apparent assumed he was above suspicion. However, recalling the near blackout conditions, the passage to the Orangerie as well as the theatrical costume the killer wore, I could not swear I saw any of my companions in the room during, or immediately after, the attack. Major Bly certainly wasn't bellowing about revenge then. Memory is never totally trustworthy especially under dramatic circumstances. Ask any prosecuting or defending counsel or a bobby with any sense. Things get out of order. Suppositions become rock-hard "facts." Human memory, even that of the relatively observant and practical among us, is fallible.

Mr. Hood was frowning and chomping on his cigar a good deal. He was getting pessimistic about returning to his business interests in America, if the case weren't resolved "pronto."

Mrs. Brown had stopped blubbering, but looked quite pale and strained. I wish I could be sure who screamed. I am only positive it was not I. It certainly sounded like a woman, but Professor Lawless's voice is fairly high-pitched. And even with deep voices like the Major and Hood, they don't necessarily sing low as it were. I am not so prejudiced that I cannot conceive of a man screaming. My opinion is that it was Brown, however.

Mary was holding up very well. I believe the work was steadying her.

Grace Leigh, in a dress that complemented her auburn hair, looked relatively stone-faced. One couldn't tell if she was numb with shock or grief-stricken but holding it inside. Or for that matter a resourceful, watchful murderess.

When Mary was just finishing serving the rest of the upstairs party, Professor Lawless returned with Georges and Jeffries on his heels.

"You look weary, Professor. After removing that bulge—the revolver?—from your pocket and returning it to its owner, do sit down and take refreshments. Georges, Jeffries, I'm sure Cook has something similar awaiting you and Mary once you have made your report."

"I am a little tired," the Professor admitted. "Here's your Webley, Major." He handed over the revolver before taking a seat beside the officer.

The Major turned a frowning, puzzled visage from the gun to the man who had handed it to him. "This is not my gun; it's Charles'. Surely you got it from the top drawer of his desk? These notches on the butt are for Huns and fleeing cowards he bagged with it. Mine merely has my initials, S. W. B., etched into the same area."

"Georges took it from your nightstand," said Lawless. "Jeffries and I both saw him. Then he handed it to me." The male servants nodded agreement to his account.

"Perhaps when you were last both target-shooting with them at the cliff," I said, "they got mixed up, Major?"

"Impossible," he dismissed. "We both always clean ours together after that in the Office and check the notches and initials." He displayed the butt to Patrick Lawless. "It bears Charles initials too. See, C.J.B. for Charles Jacob Mortlake. The Jacob was after his father."

"Another mystery," I commented. "Everyone in the house probably knew where they were kept from conversations the past days. So it doesn't eliminate anyone.

"Well, gentlemen," I said, addressing the search party, "did you find anyone or anything else of interest?"

"I'm afraid not. No lurkers were found. Though the french windows in the Orangerie were open. The pane by the handle is shattered. Jeffries will put something there to block out the rain temporarily before effecting a permanent repair when the storm passes. We presume that's how the gunman got in." The men indicated agreement.

This led to the interesting point as to where this hypothetical gunman of the Professor's imagining might be hiding and how he expected to get off what was effectively an island. Though highly skeptical, I suggest closing and locking the iron gate by the causeway and stationing the male servants in the Daimler there in case the storm receded enough by daylight for crossing the causeway, or rowing a boat to Morthead Minor. But I had them search the secret passage between the Office and kitchen before hand. I thought the one between the sitting room and Orangerie best left to the gentlemen and myself, or the police.

Fortunately, the Major agreed with this scheme, and in fact congratulated me. Somewhat unusual for the old fellow. He can be tiresome at times. It must have been the shock.

"I am afraid there is a rather delicate matter which the police will bring up, even if I keep my tongue. The room was dark. There is a secret passage in the corner furthest from the fire, well-known to us all. One of us could be the theatrically-dressed killer."

No one seemed entirely surprised, though the ladies and the Major showed various degrees of concern that the matter had been broached. After all, I had sealed the entrance and had all of us sign it before we vacated the room. Hood smiled, saying, "You don't miss many angles, do you?" in a tone I took as one of approbation.

"Err, Milady," Mary interrupted hesitantly.

"Yes Mary? If you have any ideas or suggestions toward the solution of the crime, don't hesitate to let us know."

"Well, when you said that the costume was theatrical, it made something come back to me, it did. You'll remember as how the young masters used to bring down the costume trunk for charades when there was a party. I was serving once when Mr. Jack dressed up in a cap and cape just like it for a charade that was on one of them Sherlock Holmes stories."

"Very good indeed, Mary, we must examine the attic and that trunk's contents. I believe Charles even had electric light put in up there."

"Yes, Milady," Mary agreed.

"Well ladies and gentlemen, I suggest seeing to four tasks before we leave the case for the night and try to get what rest we can. We should examine the sitting room and especially the lamp cord and the overturned vase, check whether the other Webley is in the Office desk in place of Charles's, ascertain if those dressing up clothes Mary and I recall have been removed from the attic, and search the secret passage between the sitting room and Orangerie. The dress up trunk may well have included a cape and cap. As for the passage, I suggest the Major, the Professor, and I take torches to explore it while Mr. Hood (suitably armed) and the other ladies watch the Orangerie entrance. I distinctly recall two brief periods of draft while we were waiting for the lights to go on. One was after the lights fused and another some time after Charles was shot."

I sent the ladies and Mr. Hood to the Orangerie, while the two men and I went to the sitting room. As we went across the hall, I scanned the marble to see if anything unusual was on it. I was rewarded by seeing two spent cartridge cases. One was lying against the bottom step of the staircase, and the other just in the shadow of the newel post on the dining room-side. I pointed them out and picked them up with my handkerchief and put them in my left jacket pocket, deciding I could take an envelope from the sitting room writing desk to seal them for the police.

"Professor Lawless, did you and the men not use this stair going up?"

"No. We did, however, use it coming down. I suppose we just didn't think of looking for them and missed them." He frowned, possibly at the lapse.

I then unlocked the sitting room door and we re-entered the scene of the crime. Or, to be more accurate, passed through one portion of it, the other part being approximately where Mortlake's inanimate form lay on the settee. I put the cartridges in an envelope from the writing table drawer and returned them to my pocket. The Major felt they looked like a Webley's .451 caliber. I also had the rope used to tie up Mary in my pocket.

We examined the room thoroughly, but found little else of interest, aside from the blood splatter pattern in front of where Charles had been shot, and a loop of fishing line about the base of the overturned vase leading across the carpet towards the back of the room. A significant length of insulation on the lamp's electric flex had been scraped away, also suggesting forethought. I cautioned the others to not step on the bloodstains as they might be useful to the police.

The Major and Lawless in their interest at my finding the fishing line and the damaged lamp cord insulation came rather too close to the table, which still had some flower water on and by it. At least that might account for the watermarks on the Major's jacket and Lawless's trousers, the latter down the side of his right leg along the seam.

I then turned a particular apple motif carved on Jacobite paneling, and the door to the secret passage silently slid back—causing a draft, I asked the men to note—breaking the seal I had put upon it. I shone my torch across the entrance, just before the stairs. This passage led through the thick outer stone walls going over the windows via stairs between the ground level and first floor, along two sides of the building and hence to another stair where they descended to the Orangerie entrance. We saw the most significant thing from the sitting room entrance, fresh shoe marks showing in the torch lights in the thick dust of the floor. I thought it was a medium man's shoe, though one of the ladies might have surreptitiously changed into a pair concealed about the sitting room, I supposed. The Major had rather large feet. Nonetheless we followed the tracks in the dust through the passage and came out before the rest of the upstairs party in the Orangerie. I noted with approval that Jeffries had sealed the broken windowpane before going down to the boathouse and causeway with Georges earlier. We sealed the Orangerie passage entrance with paper and glue and two signatures so that we would know if it were disturbed again and locked the door. I took the key. We returned to the sitting room and secured and sealed the passage entrance and the door to the hall, again I added the key to my jacket pocket collection.

We then proceeded to the Office. Everyone crowded round as the Major—with me at his side—used a handkerchief to open the desk drawer where Charles's gun would usually be. It was empty.

"Your gun, Major, is still missing." I said, stating the obvious.

"Indubitably, Letitia. Where next?"

"The attic I think. I'll ring for Mary. I have a vague idea of its location, but haven't been there in twenty years. The boys used to carry the trunk up and down. Between the two of us I'd wager we can find it with relative expedition!"

Mary soon appeared, and the party trailed up the stairs—Mary led and I played sheepdog, making sure no one lingered to tamper with any evidence. I noticed Grace Leigh was leaning against the Professor, smiling up at him. His arm was carelessly draped across her shoulders in a proprietary fashion. I had whiffed romance there before, but with Charles gone there was no obstacle to it. Grace, Brown, and the Major all benefited financially from Charles's will, if they were still in his employ (except in the Major's case) when he died. I believe significant annuities had been mentioned, and in the Major's case perhaps even the Manor. And Hood, like the Professor of modest shoe size, was a partner with Charles in London nightclubs, so might well benefit, depending upon the nature of the partnership.

We had to use the back stairs. The attic was reached by means of a railed stair, little more than a ladder from the corridor with the servants' bedrooms, the bathroom, and WC Charles had kindly installed. Much superior to the former arrangements and suggesting a kind streak, showing Charles's gentlemanly side. We mounted the steps, I last.

I emerged between floor boards with the rafters holding up the roof leads above my head. We used this area to store old furniture, broken hobbyhorses and other things one is attached to and doesn't want thrown away, but never gets around to having mended. The boys used to consider it a treasure-trove and spent hours getting dusty up here on rainy days in the holidays. You too, as I recall, Theresa.

Mary and I found the trunk. Sure enough, using the torch and crouching down, we could clearly see footprints in the dust, this time several sets. The size looked like medium men's footwear. It seemed the killer had poked about up here quite a bit.

"Now I remember! Mr. Hood, did you not ask me about the old days here the other evening at dinner?"

"Yes ma'am, I sure did," he said.

"And did I not mention dressing up and a trunk in the attic?"

"Come to think of it, you did! Told something about charades and plays your kids got up."

"So we all could have known of the costumes."

"That's right, ma'am."

Avoiding the sinister footmarks as much as possible, we went over to the trunk. Unlike most other surfaces in the room, it had been wiped free of dust. With Mary's help, I opened the lid. I had asked the party to wait on the way up while I got some gloves from my room. So Mary and I wore my evening gloves to leave no prints. We searched right to the bottom. The cloak and hat I recalled were no longer there. They had been there during the War on one of John's leaves as far as I could recall. Slowly we went downstairs. Brown, Lawless, and Grace Leigh pled fatigue and retired. Lawless, however, went off in the direction of Grace's bedsitter, not his own guestroom.

Once they were gone, I had an idea as to where the clothes would be. With Hood and the Major as escorts, we returned to the Orangerie. There was a rack of tools behind the door; on the back there was a coat hook, from which I hung an old car-coat I use to protect my clothing while gardening. The clothes were not abandoned in the passage. When we looked at the back of the door more than my coat hung there.

The cape and hat had been left on a hook as I had suspected. We examined them and found Charles's gun in the cape pocket. It had been recently fired as we could tell by smelling the barrel. The Major recounted that it was kept fully loaded, as was his. Two bullets were missing. We concluded that we had the murder weapon. The black or dark gloves Mary recalled were unaccounted for.

One other interesting fact, my dear Theresa. We noticed the lining of the right side pocket of the cape was quite wet, possibly from the clothes rope used to tie up Mary?

Can you guess, my dear, who was responsible for Charles's death?

Perhaps I shall be horrid and send the answer in my next missive.

Love to you and all your family!

Your affectionate,

Aunt Letitia

The Lodge,
Morthead Minor,
Devizesshire
May 19, 193—

My Dear Theresa,

I decided I shouldn't leave you hanging hence this letter by the next post. I am sure I have been heavy-handed enough with my clues to let you guess quite easily. The Major was ruled out by his size-twelve boots. I never seriously considered Brown or Grace slipping on a pair of men's shoes in the dark. Because I knew it was not me, logic dictated Hood or Lawless. Fitness would be needed to dash along the secret passage by torchlight without mishap and along the corridors, don the outfit complete with gun and rope, dash along to the library, shoot Charles, dash back to the passage, discard the outfit and weapon, secret the gloves in a jacket pocket for later burning perhaps (as they were never found), dash back along the secret passage, and resume his innocent, shocked pose. Probably only Hood, Grace Leigh, or Lawless could have done it. Hood did seem to have a motive of sorts (though it turned out he didn't; Charles's bank had just loaned him money for his nightclub venture). Lawless's was a bit tenuous, however, he clearly wanted Grace Leigh as a wife. A wife with an annuity was even better for a poor don. Charles Mortlake didn't let go of his friends easily, as shown by the forfeit provisions of his will in regards to annuities. Lawless's damp trouser leg was highly suggestive, together with the wet rope and cape pocket. That he was Grace's lover might also have rankled. The storm blew itself out overnight and, briefed by the Major and I, my old friend the Chief Constable soon arrested Lawless. I wonder to this day if Grace knew about it. I think not, but one can never be certain when money and romantic attractions are involved, can one? In any event, she got her annuity, and married a lawyer, one of the solicitors in the firm who unsuccessfully defended the Professor.

Your affectionate,

Aunt Letitia

Not in My Kitchen!

Morthead Manor,
Morthead Minor,
Devizesshire
October 1st 192—

Dear Annie,

Sorry I've been so long replying to yours of September 7th, but things have been topsy-turvy like around here and soon Lady P's likely going to find me a new situation. Unless whoever takes over wants us to stay, and I find them satisfactory and more respectable than Mr. Mortlake turned out to be!

As you will have guessed from what I've said, Mr. Mortlake "died suddenly," as they say. To put it in plain terms, he was murdered.

And not only murdered, but the black-hearted killer had the nerve to do it in my kitchen! You would not believe the mess all over me kitchen table and the floor! Some people, as you in your situation well know, have no proper respect and deference for our station in life and consequence as upper servants! It made me blood boil, it did.

Not that I believed it 'twere murder when Gladys woke me up all agog, and without me cup of tea as is her duty too! The poor simple thing hadn't even had the sense to make sure the Master was dead, just saw him slumped over the table—in me own chair too—and ran up the backstairs and woke me twenty minutes early. I could tell there was something more wrong than the Master sleeping it off.

Not that that were unknown, I'm sorry to say! And sometimes his "friend" Major Bly too, who lives with him—I have me suspicions about funny business between them! I ask you, if a man has not one but two mistresses on the premises, you don't expect other "fun and games" too! Our so-called housekeeper, Mrs. Brown, who hardly works and leaves it all to me, was his old mistress. She may still be for all I know. Miss Leigh, his "private secretary" seems to be his new squeeze, like I told you before. It's only suspicion, mind.

But Master sleeping off the drink outside his bedroom was rare enough that I didn't feel it made the house disreputable-like, or I'd have to give me notice. Usually it would just mean Mary found Master asleep in a chair or on the sofa in his Office, or perhaps the sitting room, when she opened up the curtains and doors in the morning. He stayed up all hours, didn't sleep much at night, but snoozed during the afternoon. Or so he *said*. He may have been up to funny business with Brown, the Leigh woman, or elsewhere, for all I know!

All I felt that morning was uneasy-like, what with Gladys refusing to go back down and get me me morning cuppa. Usual she's a biddable girl and if you've patience with her she can be taught things like she had all her marbles. So I made her wait, took time for a quick wash, put in me teeth, threw on me clothes and shoes, and went down with her, mildly scolding her for being fearful over nothing. It seems she'd only just taken one glance at him from the doorway and "felt something weren't right." Didn't even get near him!

When I entered me kitchen, you could have knocked me over with a feather! She hadn't had the sense or the courage to investigate, but the Master certainly didn't "look right." I thought she meant he might have taken off his trousers or shirt or something silly men sometimes do when they've got spirits in them. But he was bloody-well dead, if you'll pardon the French! He was lying face down on me new clean table. Me old faithful one was relegated to the attic despite me protests as you may recall. He had his arms about his head.

He wasn't sleeping. There was no sound of breathing, for one thing, and blood was spilled and starting to go solid like over tabletop and onto the floor where it lay on the stone flags in a pool. Gladys scrubs the floor every evening. He was so still, I remember thinking, "He can't be alive." But I went to check for a pulse anyway. I knew as soon as I touched him that he'd passed on. His skin was so cold. It gives me the shivers just thinking about it. I'd never touched Mr. Charles before or since.

I went upstairs to wake Lady Parrot.

Of course maybe I should explain why she was here. She'd been asked to dinner, seeing that there was an American partner of the Master's who runs nightclubs in London—and in New York and Chicago too, despite that Prohibition against drink I hear they have over there. Not sure he might not be a bit of a sharp dealer, if not worse. Though he's got this Yank charm to him, I will say.

That Professor Lawless, who's sweet on Miss Leigh, was down here again too. This time it weren't to advise on "restoration" and "tasteful renovations," like early on. Oh Lord, did we have them builders under our feet! It seemed they'd never go away—you'll recall me writing you about it! Not that it weren't worth it, seeing the place looking so fine again and having electric light, W.C.'s, and running water too! No, Prof's not here for that, nor to poke his nose into our secret passages neither, but to catalogue the books in the library and arrange to get them valued for the insurance.

Big on insurance, Mr. Mortlake was. He was careful about things like that. I suppose it was being a banker. He inherited it all, so it's bred in the bone, and you know how hard that sort of habit is to break. At least he wasn't stingy on the housekeeping, or my side of things anyway. Liked good food and drink, he did.

I have me suspicions his Brown woman was taking back-handers from the tradesmen. She used to be an actress and is no better than she should be, to put it mildly. It shows they're right about stage people, don't it? Least the lesser hangers-on like her, I dare say. Got by on her looks, but they're going to seed now. And then there's his secretary, Miss Leigh, a nice decent girl basically, but he seduced her, I'm afraid. And if you get into that sort of wickedness where does it go? She's not in the family way, thank God! Least not that I know. I'm surprised any self-respecting bloke like the Professor would put up with it. But as I say, he's sweet on her. She is a looker! It helps her frocks and blouses are all of the best, courtesy of the late Master.

And Lady Parrot's just like her old self, just a bit wistful about Sir John and the boys. She's really glad now she sold. Says it was a Godsend and you don't argue with the Lord's mercy. Very pleasant to Mr. Mortlake she was, despite all of his goings-on. She has taken the odd quirk of calling herself "Mrs." Parrot, now that the baronetcy's "extinguished," like they call it when there's no son or cousin to take it on. But I don't pay that no mind. Nor do most folks about here. She came here as a bride, as Lady Letitia Parrot. Clergyman's daughter she was.

Where was I? Explaining why Lady L. was staying at the Manor. She was over here for a dinner party, and then a big storm hit, and you can guess the rest—the causeway was covered and the waves were too rough to get a boat over to Morthead Minor. So we was marooned on this headland and Mr. Jeffries had to put on the electric generator—petrol-powered, it is, like these newfangled cars. The telephone lines across the causeway went down too. Same as usual, once or twice a year at least.

I woke Lady with a cup of tea. I'd taken time to have a very sweet one meself with Gladys, to get me breath back and wits about me. I told her what we'd found. She came down right away, in her dressing gown.

She said the police would prefer to have him left where he were, but saw reason when I said I couldn't get on with cooking, much less us servants eating our meals, with the Master dead in a pool of blood on me kitchen table. She sent Mary, who had come down to make her rounds, drawing curtains back and make the posh rooms ready for the day, to go up, tell Agnes, and to have her get the Major and to ask Monsieur Georges to come down with blankets for a stretcher. Meanwhile she sent Gladys for Mr. Jeffries.

Practically as soon as Gladys had time to get to the outside scullery door she screamed and came running back in the kitchen like Bluebeard were after her!

It took a few minutes to get it out of her, but she'd went to get her Mac, 'cause of the storm, and found it were covered in blood! We all went back with her into the scullery. She'd dropped the raincoat on the stone floor. Lady stooped and picked it up, then held it out to inspect it and let me look at it. The blood had mostly dried and there were some drying on the floor beneath the peg it hung on. Lady L. suggested that the killer may have worn it to protect his or her clothes, perhaps putting it on with the excuse of being cold.

We finally convinced Gladys to get Jeffries and I told her to use me coat. Then we found my coat was smeared with dried mud all along the left side and at the left cuff besides. It were clean last I wore it, just as the rain was starting, when I helped Gladys get the wash off the line. No one knew what to make of that, but Lady L. felt it could relate to the case, so we told Gladys to put it on the stone bench in the corner of the scullery by where Lady said the men were to put the bloodied table out of me way. The men were to bring my old table down from the attic for use until the police had done with the other.

About then the Major came into the kitchen. Lady L. and me went back to see to him. He'd come down in his P.J.s and gown, too. He hadn't stopped to comb his hair even and it was all rumpled. He looked like a boiled lobster; his color was so high you could have taken him for a Red Indian! At first I thought he were going to have a heart attack. He went pale and had to sit down and take some sweet tea. Almost thought he'd cry, the shattered look on his face.

Then he got his colour back, put his monocle in, and got a grip on himself. Started sputtering about an outrage and how the policemen ain't doing their jobs when a man can be surprised by burglars and killed in his own kitchen! Lady pointed out that while Gladys had found the scullery door to the kitchen garden left close to, that what with the storm, it seemed unlikely that anyone could get at us from the mainland, like. She agreed that he should have Jeffries secure the gate at the causeway just in case to make sure no one left the headland when the storm subsided unnoticed.

Lady then filled him in about the Mackintoshes and he went to see them himself, carefully avoiding looking too closely at his pal's body lying there in its own blood as he passed to get to the scullery. He agreed with Lady's idea about the killer using it to protect his clothes like.

"The blighter must be a small man if he could put on Gladys' coat and button it up. Small shoulders," he said in that plumy voice of his. Sound like he had pebbles in his mouth. To me it sounds as if he didn't grow up talking that way. When he were flustered I heard some Yorkshire in his words. "There's no sign of strain at the seams." He put Gladys' coat down and picked mine up. "Mrs. Stout's is larger all over but he still couldn't be a broad-shouldered fellow, more like a little runt from some back slum! Must ask the servants if one of them borrowed it and fell or something."

"That must be eliminated, certainly," said Lady L. quietly, like there was something else on her mind. "Mrs. Stout, will you see to it and alert the Major and I if there is an innocent explanation."

"Yes, Milady."

"The point about the killer's size is a good one," Lady L. agreed. "It narrows the possible field." I could see what she meant. I looked at the Major. He was a big-framed man, broad-shouldered, though going to fat. I doubted the blood could have been smeared on later as a ruse; there was so much of it. And when we looked for them there were drops here and there leading from Mr. Mortlake to the coat pegs.

"Must have been hiding in the outbuildings, my dear Letitia, and seen his chance to get some food. Charles let him in out of generosity and got killed for it! You wouldn't know about such matters. The British Tommy under good discipline can be the best fighters in the world, but now so many veterans are out of work and roaming about, it seems even the countryside's not safe! We trained them to kill too well. Now they bite the hand that fed them.

"Being a clergyman's daughter," he added, "you wouldn't know about such things. Think the best of everyone, what?" He spoke like he was talking to a young miss and not a gray lady of the manor who knows what's what more than most men I can think of!

Lady took this nonsense calmly, but I saw from the narrowing of her eyes that she was going to get hers back, but in her own, genteel fashion.

"May I suggest, Stephen, that we for the moment refrain from speculation and see to practicalities. The servants have a house to run. Cook can't prepare our breakfast or any other meals with blood all over the kitchen floor and table and the Master dead in front of her. Unfortunately—for the police will disapprove, I am sure—Charles will have to be carried on blankets up to his bed and the table moved to the scullery. Mrs. Stout tells me there is an older kitchen table in the attic. Perhaps you can organize Jeffries and Georges to move the tables and the body as soon as possible? Then the room can be made workable and Cook can get your breakfast. We can make a preliminary examination after we have eaten. Miss Leigh, as a former VAD nurse during the War, can be of considerable assistance, I am sure."

We filed back into the kitchen.

"From a preliminary look, Charles had his throat cut, probably with a carving knife. I do not see one lying about," said Lady P. scanning the room. "However, I can see one missing from the rack, and neither Mrs. Stout nor Gladys know where it's gone. Gladys swears she dried it and put it back last night. He has been dead for quite some time, as he seems to be at room temperature or only just above. I took the liberty of inserting the thermometer from the first aid kit into his mouth for a few moments, and I've recorded the temperature in my notebook. Once the men are here, I want all of us to take a careful look at the body and the scene before he is disturbed so we can have several accounts for the police. I shall take initial statements later in the day from the servants while their memories are fresh and write out my own account and I suggest, Major, you prepare your own."

Lady had me look at the body. Mary too. Though knowing Gladys, she let her off.

Then Monsieur Georges came in from the backstairs way, looking as neat as ever, not a hair out of place. He took it calmly, I must say. But there again he's a foreigner when all's said and done, and was a soldier in the War, so he's likely used to bodies. Mr. Jeffries too. He came in just then, Gladys shuffling in behind him. His hair was a bit disheveled; he'd likely hung his cloth cap on the row of hooks by the scullery door. He wasn't tall but he was broad, used to physical labor. While Monsieur Georges was valet he was of similar build and well set up. It seemed he had some news to report. Both had been in the war when Charles met them.

"Milady, Major," he said, bowing, after taking a good look at the Master and swearing in French, which I won't have in me kitchen and well he knows it! He apologized proper to me, Gladys, and the gentry, when I reminded him. "There's some strange tracks all over the beds in the kitchen garden, going out the gate and heading for the causeway, far as I could tell from the windows above. Odd that whoever he was he didn't just stick to the path. Peculiar looking. Filled with rain water."

"Exactly as I said, Letitia," said the Major triumphant-like. "The man was so scared after what he'd done he hightailed and ran. Is the storm still severe enough to prevent escape?"

"I believe so, Major sir, but as Milady had Gladys summon me," said Jeffries, "I haven't been down to check."

"Well, do so as soon as you're done here. Take a stout stick or poker with you and watch yourself. He might be pretty desperate. And secure the gate at the causeway too so no one can get away."

"Yessir!"

"Good chap!" said his old commander, punching him on the shoulder. "You know Letitia, I've an idea about these Macs. The prowler must have put the first one on to protect his clothes, or perhaps to warm up, as it's not stopped pouring out and chilly with the wind and all."

"Possibly, Stephen, but we must not close our minds to alternatives. The police won't. It also does seem funny if your explanation is right, why Mrs. Stout's coat isn't simply missing."

"Perhaps the prowler realized the coat would identify him with the house after he fell as suggested by the mud and brought it back."

"Perhaps, Stephen," Lady said with patience. I could tell from her voice that she didn't believe a word of it. "Would you arrange the matter of the tables and the removal of the body, Stephen?"

"Ah yes!" said the Major, he turned to the men servants. "Gentlemen, as you see the Master has been killed in the veritable center of our good Cook's domain.

She cannot prepare our food while he is left so. Please respectfully move the Master's remains up to his bed. Use some blankets as a carrier. Then please carry the table into the far disused corner of the scullery until the police have done with it, and bring down the old deal kitchen table from the attic. While you are doing that, Gladys can clean up the evidence on the floor after Lady Parrot sketches it and I take some photographs with my Brownie. Then Cook can start breakfast without being haunted by a corpse."

It didn't take them long. The Major went with the body like an honour guard, practically weepy again, and then retrieved his camera and took some snaps before going up to get dressed. Lady made a very good drawing of the blood splattered on the floor. She's made painting and sketching a principal hobby, along with gardening, her real passion. Quite a green thumb she has too as well as being very good at art. She had me and Gladys look at it after she'd done and sign our names that it was exactly like the patterns we saw. It was too.

After the Major took his snaps and before the bloody table was taken off she also pointed out what looked like a brown milky liquid mixed with the blood near where the Master's right hand had been. Like his fall had overturned cocoa. When we checked the icebox, I was pretty sure enough milk for two mugs was missing. Lady concluded he, or the killer, had made cocoa for them both and washed up the pan and mugs. When we looked, all the saucepans were hung from the right hooks, but two mugs were put back careless-like. I make sure Gladys always leaves them neat. Upon later inquiries, as they say in the thrillers, no one admitted to making cocoa the previous night.

"While I've known the Master, or the Major take things from the larder," I said, "I doubt either of them knows how to use me Agga. Miss Leigh or Mrs. Brown or you, Milady, sometimes make cocoa or hot milk if none of us is still up, but not the Master for himself. Mr. Hood or the Professor might know how to do for themselves. Mr. Charles or the Major'd always ask Mary when she was locking up if they wanted something like that 'stead of spirits. Not often, that is!"

After the corpse and table was removed Lady L. and I persuaded Gladys to get out the pail and water and the scrubbing brushes. The Lady was kind to her. I had to be a bit harsh; she's always been squeamish about blood.

Then Lady went upstairs to bath and dress and I went about my duties, without Gladys's usual help. Once she'd started I'd never seen her scrub and mop so hard and fast in me life. Soon the men had the table down from the attic and Gladys had finished the floor. I put her to dusting off the table, sweeping up the result, and giving it a good scrub with boiling water and vinegar.

I wasn't there at breakfast, but Mary was back and forth and she's good at telling a tale, even though she, Agnes, and Gladys are all Morthead Minor girls and have little schooling. They know their letters and 'rithmetic, enough to read and add up bills anyway, but not much more, but they're a mine of information about the village, the coast, and local goings-on and relationships. Like local encyclopedias, they are.

The Major was down first and Lady just behind him. The Major ate a good helping, only about half as much as usual, though, and no seconds. The Lady took her usual bread with butter and marmalade plus a nice boiled egg with her tea. Then Mr. Hood entered the room. He seemed pretty calm about it. Said something about wondering if it had been a "hit," just like them gangsters say over in America, or an accident. Real calm-like. He were also worried in case he missed his steamer back to New York. Seems he was set to sail off next week.

Then he filled his plate from the chaffing dishes on the sideboard and sat down cool as a cucumber, Mary said. Made a good breakfast despite the news. As him and the Master were partners, I wonder if he benefits now he's dead? Maybe he'd get control of their nightclubs or something?

I knew "Mrs." Brown, Miss Leigh, and the Major benefited. 'Twere no secret the "ladies" got an income for life from the will—an "annuity" I think they do call it—if they were still in his employ. The Major was set to get one of them too, as his bosom pal.

I'm not saying definite one way or t'other, but something Lady Letitia said after Mr. Charles was dead made me think it could have been more than friendship between them, if you get me drift. For all his blarney, handsome face, and being a well set-up man for his age anyway, Mr. Mortlake was sinful with the ladies at least. I been worried he'd start on Agnes, her being a bit of a looker, and told her to avoid being alone with him as much as possible and tell me first thing if anything like that happened.

I think he liked to control women. And I suspect he was rough sometimes too. All that makeup Brown uses—like a regular Jezebel—could hide bruises. And she sometimes gets up and walks very careful-like for days at a time. That's what makes me wonder, considering she hardly does a lick of real work. And Miss Leigh, who wasn't made up much before, started using it practically as much as Brown, once or twice before he died. So maybe he started being heavy-handed with her too.

I know most folks think men got a right to hit their wives and kiddies now and then. But I don't think it right meself. Makes me glad in a way I lost me beau in the war. Not that I'd think he'd do that—he were so gentle and kind, didn't even like to see horses whipped. And Mr. Charles weren't married in the sight of God or man to either of them. Men can be beasts sure enough, despite good looks and smooth tongues!

Anyway, getting back to the breakfast table, Mary said the Prof came down with his arm about Miss Grace.

She looked pale and had dark marks under her eyes and only nibbled at a slice of toast and butter. The Professor fussed over her like he was her boyfriend. He said the proper things, about how awful it was, but didn't seem that taken aback. Maybe bookish people like him are reserved-like. Keep it all inside.

Brown came in last. Her eyes were red-rimmed; she'd shrieked and started caterwauling and blubbering as soon as Agnes told her. Good thing Aggie took her tea in last, or the others would have been further delayed. She tried to soothe her, but Brown would have none of it. Shrieked her head off like a Billingsgate fish-wife, swore and yelled at her to get out. Good thing she did quick too, 'cause Brown threw something that hit the door as it closed. Not at all a lady, our Brown.

Anyway she took some toast too and let her tea get cold instead of eating her usual full breakfast, looking all the time like a dying duck in a thunderstorm. Still, she could have been playing up to the occasion like she often does. Probably comes from being a Music Hall "*artiste*" as she refers to her "career." Makes it sound like she were Sarah-blooming-Bernhardt the way she talks about it in that fake posh accent, like she had a mouthful of pebbles!

After breakfast all of the upstairs party went to view the body. Monsieur Georges was there and gave us a full account at elevenses. He talks English a bit funny, but you can understand him like, once you get used to it.

The gentry all trooped into the room. Mr. Charles was laid out on the bed still in his blood soaked evening clothes. They'd had to carry him up on his side and leave him that way on the bead, 'cause he was ever so stiff. Lady had said it was "riggermorts" or something like that had set in afore he was taken up. Whatever the posh word is, we all know corpses get stiff for a while. That's why we lay them out right away, when it's a normal death.

Major Bly looked at the reddish-purple skin on one side of his face and said something about how the killer must have beaten him before cutting his throat. Got upset about it. Then puzzled. He said something, according to Monsieur Georges, about how could a little man do that to a big fellow like the Master.

Miss Leigh put him right. Said it wasn't bruising at all, but what's left of his blood. It seems it pools at the low points in the body and stays there if the corpse is left in one position for a while. She said he must have been lying on that cheek on the table. And his head was on one side when we'd seen it.

And that was more or less it, except they decided the right side of his throat behind the ear had been cut, severing the main artery to the brain. And with me missing carving knife! Some folks have no respect for a body's tools. And a fine sharp one—Gladys hones it each day—with a nice bone handle that fit me grip just right too.

Next all six of them separated to put on their outside shoes, coats, and hats and went out to look at those footprints. Monsieur Georges was sent down to tell Jeffries he was wanted and keep watch at the landing while he was busy. Mary saw Lady L. come out of the Office with the Master's binocular case around her neck and a yardstick under her arm.

They all came into the kitchen in their rain gear. Jeffries was told to meet them in the scullery. I saw my lady slip her notebook and a pencil into an outside pocket as she passed and heard the Major ask her what she was doing with the yardstick.

"Well, Stephen, tracks are vulnerable things in this kind of weather, and we should do everything we can to assist the police in apprehending the criminal. We can measure his or her stride for example, and also the length, depth, and width of the prints, and I'll sketch their outline annotated with the figures. Then we can have Jeffries put garden pots or buckets or something over them to protect them from the elements, at least till the police arrive."

"But why the binoculars?"

"Georges reported the prints went towards the causeway and boathouse. If one of the rowboats is missing, we may want to scan for debris. We also might give Jeffries the task of checking the perimeter of the headland and what he can see of the coastline, too. For instance, I have an idea that any boat out of control or just set adrift would wind up dashed against the rocks on the southeast part of the cliffs."

"Good thinking, Letitia! If you were a man, you'd have made a fine staff officer."

"Why thank you, Stephen."

Jeffries soon arrived and they all went off.

He told us later that before leaving the relative shelter of the kitchen garden walls, Lady had done her sketch of the prints and they'd measured both the prints and the distance between them. The prints were an odd shape, more like a Dutchman's wooden clog than a shoe. We have a pair of them clogs or patterns in the billiard room, on the wall, ornamental-like. They also looked to be of medium size, allowing for the thick walls of such shoes, to give more float power in soggy fields. The Major's clod-hopping boots were larger. So that seemed to let him off.

As Jeffries told it over a late tea, the tracks led through the latch-gate and headed straight for where the wave-covered neck of low land with the causeway came out onto the graveled drive to the front door and round to the stable yards. The boathouse was just by the causeway, outside the iron-gate and walls.

They'd been following the tracks for awhile, pausing now and again for him to measure the stride, Jeffries told us. It didn't look to be long enough for a tall man. Lady L. recorded the figures in her notebook with a pencil, back to the wind and rain.

As they neared the boathouse, I'm told she spoke out, raising her voice against that rain and wind—coming down in torrents it was at times while they was out, rattling me windows something fierce. Said to look how the prints avoided the gravel path and used the mud. Even in the kitchen garden them footmarks only used the path at the gate. Lady said it were like a trail set to mislead, she thought.

Major yelled back something about can't be sure. Sticking to his pet idea, stubborn as a mule as usual, or so Jeffries said. Lady also pointed out where someone could have taken clogs from the house, the billiard room pair I already mentioned. Mr. Hood suggested if they were where they should be they'd have to have been scrubbed and show signs, and if they weren't there that would also make it pretty certain.

It turned out Aggie found them with mud drying under Brown's bed. Lady L. had asked that she and Mary take a look about likely hiding places in everyone's room—hers included— while they were out.

When they reached the boathouse the prints went in the land doors, Jeffries told us. The doors had been left open and latched back on either side against the wind. The motorboat and one of the rowboats were there, but the second rowboat was missing.

Inside the boathouse Lady L. said all anyone pulling a fast one had to do was push the rowboat with an oar or a boat hook. That would do to get it out the water doors, which they also found open. And the wind and the current would take it away and make it look like someone had tried to escape. It would also supply smashed up wood to suggest to the bobbies they'd floundered and likely died. Jeffries said the Major was stubborn again. Saying the tramp could have been crazy-scared or foolish enough to risk it.

There didn't seem to be any wreckage near the boathouse. So Lady L. arranged to have Jeffries take the binoculars, and look about the coast. Later he saw some floating boards and part of an oar beneath the cliff, amongst the rocks.

After the party got back from the boathouse, Brown abandoned the rest, saying she was cold and wet. She stamped through the scullery into me kitchen and got wet, muddy footprints over my floors. I heard her muttering about changing and ordered that a hot whisky be brought up to her room. I sent Gladys running upstairs, to make sure the girls were out of the way, but they'd finished by then.

Lady Parrot led the others round the outside of the house to see if there were any signs of someone coming back, Jeffries said. I think she was remembering the mud on me Mackintosh. They found no tracks leading to the house—the south approaches are turfed near the house, except for the flowerbeds and gravel paths. But they did find a hand or glove print, an impression of part of a body, and a knee and the sole near the toe of a smallish-sized shoe in the flower bed on the left side of the Master's Office as you approach the french windows. Someone—Lady thought the killer—had slipped when he or she were almost home and fell, partly on the grass and partly on the flowerbed. He'd pushed himself to his knees and got up. Lady had Jeffries measure the finger-lengths, the hand-span, and the depth of the handprint, and wrote the figures down. Then she directed him to cover these prints and several of the clog ones in a row with upturned pots or pails before he went looking for boat flotsam. There was some mud on the flags in front of the french windows and the grass nearby, like someone wiped off the clogs on the grass after the fall? That's what it seemed like to Jeffries, and Lady pointed it out to the rest.

Mary cleaned the shoes. She said if the shoes were small, amongst the men Mr. Hood and the Professor had small to medium feet. She hadn't cleaned any of theirs with pointy toes nor seen any while searching neither. Aggie hadn't seen any like that in their rooms either. Mrs. Brown and Miss Leigh had regular shoes for women. Lady P.'s shoes were on the mannish side.

Agnes also found traces of muddy grit in the bath and hand basin not far from Lady's room. Lady told her when she reported it quiet-like later, she remembered being woken up because someone was running the taps, about 3 o'clock in the wee hours. Brown and Miss Leigh were all quartered along this corridor, the men in the other one. The bathroom was between Mrs. Brown's sitting room and Miss Leigh's bed-sitting room. Lady L. suggested soiled clothes as well as an individual had been washed, reasoning at least stockings or trouser legs would have been muddied as well as my Mac. Of course, it didn't have to be an inhabitant of the corridor, as she put it, who used the bath. A man might have done it to throw sand in our eyes.

The killer had gone back to the kitchen, hung me Mac back up, washed and dried the saucepan and mugs, and put them away. Gladys found a few pieces of mud in the cracks between the stones when she was sweeping the scullery and kitchen. Didn't think nothing of it at the time. Maybe it fell from me coat. Mary found some when she swept the inner hall floor and on the carpet in the Office. Likely fell from the clogs or the shoes. Lady said the killer would have to have taken off both shoes before stepping inside, or the muddy one would leave tracks.

That's how it was left for the police, who were summoned the next day when the storm had passed on.

Well, as you've probably guessed by now, it was down to Miss Leigh or Mrs. Brown unless one of us servants did it, and of course we didn't. What good would it do us? And we're all good Christians—excepting Monsieur Georges, who's Catholic. And he's a decent enough bloke anyway, even if he do talk funny.

The clogs under Mrs. Brown's bed, when everything else had been so careful cleaned up, made them suspect Leigh. She was examined by the police surgeon and a prison matron and they found bruises on her left hip and thigh. The shoe-toe matched one of hers, as did the handprint and stride, and they found traces of mud between the bristles of a shoe brush in her possession, which she had no need for here where Mary does the shoes for her. Eventually she confessed. It seemed she wanted out of her relationship with Master. He got violent and wouldn't let her go. She was afraid of him. She also was attracted to the Professor and wanted the money Master left her. So she lured him into the Kitchen, slipped on Gladys's Mac saying she was cold, and made cocoa for them. While he was sitting at the table and she passing back and forth behind him, she did it with me carving knife. Which they got out of her that she had the nerve to throw in the sea!

Your old friend,

Esther Stout

Poking Up the Fires

March 22, 192—

I never thought I would see such adventure and melodrama played out at John's old family seat, Morthead Manor, namely murder! Aspects of the secret passages of which we were in total ignorance! I feel the only place I may relate this tale is here, in my journal.

It's the stuff of the pleasant type of thriller. Perhaps something by Dorothy L. Sayers or Mrs. Christie or Georgette Heyer! But for it to be true, and to take part in it one's self, was truly a peculiar experience.

After that introduction, the actual story itself will seem too prosaic for words and be a bit of a bore if anyone reads these diaries, perhaps a relation or an archivist.

And in a peculiar way, it was. It seemed so like a play—the sort of farcical send-up one might go to for light amusement when in town—in which we were all playing our parts, that I hardly felt in any danger even after the guns came out and we were more or less kidnapped. Even stranger was how kidnappers and murder suspects allowed me to look into the later crime for which they denied responsibility. But there again they would, wouldn't they?

I was marooned at the Manor by a storm—the sort that strands the inhabitants of the house two or three times a year for a few days. I believe when I was a girl one spring, I had been meant to go to tea with the Parrots. A storm hit as I was being driven there and when we got to it, we found the causeway submerged on its low neck of land, the sea too rough for a boat, and we had to turn the horses around and head back to the village. That was before anyone in Devisshire had a motor car or dreamed of one. I remember John and his father, Sir George, in a yellow oilskins and sou'westers waving from the other shore between the gate posts and we waving back.

I believe that was the first time I was aware of the potential for isolation of my future home. It may be the first time I recall seeing my future husband too, come to think of it.

Getting back to the recent drama, we woke to the shocking news that the current owner of the Manor and our host, Charles Mortlake, had been found slumped over his desk in the Office with "his head bashed in" as Agnes put it, while drawing the guest room curtains and serving my morning tea. Not exactly the chatter one expects first thing at a country house party, even an enforced one. I ordered that the Office be locked and then indicted we would look at it after breakfast. I told her she had better put it as my "suggestion" to Major Bly, Charles's bosom friend and constant companion, who would no doubt want to "take charge." He is not one of the brighter sort of retired military men. Wisely he agreed—as I knew he would. His love of food shows in the steady increase in his girth, even though he is a tall man and weighed heavy even when I first met him a few years ago.

At breakfast, conversation was naturally subdued and we women, at least, made a poor meal of it. The three men ate their normal fare, though two of them seemed distracted and not noticing what they put in their mouths.

The upstairs party comprised three inmates of the house and three guests.

First I shall introduce the inhabitants. Major Stephen Bly, Devizesshire Foot, retired, I have already mentioned. He helped Charles with estate management and I believe was a younger son of a genteel family with practically no money, but a mortgaged estate in Devon. "Mrs." Hettie Brown, the "Lady Housekeeper," was once a music hall *"artiste"* and, I inferred, had been Charles's mistress since before the War. Miss Grace Leigh, a young lady of good manners and respectable, though middle-class, parentage, was Charles's "personal secretary." Her one failing so far as I was aware is to have succumbed to sustained pressure and become Charles's new mistress, or so I have it on good information.

The other guests (besides myself, relic of the last baronet Parrot) were two "gentlemen." The term applied in varying degrees, at least as far as I knew at this point in the story. Professor Patrick Lawless was an Oxford History don in his thirties (though of a grammar-school background) who advised Charles on his extensive modernizations and renovations, and was an expert on priest-holes and such things. He was currently cataloguing the library. Mr. Jack Hood was an American from Chicago. He presented himself as owning nightclubs or "speakeasies" in that city and New York (despite the current Prohibition), and of being backed by Charles in one in London.

After breakfast, we proceeded to the Office en masse. On my instructions, Mary had secured the door and pasted a signed piece of paper across the entrance to the secret passage, which led only—as I then thought—to the scullery. I have always subscribed to the maxim "better safe than sorry," and some guilty party amongst us might have wanted to interfere with the evidence or to make sure nothing incriminating had been overlooked.

Mary unlocked the door and we paraded in. Charles was indeed slumped as reported with the back of his head rather gruesomely like it had been struck by a heavy thin object. Looking about the room, I noticed the poker was somewhat out of place on the rack of fire irons in the grate.

"Perhaps the poker is the murder weapon?" I said. Professor Lawless and I moved over to examine it.

The Major started on an anecdote about an adventure during the lateWar as was his tiresome wont. "Charles was in action once during the War. It got pretty furious. Our boys were actually fighting hand to hand in a burned out farm house the Hun's were using as cover. Charles led the men. He had his Webley revolver knocked from his grasp as he was thrown to the ground by a gorilla of a Hun noncom with a bayonet. He thought he was done for. But the Hun, likely pausing to play with him, allowed him to scramble to his feet. As he pushed himself up from the mud, his hand miraculously found this rusty poker. He managed to get under the surprised Hun's guard and killed him with a blow to the side of the neck. Then he retrieved his Webley.

"Strange if a poker like that which saved him was destined to be the instrument of his own demise!" The old soldier was deeply moved and could barely maintain his composure, taking refuge behind a large handkerchief and blowing his nose energetically.

"Yes, Major, ironic," I said. "Though the German might see things differently, of course! It does seem a likely murder weapon from the appearance of the wound and its shape."

I took out my own handkerchief and picked the instrument up. The old officer came over to look closely at it with Lawless and I.

"It seems if it did kill him that efforts have been made to wipe it clean," Lawless observed.

"Yes," I agreed slowly, but took a closer look at where the hooked end was rough and irregular. I thought I saw something. "Get me a magnifying glass from the desk will you Miss Leigh?" Once she had brought it, I confirmed what I thought I had seen. "See here," I pointed out, "blood, a minute bone splinter, a few white cotton threads, and a few brown hairs, probably from Charles."

Lawless and Stephen Bly took turns at the glass and agreed. We heard retching sounds from behind us.

Turning around, we saw Hettie Brown doubled over and being sick over the Aubusson carpet. She retreated hastily, hands over her mouth, presumably to the W.C. behind the stairs. We turned back to our investigations. I placed the weapon on the desk, and considered the rest of the room.

"The french windows were bolted, Mary?"

"Yes, Milady. I didn't check the first time when I found him, but I did when I went back to lock up and seal the secret passage as you and the Major said to."

"Did you handle the french door with your bare hand?"

"Last night, yes. This morning I just looked and saw it was bolted."

"The curtains were over the window this morning?" I gestured to the heavy red damask draperies now pulled back.

"Yes, Ma'am. The electric light was still on—the lamp on the desk and the standard lamp behind it. I drew the blinds back and switched them lamps off." The floor lamp stood near the wall on which the fireplace was, placed to throw light over Charles' right shoulder. The desk was a few feet out from the same wall at right angles to it, some six or seven feet beyond the mantle place, with the french windows at the chair's back. The rain continued pelting against the panes of glass. The entrance to the secret passage was in the corner behind, and to the left, of where Charles was seated.

We carefully looked about the room, including the floor, for possible clues. The deep-piled royal blue carpet revealed nothing. It seemed Charles had been working on some papers when he was struck down, as his gold fountain pen lay on the blotter to the right of his arm, as if put down when someone had entered. The three cushions on the couch facing the desk on the opposite side of the hearth were all at the left end and flattened. I asked the Major if they were like that when he left last night.

"No. I sit at the right end generally with one cushion at my back. The end table and magazine rack are handy, and generally the other end is too near the fire." He gestured to the end where the ottoman was, though it had been pushed in front of the end table and was not parallel to that piece or the couch. "My footstool's been moved. Usually it's in front of where I sit," he added.

When questioned, Mary confirmed that the furniture had been as the Major described it at about ten forty-five when she checked to see that nothing more was wanted, and bolted the french windows for the night. She also reported she saw the Major start up the stairs a few minutes later as she left the dining room. Miss Leigh said she had gone up to write letters about nine forty-five, ten minutes after I had left the sitting room when Hood and Lawless went off to the games room. Brown had left the company earlier and claimed to have gone up towards ten. The remaining gentlemen asserted they had gone up at about ten-thirty.

There seemed to be an elusive odor in the air. I remarked on it.

"Perhaps it is . . . " the Major said, trailing off, gesturing to Mrs. Brown's breakfast on the floor.

"No. Not like that, though that makes it difficult to smell. Perhaps a trace of cologne or perfume? Sweet and flowery, but I can barely smell it."

"Oh, it's probably just the brilliantine Charles uses to slick back his hair, and his after shave or perhaps one of the other gentlemen's," blurted out Grace Leigh. "That Charles used, I should say."

I took a good look at her, but reserved my judgement. After all, she and Hettie Brown would both be far better qualified than I to testify to that! I walked back over to behind the desk and leaned over the corpse from the left side to sniff his hair. There was an odour true enough, but nothing like the one I was speaking of. I expressed this conclusion. After sniffing each gentleman, we were no further forwards. Miss Leigh's perfume, which she seemed to rotate daily, was overpowering the scent in the closed room anyway.

I went back to the couch and smelt the cushions closely. The same scent was stronger here, along with a scent of human animals *in flagrante delicto.* I had the others smell the crushed cushions, too. Hood, Lawless, and the Major agreed with my sense of smell, somewhat embarrassed at my plain speaking. Leigh expressed doubt and Brown, who had re-joined us, excused herself, saying she still felt queasy. She also had on a perfume, which clashed disagreeably with Leigh's. Neither matched the cushion scent, but they were more like it than the hair creams and lotions of the male members of the party. I use just a dab of lavender water, and often not even that. I hadn't used it that morning for the simple reason I had none with me.

Having obtained an electric torch from Mary earlier, I proceeded to open the secret passage by turning the pear-shaped boss in the paneling in the corner. The door slid back, breaking Mary's seal in half. I switched on the torch and played it over the floor, Major Bly and the ladies were peering over my shoulder. The remaining gentlemen were somewhat behind us.

"Why, look at the dust!" exclaimed the Major. "I didn't think anyone had been in here for months. But there are footprints all over the place, going both ways. Whatever can it mean?"

I distinctly heard two metallic clicks behind us. Apparently so did Stephen Bly (despite his slight hearing loss), Miss Leigh, and Hettie Brown, for we turned about as if one.

"That," said Mr. Hood, "is a good question, but the answer to it is: none of your business. You shouldn't have stuck your noses into it."

We turned around slowly, and found ourselves facing not one, but two, revolvers—one pointed at us by Patrick Lawless and the other by the American.

Whatever interest they had in the passage had not been legal, it appeared.

"You foul murderers!" yelled Bly. I glanced at him. His color approximated that of a boiled lobster. Clearly he was upset. "Having the infernal nerve to kill Charles, your host and benefactor! Which one of you did it? I'll see you hang one way or another!"

"Cool down, Gramps," said Hood, pointing the barrel of his gun at the Major's chest. "We were Chuck's partners in a little smuggling racket. Him being a corpse puts the kibosh to a good business venture. I didn't kill him, nor did Paddy here.

"When he caught it we were somewhere in the really secret tunnel, seeing to loading his motor launch for a run to France once this storm lifts, to exchange some merchandise. We found him like that about three a.m. We'd been down there since just after you left him, Grandpa, so don't sweat it or try nothing foolish.

"If the cops really look for it, they'll find our secret passage and smuggler's cave beneath the cliffs. Chuck had them restored during the 'renovations.' Paddy found out the Mortheads – the guys before the Parrots -- were into smuggling priests and Catholic agents in and out of the country, maybe some duty free goods too. King James's folks sealed up that part of the tunnel, filling in the first part with rocks before they sold it and a baronetcy to the first Parrots to live here.

"The cops'd find our prints all over the boat and traces of cargo if they really tried, and assume we had a disagreement with Chuck here. We didn't. But cops like easy answers. None of us wants to hang. So if you folks behave yourselves, you'll be inconvenienced till after the storm lifts, but be fine in the long run once we've gone on the lam, out of this nice country of yours.

"Now what will we do with you for now. Any ideas, Paddy?"

"Perhaps tied up in the dining room?"

"Yeah! I like that idea. Then only one or two of us would have to guard them at a time. From the radio, sounds like it'll be just the one night."

"One or two, of us?" I asked. "I take it that means there are more conspirators in this house?"

"Yeah, Georges is one of us, and Jeffries too. They were 'downstairs' with us too. Both were in on the black market games Chuck got into during the War. I connected up with them then. As I have experience distributing illegal stuff through my nightclubs stateside, Chuck made me an offer to set up an operation here for him. We still sell to middlemen, but selling direct we get more of the proceeds. That was just about done. His bank isn't doing as well as it appears on its own account, see. A bank's a good way to turn money legit. No one thinks anything of banks making money. That's what they do."

The Professor went to fetch Georges and had him get rope. Once this was accomplished, we were escorted to the dining room and tied up. Georges and Lawless were to keep an eye on us, Mary, and Agnes, while Jeffries took first shift at guarding Cook and Gladys, who were allowed to go on preparing food, as the gang wanted to eat. We were to be hostages for their good behavior. Hood—if that was his real name—was about to leave us when I had an idea.

"If, as you say, none of you killed Charles Mortlake, it would be in your interest for all the evidence to be collected as soon as possible. Why not let me help you keep clear of the murder charge at least by looking into it. I do know a good deal about this sort of thing from reading crime reports and fiction, and the stories my friend the Chief Constable has told me over the years. The others will still be here as hostages. In fact, we can start without you even untying me, with Mary, Georges, and Agnes here, though we may have to go elsewhere later on."

"She could be right, Br—" "Hood" looked daggers at him. So "Jack Hood" was an alias. "Jack, I mean," said the Professor, correcting his *faux pas*. "We don't have anything to lose. None of us are guilty. Any evidence she finds will likely point towards that. And keep the hanging offense off the warrants for our arrest."

Hood thought about it for a minute. "Yeah. I kind of like the idea, lady. You said you could start here. Go ahead."

"Georges, when did you last see Mr. Mortlake before going through the Office to the secret passage?"

"It was just as he finished dressing for dinner. I was dismissed for the night. We always stayed in -- how you say? -- our 'roles' in case anyone overheard. He was early. That either meant he wanted a drink, or he had an amorous rendezvous."

"I was down early too," Stephen volunteered, "just before Mary prepared the drinks tray. I was there, wasn't I Mary, when you put it out?" She confirmed this. "Charles didn't appear until just before the dinner gong. You were here, Letitia. Miss Leigh had time to finish her cocktail and I refilled it for her. I believe Mrs. Brown came in only just before Charles."

"Last minute instructions to the servants," Brown explained.

"Which ones?" I asked.

"Err, Cook, I think," she ran her hands through her bleach blonde curls. Convenient that Cook was not present?

"Come on, Mrs. Brown, this is a murder we are talking about. It is widely known you and Charles were more than friends for a long time. It won't sully your reputation to admit a rendezvous."

"Oh, very well, you old tart!" she said crossly. "Charlie 'ad me. Just a quick one. 'E didn't take his shirt, nor even 'is trousers and underwear entirely off. He was pretty rough as usual, but at least 'e didn't beat me like 'e does sometimes since the War. 'E's got a mean streak does me Charlie. Or he did." She broke into tears and sobs. They seemed genuine, but I recalled her experience as an actress of sorts and withheld judgement.

"The rotter!" exclaimed Leigh. "I must have just left when you came along! No wonder he was almost late!"

"So Grace, you also say you, to be blunt, copulated with Mortlake before supper?"

"Yes. Yes, I did."

"You look puzzled, Mrs. Brown," I prompted, noticing her raised eyebrows.

"Well, if Miss Leigh says so I guess it's true, but even in the old days, he had trouble doing it soon after 'aving a go. Usual 'ad to wait an hour or two."

"He wasn't that way with me!" said Leigh. "Maybe it excited the bastard, having us one after the other?"

"Could be, luv, but I still think it's strange. That's what it is. And I've known Charlie for near twenty years," Mrs. Brown said, still skeptical.

"Did either of you have a liaison with Charles in the Office after his associates had gone about their business?"

"Not me," said Brown. "If Charlie wants me 'e either tells me where and when to come or 'e knows where to find me bed. Sometimes 'e wakes me up in the wee hours and 'as me. Sometimes, like yesterday, 'e lets me know and I meet 'im."

"Miss Leigh?"

"Why no!" she said, wide-eyed. "Charles didn't ask me to come to him or anything." She turned her attention to her long, red, manicured nails. "I was probably getting my beauty sleep when he got his comeuppance."

I wondered which one of them was lying, and whether the liar was also the killer. As Charles let it be known that both of the women stood to inherit generous annuities if still with him upon his death, they shared a motive. For that matter, Stephen Bly was also said to be in for one and there had been hints about the estate too;

not that in the normal course of things he would have inherited, being about a decade older than his former subordinate and friend.

I began to think of perfume. Leigh wore several different ones and seemed to change them daily. As far as I could recall, Brown wore just one or two, and they tended to be older established scents of pre-War vintage, though Parisian and likely supplied by Charles. Yes, that would bear investigating.

"Stephen, Miss Leigh, Mrs. Brown, did anyone see you after you were upstairs, while on the way to, or from, the lavatory or bath, for example? Or did anyone call for a servant?"

"Well," replied the Major, "as you know Mary saw me heading up. I believe I passed Hood on my way to the bath, and Lawless returning from the toilet. Lawless wore pajamas, slippers, and a dressing gown, by the by," he glowered at the gunmen.

"That's true," agreed Lawless. "Jack and I made a point of being seen prepared for bed and actually getting under our sheets, before redressing and heading down below. So did Georges."

Georges and Hood agreed. Mary had seen Georges similarly garbed as she went to use the facilities after locking up. She gave him a black look, to which he responded with a smirk.

"I popped me 'ead in," said Brown, "and checked up on 'ow Cook and Agnes were doing before I went up, about quarter to ten. After that I think, Lady Parrot, you saw me coming out of the bath in our hallway."

"Yes, I did. It was about half-ten, just before I retired," I agreed, trying to recall the precise time. "We were both dressed for bed."

"That'd be about right," Brown agreed.

"Well, I saw Mrs. Brown coming out of the bath just as she slipped back into her bedroom. I was just coming out of my room. Do you remember?" asked Miss Leigh.

"I think I caught a glimpse of you. You were in your yellow and blue kimono over one of them filmy negligees Charlie bought you. Where you were going, I 'aven't a clue, though I think I did hear a door close soon after so it could have been the loo."

"Thank you all for your cooperation," I said. "Now if someone would be good enough to untie me, I think we should examine some of the rooms upstairs and take another look at the Office. I would appreciate it if you let Agnes come with me. If all are willing, it might be good to search all our rooms, and I'm not as spry as I used to be."

Hood undid our bonds and he and Lawless escorted us upstairs, while Georges watched the others.

We searched the men's rooms first. It seemed Major Bly's Webley revolver had been confiscated, for it was not in its reputed normal place in the bedside table drawer. Not that I had been intending to try anything so foolish, but one does consider possibilities . . . Lawless and "Hood" were already almost packed, except for some dirty clothes. They allowed us to examine the contents of their drawers, wardrobes, and cases, but we found no traces of blood, even on handkerchiefs. Of course the assailant would likely have burned anything incriminating given a chance as all rooms had functional fireplaces and coal scuttles, but Agnes reported she had noticed nothing unusual when she cleaned out the ash and prepared the evening fires for lighting before time to dress for dinner. We did, however, find a snuffbox filled with white powder in Charles's bedside table. This "Hood" confiscated, frowning and muttering about fools who try the goods.

The women's rooms were more intriguing.

Secreted amongst Leigh's underwear and frilly hankies, Agnes found a powder compact, which also contained the same white powder.

"Hood" didn't confiscate it, as it was evidence against an outsider, though Lawless argued with him on this point. It seemed the Professor was not immune to her charms. From the exchange it seemed Charles had introduced her to "the stuff" and was rationing her, mainly to time around when they had sex, otherwise he kept her on a strict ration. I felt some sympathy for the young woman caught in the toils of drugs—no doubt one of the ways Charles Mortlake used to seduce and then control her. I put it in an envelope from a supply I had secured from the Office on our way up for evidence, sealed it, indicated location and time found, dated it and had Agnes, Lawless, and "Hood" add their names to mine as witnesses.

On her dressing table there were seven bottles of expensive, fashionable perfumes from Parisien Passion to Ambrosian Dew. I sniffed each and though I couldn't quite be sure, felt the latter was close to the scent on the pillows in the Office, suggesting the girl was lying, whether out of foolishness or guilt, I could not tell.

I also had Agnes search my room for the sake of fairness, though it would be absurd to think of Charles Mortlake taking a second look at me, or my succumbing to his advances if he did!

When we looked through Hettie Brown's room, I found her underwear and handkerchiefs surprisingly conservative, as was her nightwear, though she did have one or two frilly nightgowns. She also had two well-known perfumes on her table. Neither resembled the scent in the Office.

We quickly searched the servant's quarters, finding nothing that seemed pertinent, and then proceeded downstairs to re-examine the Office.

I asked that Mary be present when we re-examined the Office, so poor Agnes was tied up again, and Mary released from hers.

I had the Professor lift the body. Taking a closer look at the corpse's clothes Hood, Mary, and I observed both blonde and auburn hairs on Mortlake's evening jacket. The auburn ones —Leigh's color—very much predominating and overlaying in places the former, about the collar, neck, and chest. The blonde hairs had darker roots, consistent with Mrs. Brown's peroxide blonde hair.

We then took the magnifying glass once more to the murder weapon. I wanted another look at those threads on the poker. Mary helped me search the room thoroughly, wearing pairs of my evening gloves collected from my room while we were there for the purpose. Under the desk, Mary found a scrap of lace. It matched the threads caught on the prong of the murder weapon. There were also blonde and auburn hairs on the settee back.

"Probably this hooked end of the poker with the rough finish about it tore the lace off the handkerchief used to wipe it clean of prints."

"Milady!" said Mary, who had gone over to the fireplace and began pushing ashes about with the tongs. "I didn't clear the grate this morning in the kerfuffle. Look at this. It's only partly burned."

She found the charred, partly intact remnants of what seemed to be a lady's handkerchief with lacy edges.

That was all we found. Our captors got away early the next morning. Lawless had offered to take Grace Leigh with him, but she had indignantly refused. A few hours later the Major managed to loosen his bonds and free us.

Miss Leigh was too hasty in refusing Lawless's offer. Not only did she not know that the cocaine had been found in her room and the auburn hairs on the evening jacket, she also dismissed the scent, and believed the handkerchief had been consumed by fire. As I reported, she favored frilly handkerchiefs and Mrs. Brown, surprisingly, preferred practical ones without a lace border, as do I. It was the lace and the remains of the bloodstained handkerchief that may well hang her. The scent proves her presence in amatory activity with Mortlake. The relative position of the auburn and blonde hairs suggest she was the last to "neck" with Charles on the settee (to put it politely) rather than Brown. The flimsy pieces of cotton lace link her to the murder weapon.

—Letitia Parrot

Agent on the Case

Mr. Gregory O'Grady,
Pinkerton Detective Agency,
New York,
New York, USA
November 5, 192—

Dear Boss:

Me again dashing off a quick account as directed by cable. The full field report in proper form will have to follow. With the English cops getting involved both over Mortlake and the clubs, things are pretty hectic for Hammet and me. I no longer have to impersonate Jack "Cutthroat" Hood.

As Operative Hammet's telegram told you—once that darn storm blew off and we were no longer marooned on the headland where Mortlake's mansion is—the Mortlake aspect of the case is over because, in a manner of speaking, so is he. Kaput. A corpse.

He got himself killed during the storm.

I had to blow my cover in confidence to the local cops. Our Scotland Yard contact made it okay when they telephoned him for confirmation of the operation. At least we've got enough evidence here to help our clients make their case against his American associates and his other illegal ventures here to make the Brits cooperate (maybe) in cleaning up the Bermuda end of the thing, despite their usual winking at it. Our Scotland Yard contact certainly appreciates my discoveries in our little amateur murder investigation.

Now the Brits are thanking us instead of frowning on "agents employed by a foreign power" (referring to, of course, our ATF clients).

As you already know from my earlier progress reports, Charles M.'s little secret about the uses to which he wanted the nightclub put totally changed our Scotland Yard contact's patronizing, uncooperative attitude. And discovering a bit more about the subject's illegal activities has changed their attitude to his Bermuda-U.S. activities, "don't you know."

I say "us" not because Hammet was here where he could have been of some use, the way things played out, but because it was really this old Lady (yes, that's lady with a capital "L," though now her old man's kicked the bucket she prefers Letitia or Mrs. Parrot), one of the local nobs. Hubby used to own this joint and she got stuck with it till Mortlake bought it and left her in clover. She really caught the killer with help from yours truly, and in the course of the investigation found out about the other stuff.

It was really Mortlake's complex "domestic arrangements" that killed him and helped us out too. Well, I'd better get down to brass tacks.

It looked like another good morning to linger in bed. The storm was rattling the windows—there's been wind like you wouldn't believe and pouring rain too -- cats and dogs—and it was real dark. I didn't realize till I got to this little island that rules a quarter of the world (bloody colonizing bastards, I'm thinking) it would be so wet. But they seem like nice folks, once you get to know them. They're very standoffish, 'least the upper-crust, monied types, and even the professional guys ("aping their betters," I guess) till you are "properly introduced." Then they can be real pally. Those intro letters ATF took off Hood as he got on the boat and carted him off quietly worked a charm with the local criminal element, Mortlake included.

Not that the cops thought he was one of the bad guys. Nah. No way. They were amused at the thought of a rich banker, who inherited his money, "stooping so low," the toffee-faced guy said. Like the Social Register types and the Boston Brahams can do no wrong, but the whole country's like that, least the haves. And the working stiffs have to bow and scrap and put up with it.

That was just before he read me the riot act and gave me about half an inch of rope, saying he'd come down on me like a "ton of bricks" if I got into anything shady. Changed his tune pretty quick when we produced the lowdown on the club scheme, then it was like he was the client, not ATF.

Anyway, like I say there really wasn't much to do, me and Mortlake started discussing our supposedly mutual plans for supplying Hood's speakeasy clubs in the U.S. from his organization via Bermuda. Then the storm hit and everyone in the damned mansion was incommunicado and forced to stay put.

The morning Mortlake's death was discovered Agnes, the chamber maid, came in with my morning cup of coffee. It took me a few days before I got them to heat me up some coffee saved from the previous night. Waking up to tea is the custom. While I was getting an eyeful of the scenery (a real looker, Aggie) and wasn't paying attention at first, she poured out the story, breathless, of how Mortlake was dead with his head bashed in, on a bench in a little workshop nook off the scullery. Gladys, the little buck-tooth rabbit of a teenager who's kitchen maid, found him and screamed her head off. I was ready to jump up and go look, but Agnes said that Lady Parrot (whom all the inside servants except Georges, the so-called valet, used to work for) and Major Bly -- an old bore and best buddy of Mortlake; I haven't got anything on him, but they were close as shadows so it's incredible he knew nothing about the shady side of Mr. M. -- had decreed that inspection of the dear departed would wait till after they "broke their fast" and that no one was to go near the area till then.

I thought of sneaking down and going round outside to get a preview, before clod-hopping amateurs messed up the scene, but then I heard it drumming on the roof like a Niagara above me and thought better of it.

Next chance I got at sizing up the suspects was at the breakfast table in the dining room.

I will just mention that Agnes said Mary, the homely spinster who's parlour maid, found the door by the panty ajar when she did her morning opening up routine. But I wasn't really buying the outside job idea, the Major was trumpeting. We were marooned on an island practically with the causeway on its low neck of land washed by giant waves. And Jeffries -- the guy who lives over the stable, is the "Master's" chauffeur and handyman (and really bodyguard and muscle up to his bull-like neck; if it wasn't for the chin you couldn't tell where the neck stopped and the head began) -- keeps a careful watch. I wouldn't like to be a prowler meeting him up a dark alley, or anywhere else, if I couldn't run like hell, or didn't have my revolver on me. Big guy. All muscles and likes to flex 'em.

Oh yeah, the suspects.

There was Lady Parrot. I kind of liked the old broad. She had a sense of humour, I suspected, and didn't take all this title stuff seriously. The servants thought she walked on water. I couldn't figure out a motive, unless Mortlake -- a guy you definitely didn't want to leave alone with your looker of a sister -- had been feeling up Agnes, or raping her, or something. And there were no signs of it I could see. Otherwise I suppose she could be batty and resent anyone who lives in her old home or does "immoral" things there. But if I were a betting man, I'd put my money against her rubbing Mortlake out. She was very composed, but thoughtful and watchful (without being obvious about it like most amateurs). Took her usual toast and marmalade with tea.

Which brings me to his "housekeeper." "Mrs." Brown had been with the Mortlake for fifteen years or more. She was really his old floozy; used to be a showgirl and still a bottle-blonde; uses a lot of makeup. Maybe Mortlake was beating her and she snapped? I wouldn't put it past him, but if she'd put up with his ways for so long, why now? But she gets an income if she's still employed by him when he dies. Could be also she'd been caught cooking the household books more than he would put up with, or had another business disagreement with him. Could be part of his gang. Don't know how much she knows. She's called Hettie by her pals like Chuck and the Major. Don't know if Chuck shared her now-fading charms. Doubt it. I see him as territorial.

She was very quiet at table with dark circles under the eyes. Looked like she was crying almost silently, dabbing her cheeks now and then, sniffing and blowing her nose. There again she had been an actress and maybe could fake it convincingly. Shaking hands too. Took black coffee and toast with her left hand. The only southpaw in the house and Jeffries looked like a regular pitcher too. Don't know how much she knew, but probably more than the "secretary," the new girl on the block. Usually has a full breakfast.

Which brings me to Mortlake's (higher class, younger) floozy, his "private secretary." Maybe she was his typist at first, but she's got a body, and I've observed when Mortlake sees one he wants, he'll buy it. She sure does have fancy clothes and jewelry, courtesy of Chuck, naturally. Name's Grace Leigh. Daughter of a government clerk, respectable but not one of the nobs, just a white-collar Joe. She gets income too once he's bought it. Said to be same deal as Brown. Could be one of the gang, but I don't think so.

Jealousy rearing up on its hind paws? Or good old greed?

Then there's the Major. Stephen Bly. English. Retired. Used to be Mortlake's boss during the War. Stupid as sin in many ways, or so he seems at first. Always telling the same war stories. Spends most of his time with Mortlake. Don't know if there's any shady business between them, but it seems a strange friendship for Mortlake, if you ask yours truly. Still the old boy knows something about landed estates and ran that side of things for the Man. Maybe he just fakes the old fart bit. Could be involved in the racket. No proof though. Also gets lots of pounds at five greenbacks each after the funeral.

Again could be money. Jealous of the gals Chuck had? Or maybe he sniffed me out and felt it time to take the inheritance and kill the only one who could rat on him?

He had on a long face at breakfast and loudly expressed his view that "gentlemen" were not safe from vagrants in their own homes. But he shoveled down the grub like usual. Getting fat, though a tall guy.

There's also this Professor Patrick Lawless. I haven't had a chance to check him out yet. Don't know if he's a real Oxford Professor, but it'd be pretty easy to check out. I also have not determined if his activities match his name. He acts enthusiastic about history and knows a lot — I suppose he could be faking it like me for all I know about it. Could be a member of the gang using the name of a real Oxford guy. Hence the ratting motive might apply. Mortlake seemed to be real chummy with this character too; not Siamese-twin style like the Major, but on good terms. The Prof supposedly advised him on tasteful restorations and renovations.

I think he's sweet on the Leigh woman. Could be a motive there. If he's in the gang it could be a business disagreement. Meant to be here to catalogue the library and seems to be doing it, but what do I know about cataloging? He's writing on index cards while looking at books and filing them in a cabinet.

Very interested in secret passages. Before Mortlake's death I only had the chance to check out the one between the sitting room and the Orangerie. There's another between Mortlake's Office – *de facto* the Major and Chuck's cozy private sitting room, all others by invitation only -- and the scullery off the kitchen as you will see. No signs of recent activity in the first one: the deep dust showed no footprints.

Lawless ate more or less the same as usual at breakfast, but so did I. Another thoughtful, watchful one, but a bit more obvious than Lady P. or me.

I doubt the inside servants are involved, unless it's Georges, the French "valet." I strongly suspect he's part of the gang and there's a connection with French crooks. Muscles Jeffries is in the thick of it, of course. Falling out amongst thieves? Bribed by a rival gang?

Breakfast finished, we guests and Mary were on our way to the scene of the crime through the kitchen. Brown's housekeeper office was on the right of the passage between the green baize door marking off the servant's premises and the kitchen. In the kitchen Ma Stout (the Cook) and Gladys, the kitchen helper were at their work. Lady P., our self-appointed leader, paused by them.

"Gladys, Cook, would you mind very much coming with us?" said Lady P. politely. And then we were nine, all trooping through the scullery proper. There we stopped by the garden door (adjacent to the secret passage entrance) for Parrot to grill Mary.

"Now, Mary, would you please just show us how the door was when you found it and what you did."

"It was just open a crack like this, Milady," said dutiful Mary. "It's sheltered from the wind on this side of the house a bit and the kitchen garden walls help, or it would have been blowing back and forth all night, I daresay. I thought it was strange, but that perhaps Mr. Jeffries had come in for some tea after a late round, didn't pull it all the way closed, and forgot to lock it. It doesn't seem like him to be careless, though. I was going to report later, but Gladys fetched me, started screaming something awful. Cook not being quite down, I went to her. Mrs. Stout came down the back stairs as I took Gladys back into the kitchen, so we told her what Gladys said she'd seen. Then, Cook and me went to look ourselves, after giving Gladys a biscuit and a cup of tea and telling her to have a sit and calm down. She was shaking something fierce from the shock like."

"Thank you Mary. Let us proceed. You can tell us the rest when we are there."

We went back into the scullery proper.

"Now Gladys, come to me," said Parrot. "You are perfectly safe with us here. Nothing can harm you. Please tell us where you were when you first realized something was wrong."

The gawky teenager came forward, dragging her feet, but like she was Doc Pavlov's dog, having heard the bell. She gulped, her prominent Adam's apple beneath her negligible chin bobbing up and down, before beginning. She kneaded her apron in the hands without seeming to know it.

"Well, Milady, I'd come into the scullery to get to the pantry. We'd finished the last of the tea in the caddy last night and Mrs. Stout had told me to get some more from the pantry, but I forgot, so when I'd opened it this morning, 'twas empty. So I guessed I'd forgotten. So I took the caddy to the pantry and filled it with the tea. I didn't notice the door was ajar. Just thought there were a draft or something, though I'd never noticed one there afore. I guess I was feeling worried Mrs. Stout would find out I didn't do it last night and scold me.

"Anyway, I was coming out of the pantry and crossing back to the kitchen doorway when I saw something at the far end out of the corner of me eye, over where Mr. Jeffries fixes things that don't need no big cutting tools or nothing that makes too much mess. 'Twas on the stone bench, by the old hearth, the part that used to be the kitchen hundreds of years ago, like. But there I go babbling on again like Mrs. Stout tells me off for when she's busy," she smiled shyly and giggled. "Not that she means anything by it, but it means she's in a hurry and don't want to be distracted.

"Well, then I looked and thought there was a black and white bag of something on the bench. I went over and I saw it was a man with his forehead bashed in. Then I ran screaming till Mary gave me a slap and told me to calm down and tell her what's the matter."

Lady P. took a few steps past the secret passage entrance panel where there was a line of sight unblocked from the pantry entrance and asked, "So you were about here?"

"That'd be about right. I know I'd just passed the secret passage 'cause I'd wondered why there were a piece of paper caught-like in the corner of the sliding door." Everyone turned around and saw that there was indeed some paper stuck in the usually invisible line where the oak panel concealing the entrance met the wall. Just a corner stuck out and marred the invisible effect. "It took me mind off Mrs. Stout. Then o' course I saw the body and forgot about the paper until just now." The girl giggled, laughing at herself, a bit hysterically.

"That's fine Gladys," said Detective Parrot. "We'll see about that in a minute. Thank you for drawing it to our attention. Now, when you went over to the body did you touch or move anything?"

"No, Milady, I was too scared," the girl answered.

"Go back with Mrs. Stout now. I don't think you need be with us any further just now."

"Yes, Milady! Thank you, Milady!" she said, relieved, and skedaddled off through the kitchen doorway followed by the cook.

"Shall we investigate the vicinity of the body first?" The way she said it, it wasn't a really question. So we all wandered over through a sort of archway. It looked like the house was originally smaller than it is now. There was this big fireplace dominating the far wall. The kind you could walk in if it wasn't for it being bricked up, with a little door to the side, maybe for bread making? I imagined a whole pig roasting on the spit over a log fire way back.

The body was on a bench coming out from the right-hand wall, halfway from the former hearth to the arch. I guess it was the original kitchen counter where they'd chop things up and stuff. There was a stone sink in one end and a pump handle beside it. Along the wall on the far side by it was a wooden rack for tools on the wall. Screw drivers, hammers, drills, a plane, wrenches, crowbar . . .

We focused on the other end. I only half registered the background at first. 'Cause the principal subject, a.k.a. Charles Mortlake, lay like a rumpled, spread-eagled penguin in his society evening get-up on a quilt, with the top right part of his face a shattered mess. Not a pretty sight. Before, Mortlake was a handsome man, not like me, or you, boss. No more. Let us say he was a disagreeable sight with blood, skin, bone, and gray matter sort of mashed together and looking kind of squished. I wondered about the comforter.

Brown covered her mouth with her hand and turned her back on it. Leigh, who'd been a front-line volunteer nurse during the war—VADs they call them, middle-class gals getting their hands dirty amongst us lower order types as imitation Florence Nightingales—looked more professional than usual, though a bit grim around the mouth. The Prof and me, we'd been in the war too and it wasn't new. The Major stood stock-still for a minute, then I saw tears dripping down towards his open mouth; then the mouth shut, his gray head bowed and he said a prayer (out loud) for his "dearest comrade, so foully done to death." So the rest of us sort of went along, till he got a grip on himself. Then we got back to business.

You didn't have to be a pathologist to tell this guy was dead. Still Leigh felt for a pulse, and tried to move his arm.

"He has cooled to room temperature. There is no pulse and rigor has set in. Death must have taken place some hours ago. At least five or six," she pronounced, like the doc in a detective novel. I had no idea what her opinion was worth, but it was the only thing we had and it seemed to make sense to this gumshoe. I glanced at my watch. It showed about ten, and we'd rushed through breakfast. These folks don't exactly keep workingmen's hours. Her estimate would mean he had died by five a.m.

"Look at his trousers," said Parrot, after looking the corpse over good, even leaning down to look at the bottom part of his clothes from the side. "The buttons. Some of them aren't properly done up."

"Maybe the guy fluffed it when he last went to the john." I suggested.

"That is an idea certainly," she replied, "but you will also note that the trousers are badly creased and I noticed nothing amiss at supper."

"So he took a long time in there," I countered.

"Possibly, however, I suggest we look at his underwear. The trousers don't seem properly pulled up at the back. They are barely over the buttocks. As you can see, the tails of his evening jacket are doubled up under him. The quilt looks rumpled too, as if it's been pushed up. I suspect he was killed partially disrobed, perhaps for amorous purposes, and the killer was going to straddle him or, um, was to use his or her mouth."

"Letitia! How could you say such a thing? I always assumed ladies didn't know about unnatural practices, unless they were, err, professionals. And as for suggesting Charles would demean himself with a rentboy or a 'gentleman' imitating one — Preposterous!" The Major had gone an alarming shade of red. Amused, I watched eagerly, to see how Lady P. sorted him.

"Of course ladies know of such things, my dear Stephen, they only don't talk about them under normal circumstances with men, unless they are their husbands or lovers. As for the idea that Charles could have a sexual interest in men as well as women, let us put it to one side for now. Men get women to perform such acts as far as I understand. Such cases even figure in the police reports in the newspaper occasionally if you follow them as *fellatio* if I am not mistaken. The police will certainly not eliminate the idea of a male killer, or a female one. But before bursting a vessel about it, let us examine his underwear and his genitalia. There may be some suggestive traces."

The Major was left speechless, gap-mouthed and blanching at this plain speaking?

The old broad was "spot on," as the Brits would say. The Professor and me did lifting honours. Lady P. drew down his pants and drawers. While examining the inside of the latter, we all saw more than we wanted to of the corpse's equipment plus some brownish stains on the inside of his white shorts around the fly.

The killer must have caught Mortlake when he was expecting something quite different. Perhaps just after he fooled around with . . . presumably the killer, an accomplice, or someone who had just left. Unless the killer cowed her (or him?!) into cooperation. Anyway it looked like the killer (or someone) had tried incompetently to cover up the fact that sex was involved, or had taken place, just before Mortlake was attacked. Maybe the killer gave him a farewell present and then the kibosh. Afterwards, the killer, or some one else, pulled his drawers and pants up. Someone else could have come back after the killer left and interfered with the scene, but I don't think so.

The old Major was turning purple by this time, but thankfully he was still speechless. Brown had recovered from a slight nausea attack and was staring at Mortlake's crotch like a bird at a snake. Sort of shocked looking, like she'd never seen it before. Well, of course, maybe they always did it in the dark. Or the gossip was wrong. But don't bet the ranch on it.

"I think we've seen what we need to see. Thank you, Professor and Mr. Hood. If you will lift his pelvis once more I will return his garments to approximately the position we found them in."

After we'd made the corpse "decent," the old lady turned her attentions to the tool rack. She pulled evening gloves from the left-hand pocket of her tweed jacket and put them on. Then she—and I'm not kidding—pulled a magnifying glass from the other pocket.

Then she systematically went over the tools, with me looking over her shoulder. It wasn't either of the hammers, but there looked to be some traces of blood in the cracks of the wrench. It's difficult to clean one of them in a hurry.

"There is some blood on this spanner," Parrot informed the others. "We must keep it safe for the police. Mary, some of that brown paper and the glue pot." The maid produced the items from her apron pocket. Lady P. wrapped the wrench and sealed the package, having me and the Major sign the paper over the joins. Then she put it in one of those capacious pockets.

"Now let us investigate the passage," she said.

Not without some relief we turned our backs on the dear departed, and trooped through the archway back to the entrance by the scullery. Lady P. performed the open sesame act and the wall panel slid back, about three feet of it, revealing some stone steps. As it opened, as instructed I hung onto the corner of paper stuck in the panel with my hanky. I straightened up and found a folded piece of expensive-looking, scented cream notepaper. I gave it to Detective P. to do the honours. She still had her evening gloves on.

She unfolded the letter and read it out:

Daring Stallion,
Meet me in the scullery at the witching hour.
I'll be ready and waiting, lover. Unless you
don't want a good time!
Lustfully Your Ever-loving Lonely,
Hell-Cat

"The writing is copperplate printing, except the signature which was in a rounded smooth flowing hand. Does anyone recognize it?" She showed it around to all present, including Mary. The scent seemed familiar. I couldn't recall which broad had worn it. It wasn't their everyday stuff. No one else admitted placing the writing or scent, neither.

"Charles (assuming he is "Stallion") came through the passage to keep the rendezvous with Mrs., Miss, or Mr. Hell-Cat. Mary, please bring us some electric torches from the emergency store in the kitchen."

Brown looked pretty shaky and Leigh offered to take her upstairs to lie down and they left us. Mary brought back six flashlights. We left her with two as we descended down the short flight into the midst of the thick walls, down maybe eight or nine feet. I figured the passage was lower than the floor to go under the french windows. From the dust on the floor that showed up in my flashlight beam — or really mostly its absence except along the walls—it looked like there was regular traffic. This began to look interesting from our standpoint. It certainly wasn't a short cut to the Office with all the up and down. So why would Mortlake come that way? Unless he was already down here for some reason . . . Or just to conceal his passage?

When we reached the corner, the passage opened out into a little room. Almost like a small lock-up cell except without the bars. There was a bench against one wall as we played our lights about it. All three of my companions at one time or another had been this way before. Parrot, she said, when one of her sons wouldn't come out when playing hide and seek with his brother. The Major said he took one look before the renovations, but that the Professor was the expert in that sort of thing. He wrote articles and books about priest-holes and such and had overseen the restoration.

"What's this!" said Lady P. shining her light on what looked like an iron, rust-free handle in one of the cobbles under the bench along one wall. "I'm sure it wasn't there in our day. I wonder what it accesses. Mr. Hood, Professor, perhaps you would try to lift it?"

I started to shrug out of my jacket, but fortunately the Major had turned his gaze and "torch" beam on Professor Lawless just then and I caught the movement and beat him to the draw. He was happy about the murder investigation, but not about us poking into the goods down below. It turned out there was a shipment of cocaine in a nice little sub-basement the builders had made for Mortlake—allegedly as a wine cellar -- under Lawless's supervision. So he was one of the drug and liquor smuggling gang. On my instructions, Lady Parrot took his gun. At that point I explains who I am. I still am not certain the Major was not in the gang, but he played the innocent well if he was. Behaved like a lamb. He even helped me and the ladies get the drop on Jeffries and Georges later. We tied them all up and took turns keeping watch (with Mary, Agnes, and Cook) until the storm broke and the police came the next day.

You'll want to know who killed Mortlake, even if it didn't directly effect our brief. Well, unless the gal or guy bashed him from the side while he just lay there and took it, Chuck was hit on the right side of the head by someone straddling him and holding the wrench in the left hand. Brown's the only southpaw. She's also his long-time lover and has the initial "H" for Hettie. As you know with aliases and even pet names people tend to select words with the same letter. Of course "Stallion" did not fit the same way with Mortlake (it would have with Stephen Bly), but what the hell. Also she was the most disturbed, had those dark rims under her eyes — suggesting she'd not got much sleep — and Lady P. also found the scent to match the letter on her dressing table and the note paper in her office. The letter must have slipped out of his jacket pocket just as he passed through the door and closed on it without being noticed. Maybe the killing was what kept her up all night. Or maybe it was searching for the note.

Detective Parrot and me figured Brown was tired of being knocked about as foreplay, and probably also jealous of the Leigh dame. She wanted to get the annuity Mortlake left her in his Will.

Yours Truly,

Joe Guilliani, a.k.a. Jack Hood